Nothing Like a Cowboy

By Donna Alward

Getting back in the saddle has never felt so good...

Brett Harrison tried marriage once and isn't anxious for another round. So when his meddling twin sister sets him up on a dating site, he seriously considers strangling her and cancelling. Luckily for him, he's too much of a gentleman to act on those impulses, and when he meets Melly Walker, he wonders if it's time to get back in the saddle.

Melly knows exactly where her previous marriage went wrong. She was dazzled by her ex's big-city charm and strayed too far from her roots. This time, she's going with tried and true—a dyed-in-the-wool cowboy. Her first few dates net her more duds than studs, but when she meets Brett, she's ready to get more than just her feet wet.

The principles of trust and compromise are great in theory, but when Melly discovers Brett has his eye on more than just her curves, she questions her judgment and his motives. Is Brett ready to drop his dreams for something as unreliable as love?

Warning: Contains virtual hat-tipping, real-time kissing and sexy times. Yee haw!

Something About a Cowboy

By Sarah M. Anderson

He's a man of his word...and she's gonna take him up on it.

After six years working his ranch and raising his boys, widower Mack Tucker is staring down the barrel of another long, lonely winter. Until his grown-up sons decide it's time for him to move on. They not only sign him up for an online dating site, but also screen the first batch of interested parties.

Mack is furious—until he spots one of the profiles. He's intrigued. Intrigued enough to drive three hours to Billings to meet Karen Thompson.

Burned by her ex, Karen isn't interested in diving into another marriage, but she wouldn't mind dipping her toes back in the dating waters. But this time, things will be different. What could be more trustworthy and honest than a strong, silent cowboy?

Their first date gets steamier than either of them intended, and Mack fears it may be too much, too soon for him. Torn between the past and the present, Mack has to cowboy up or lose the possibility of a future with the woman who makes his broken heart beat again.

Warning: Contains skinny dipping in public, sensual biting, gratuitous use of roses, and a red lace thong. Sometimes all at once.

Anything for a Cowboy

By Jenna Bayley-Burke

Her plan was for them to fall in bed, not in love.

When veterinarian Jacy Weston changes her location on her western dating website profile, she thinks it's no big deal. Opal Creek...Myrtle Creek...what's the difference? As little white lies go, this one barely qualifies. Besides, since her brothers have chased off every guy within a hundred miles, the expiration date on her virginity is way past due.

Ray Mitchell is not inclined to waste his time on something as unnecessary as dating, but it's much easier to take a woman to coffee than to explain to his mother why he's in no hurry to get married again. Despite NotMy1stRodeo.com's promises, he doubts he'll find any woman willing to find herself stuck on a remote ranch raising rodeo stock.

But Jacy is different. She isn't afraid to get her hands dirty. Or to get down and dirty. Ray's thinking he's found the one, until the truth comes out...and he realizes the divorcee from the next county he's been dating doesn't exist.

Warning: Contains a virginal heroine looking for the nearest exit for the horizontal highway to heaven, and a cowboy willing to go the distance for the right woman.

Not My 1st Rodeo

Samhain Publishing, Ltd.
11821 Mason Montgomery Road, 4B
Cincinnati, OH 45249
www.samhainpublishing.com

Not My 1st Rodeo
Print ISBN: 978-1-61923-094-1

Editing by Heidi Moore
Cover by Syneca

Nothing Like a Cowboy, ISBN 978-1-61922-861-0
First Samhain Publishing, Ltd. electronic publication: June 2015
Something About a Cowboy, ISBN 978-1-61922-870-2
First Samhain Publishing, Ltd. electronic publication: June 2015
Anything for a Cowboy, ISBN 978-1-61922-860-3
First Samhain Publishing, Ltd. electronic publication: June 2015
First Samhain Publishing, Ltd. print publication: June 2015

Contents

Nothing Like a Cowboy

Donna Alward

Dedication

To Linda and Debbie, for telling an awesome story and giving me such a laugh in the first place.

Chapter One

Brett Harrison stared at the computer screen in horror.

"Jesus, Manda. Are you crazy? You put me on a dating site?"

He stared at the picture of himself filling the top quarter of the monitor. It was a cropped shot from Manda's wedding last year, when he'd been dressed in a suit with a string tie and all the groomsmen had worn matching black Stetsons. It wasn't a bad picture, he supposed. But it did look like he was...well, posing for it, which made things worse. It made him look like he actually cared. Like he was serious about looking for love...when he hadn't even known the site even existed. And if he had known about the profile, he would have taken it down. Immediately. Like he was going to do right now.

If she weren't five months pregnant, he'd strangle his twin sister.

Manda perched on the side of the desk. "Hell yes, I put you on a dating site. It's time you got back out there. You're never going to get laid if you hole up in your office or in the barn or wherever."

He frowned. "My love life is none of your business."

"Right. And when you go around snapping at everyone? I want my kid to actually like his Uncle Brett. Trust me, big brother. What you need is a hot night of—"

"Of nothing," he interrupted, trying really hard not to be slightly amused. Trying to be mad. Ever since she'd gotten married, Manda had suddenly become an authority on romantic bliss. But to his mind, only desperate people used dating sites. The *facts* were just full of lies or inflated truths at best.

He wasn't that desperate. Was he? He wondered what Manda would say if he confessed that he hadn't been with a woman since his divorce. Or maybe Manda already suspected, and that was why she was pushing. Meddling.

"I can find a date if I want one." He scanned the rest of the profile and had to admit, Manda had been pretty honest. Of course, she'd only played up the good parts. He had faults. Lots of them. Sherry had been quick to point them out too. It wasn't much wonder their marriage hadn't lasted, considering how little she'd thought of him.

Apparently, he wasn't romantic enough. Didn't tend to a woman's needs. Wasn't—and this was what stung the most—smart enough. Too rough around the edges. If he'd known she felt that way all along, they never would have made it down the aisle in the first place. And that wasn't an experience he was eager to repeat. He'd almost lost his share of the ranch in the settlement. He wondered what his ex would say now that the situation had changed substantially. The ranch was in better shape than ever, and they were seriously looking at expansion.

Manda scoffed, giving him a slap upside the head to emphasize her point.

"Listen, you know as well as I do that offerings are pretty slim around here." He looked up at her. "Let's just take this thing down and forget all about it."

But Manda was stubborn, and she raised an eyebrow at him. "So which is it? You don't want a date or there's no one you like? Maybe you need to head into Gibson for a bit, hit the bar, whatever. Stop being so damned choosy."

"Manda." He was done fooling around, and he let his tone communicate that. "I don't want to be on a dating site. Take down the profile or I'll do it myself."

She grinned. "No. And you wouldn't know how anyway, because you're technologically challenged." Her expression turned smug. "Besides, you already have a date."

For five seconds, Brett was sure his head was going to blow off. "What do you mean, a date?"

Manda got off the corner of the desk and reached around him to slide the mouse over the mouse pad and click on an icon. "See? Melissa. Melly to her friends. You sent her a hat tip."

"A hat tip?"

"Well, yeah. The guys have to make the first move here, you know? See? She's checked off divorced, spring and mutton busting." She straightened, crossing her arms with satisfaction.

"What the hell does that all mean? Manda, pregnant or not, you're walking a fine line here."

"It means—" she sighed with impatience, "—that she's divorced, she's under thirty and she wasn't married very long."

He raised a dubious eyebrow and looked closer at the screen. For the love of Mike, the criteria the site used was downright hokey. His profile, on the other hand, listed him as divorced, summer because he was over thirty, and his marital experience as bull riding.

"Sounds great." Sarcasm dripped from his tongue.

"Yes, it does. Because you invited her for coffee."

He tamped down his absolute frustration at his sister's taking over the situation and replied through gritted teeth, "I didn't invite her anywhere."

"Well, I did for you. See? A coffee date. Very public place, limited time if need be, daytime. Women try to be really safe on first dates. She'll probably have a wingman ready to text her with an emergency if she needs an escape route."

It was sounding more like a military maneuver than a date. "What if I'm the one who needs an escape route?"

Manda grinned. "So you're going?"

"I didn't say that." He pinned her with his sternest glare. "Manda, you had no right to do this. To pretend to be me. To set this up. It's my life. I wish you'd respect that."

She stared right back. "I did it because I love you and I'm worried about you and I knew you wouldn't go do this for yourself."

"You're damn right—"

"And you've been licking your wounds ever since Sherry left. You need to get back out there, Brett. This girl doesn't have to be the one. But she might at least be a start to you realizing that not every woman out there views being a rancher as a handicap that needs to be overcome. This site, it's specifically for people like you."

"People like me? What on earth does that mean?" There was actually a site for hermits? Desperate recluses? Eunuchs?

"Not my first rodeo. It's for cowboys and ranchers, sweetie. And ones who've been around the matrimonial block and lived to tell the tale."

"And want to again, which I clearly don't. You forgot that part."

"You just think that." Manda frowned and put her hand on his shoulder. "Will you at least look at her profile? Buy her a cup of coffee? If you back out now, she's going to feel like crap."

"Then you can be the one to explain. I'm sure you'll let her down easy."

Manda's lips formed an ominous line. "Fine. Don't go. Whatever. Just stop moping around here and growling at everyone. We're sick of it."

She left the office, slammed the door, and silence fell in her wake.

Brett sighed, stared at the now-closed door and counted to ten. Why was it Manda always knew exactly what to say to get under his skin? Little sisters were the bane of his existence—

and he had three of them. Manda, he took great pride in reminding her, was a whole seven minutes younger than him.

Hell, they were probably all in on this. Manda was the oldest and most often the spokesperson. Particularly now that she was pregnant with his first niece or nephew. Everyone knew he was a soft touch.

He turned in the chair and let his gaze fall on the monitor again. The screen showed the messaged conversation between himself and this woman. Melissa. Melly, he mentally corrected. Who the hell went by the name of Melly?

He clicked on her name, her profile popped up, and his mind went utterly blank for a few minutes.

He wasn't sure what he'd expected, but the woman on the screen was attractive. Really attractive. The picture was casual, looked like the background of house siding behind her, and she wore a simple blue plaid shirt, like she wasn't too worried about what she wore for the photo. Neither did she wear a lot of makeup, but she didn't need to. Her eyes were an intriguing almond shape and a soft, chocolaty brown, just a little darker than the smooth waterfall of hair that fell over her shoulder. A half smile touched her full lips. What on earth was a woman like that doing on a matchmaking site? Surely she didn't have any problem finding a date.

He went back to the message window and read what she'd written to Manda. Polite, modest, and claimed that she had never signed up for a dating site before. He wondered if that were true. Wondered if everything on her profile was true. It said she was twenty-nine, five-foot-nine and taught high school English. She was divorced and still hopeful there was a Mr. Right out there.

Well, wasn't that just sweet?

Brett pushed back his chair a bit and sighed again. Okay, so the photo had caught his attention. And the details weren't bad either. But did he trust them?

No sir.

Still, his details were accurate. Maybe hers were too.

Hold on. Was he really considering going through with this farce of a date? He thought about what Manda had said. It wasn't this Melly's fault that Manda had impersonated him and set up a date. She'd be at the Daily Grind coffee shop tomorrow evening, waiting for him unless he told her otherwise. Standing her up was not an option. His mama had raised him better than that. And the idea of messaging her and calling it off...Manda was right. Canceling would probably make her feel like crap. It had to take a lot of guts to put up a profile and actually send someone a message.

He shook his head. What the hell was wrong with him? Why did he suddenly feel flattered that she'd said yes to a question he hadn't even asked?

He looked at the messages once more. "A cup of coffee sounds perfect," she'd answered. "I'm really looking forward to meeting you, Brett."

Aw, shit.

He was going to have to go through with it. But just one date. One coffee date. They could meet and be friendly and go their separate ways, and that would be that. And his profile was coming off the site as soon as it was over.

Damn straight.

Chapter Two

Melly stood outside the Daily Grind, her right hand gripping the strap of her handbag as she reconsidered for about the millionth time.

Why was she putting herself through this again? Was Brett already inside? What if he didn't show, like the last guy hadn't? What if he did but looked nothing like his picture? For a split second, she considered turning around and walking straight back to her car and heading back to Helena. Why had she ever thought that online dating would be a good idea?

But she wouldn't stand him up, because that would be rude. Besides, it was time she got back into the dating game. Sometimes she felt like she'd forgotten how to flirt. Banter. Have fun. Be herself. Fun Melly. Unfortunately, Fun Melly hadn't come out to play since signing up on NotMy1stRodeo.com. Her dates so far had been disasters.

One man had looked promising from afar, until he'd come closer and her nose had alerted her that he'd come right from the barn. There had still been manure on his boots, for God's sake. She was all for cowboys and ranchers but expected a man might clean his boots and change his shirt before meeting a woman for lunch.

Then there'd been the man who was at least fifteen years older than his picture and had only half the hair she'd expected. He'd been polite, but there definitely wasn't any spark. At all. The date had been painful and blessedly short. She'd felt relieved but also a little offended that he'd seemed to be in such a hurry to get away. And then, of course, the no-show. Wow.

She'd decided to throw in the towel, and then Brett had sent her a hat tip. She'd closed her eyes and sent a wink back to him before she could change her mind. The offer for coffee had come shortly after that. *One more try*, she'd thought. And when it didn't work out, maybe she'd let her BFF, Leanne, set her up with the gym teacher at her school. She'd been nagging Melly for ages about that—

"Melissa?"

She spun around at the sound of her name being spoken, her bag swinging with her, sliding off her shoulder and dropping to the crook of her elbow with a heavy thud. Yep, being herself sometimes translated into being a little klutzy and awkward. She scrambled to push the straps back over her shoulder while at the same time attempting a smile. Holy crap. She struggled to keep her composure, but her first thought was that his picture hadn't lied.

"You must be Brett. I'm Melly." It came out stronger than she expected, and she tried a smile with it, proud of herself. "Melissa. Melissa Walker."

The repetition of her name had probably wrecked any calm factor she'd achieved, hadn't it? She held out her right hand to shake his and *whoomp*. The bag slid off her shoulder again, jerking her hand downward. Her own damned fault for cramming it with her phone, wallet, emergency makeup and a hardback novel in case she ended up waiting...or worse. At least he hadn't stood her up. That was a good sign, right? She swallowed and held the smile, trying not to look like she was staring. Hells bells, Brett Harrison looked yummy enough to eat.

Once more, she shoved the handbag straps to her shoulder. "Sorry," she apologized, her cheeks hot, and he smiled in return. He had incredible blue eyes, she noticed. Nice and clear, with the tiniest of crow's feet in the corners and a fringe of light brown lashes. He hadn't worn his hat today, like he had in his profile picture, and she studied his hair, cut short around his ears, a little tousled on top, the same blondish brown as his lashes. The toffee-colored hair and blue of his eyes set off his tanned face, which she supposed came from working outdoors much of the time.

And his body... Well, it was impossible not to notice the tall, strong build. His stats had said he was thirty-two. Her heart gave a solid thump as she realized that Brett Harrison's profile had been one hundred percent accurate. He was exactly what she'd had in mind when she'd signed up on the dating site. A gentleman cowboy. And the way his sky-blue gaze settled on her now, a sexy one to boot. Maybe the other dud dates had been leading up to this. Who said persistence didn't pay?

Brett merely smiled at the awkward moment as she clung to her purse strap. "I have a mother and three sisters. I'm familiar with the phrase, 'my life is in my purse'."

"It really is," she said, letting out a sigh of relief now that the initial introduction was over.

Brett gestured toward the door with a hand. "So, uh, how about we get that cup of coffee?"

She nodded, suddenly shy. Brett opened the door for her, and she scooted inside and then waited as he followed and they went to the counter to order their drinks.

"What'll you have?" she asked, determined to keep her chin high and confident, even though inside she was nervous as hell. The beginning had been less than auspicious, but there was time to turn it around. Be bright and sparkly. "My treat."

"I'll get the coffee," he said, reaching in his back pocket for his wallet. He was turned a little to the left and she got a passing glimpse of the square of his back pocket, a little more faded than the rest of his jeans. And resisted the sudden urge to fan herself.

Instead, she put her fingers on his arm, only briefly as she suddenly realized it probably seemed a little too familiar. "Brett, I'd like to buy you a coffee. Will you let me do that?"

James had been a stickler about paying for everything. He'd hated her trying to pay, like it was an insult, an assumption that he couldn't afford things, an affront to his masculinity. She really hadn't realized how much financial trouble he'd been in until he'd filed for bankruptcy. Anyone she dated had to get over that sort of male-pride thing. She figured this was a good first test.

He met her gaze for a long moment and then nodded. "I guess that'd be all right." He raised an eyebrow. "This once."

Meaning there'd be a next time?

"Good. Now what'll you have?"

He grinned. "A big mug of black. I'm a man of simple tastes."

She smiled back, encouraged. "You got it."

She ordered his coffee and then her own, which was slightly more complicated as there was a flavor shot and some steamed milk involved. But within a few minutes, they were headed to a table in the back corner of the shop that looked out over Gibson's Main Street. To her surprise and pleasure, Brett held her chair for her and waited for her to be seated before sitting across from her. Good looking—check. Manners—check. She wondered what else he had going for him?

"So," she said, laughing nervously. "Here we are."

"Here we are," he echoed, one corner of his mouth tipping up a little. He raised an eyebrow. "Let me guess. You're mentally going over my profile and trying to figure out if I lied."

Her cheeks heated again. "Clearly, you didn't." Rustling up her courage, she added, "If anything, the reality's better than the profile."

His laugh was low and warm and sent tingly feelings rushing through her body.

"I have to come clean," he confessed. "I didn't set up that profile. My sister did. I didn't even know about it until two days ago."

Disappointment flowed through her, and embarrassment. "Oh. I see. And she's the one who...?" Now she was feeling foolish. Naïve. "She sent the hat tip."

"Yes. I was really mad at her when I found out."

"I can imagine." Suddenly the coffee in front of her wasn't so appealing. Was he gracefully looking for a way to exit? He hadn't even asked her here today. His sister had. "You know, I was a little worried you were going to be a no-show."

He chuckled again. "I thought the same about you. And I thought about messaging you and canceling, but I realized it wasn't your fault my sister's an interfering pain in my butt. So I figured I'd show up, see if you did too, and have a cup of coffee. What could it hurt?"

This was sounding worse and worse. Like it was a pity date, for Pete's sake. She wondered how long she needed to sit here before she could get up and leave without being impolite. He hadn't wanted to be here. He was just showing good manners.

"Melly?"

She lifted her head and looked at him, surprised when he used the preferred shortened version of her name.

"You know, I'm not so mad at my sister anymore." And he smiled.

He had a good smile. The kind that made a girl feel like he was letting her in on some sort of secret. The kind that felt like it was for her and her alone. It was intimate, a little shy, a little bit cheeky. He rested his elbows on the table and it stretched the cotton of his shirt across his broad shoulders.

"You're glad you came?" she asked.

"More every second."

"Me too," she replied and smiled back at him. Okay, so less than a stellar beginning on both their parts...but it was showing potential. It was the smiling at each other that made everything seem suddenly, deliciously intimate. Something sizzled in the air between them. Was it too soon to be feeling any sort of attraction? And yet it was there, pulsing in the air around them, a tension that was as delicious as it was unnerving. Maybe she wouldn't need Leanne's help with that date after all.

He lifted his coffee cup and took a drink. She watched him, her gaze focused on his full lips as they touched the porcelain cup. Muscles tightened in familiar places. The words *dry spell* flitted through her mind, though she found she didn't care a whole lot.

Still. It was a first date. No sense in getting carried away. Much. She raised her mug and hid behind it for a few seconds, telling herself to get a grip.

"So," he said, sounding remarkably conversational. "You're an English teacher."

"Yes," she said, following his lead in the get-to-know-you portion of the date. "In Helena. I've been renting an apartment there since..." She swallowed tightly. The dating site was for second chances after all. "Since my divorce."

"You seem too young to be divorced," Brett said, his brows pulling together. His gaze swept over her. "And far too pretty."

She absorbed the compliment and considered. How open should they be on a first date? What if there wasn't a second? She measured her answer. "I was young and a bit dazzled by him, I suppose. I met James when I was in college. He was charming and sophisticated and interesting. He liked nice restaurants and fast cars, and I guess I thought I did too. At least for a while."

Huh. She hadn't really thought about it in that exact way, but the failure of their marriage hadn't been all James's fault.

He'd lied and he'd hidden things from her, but she'd been pretending to be something she wasn't too.

"You don't like those things?"

"For a treat? Maybe. As a way of life? I'm not much into flash." She decided to keep the bankruptcy part to herself. No need to reveal everything all at once. "I'm a lot simpler, really. I'm a farm girl at heart. I realized I prefer big skies over bright lights. Food I can pronounce and identify over the latest fusion fad."

"You were raised on a farm?" Brett seemed both surprised and pleased by the knowledge.

She nodded and relaxed a little. She loved talking about home. "My parents have a small ranch about a half hour from here. I grew up growing my own vegetables and raising chickens too." She grinned. "Actually, one of the things my ex-husband was most shocked at was that the eggs didn't come out all nice and clean and white like those from the grocery store."

She was gratified when Brett chuckled. She'd far rather talk about her upbringing than James. Especially now. Her dad's heart condition made it harder and harder for him to work, and he was set on selling the ranch, no matter how much she protested. It made her heart hurt just thinking about not having the place to call home anymore.

"How about you?" she asked. "Your profile says you're a rancher."

"Yes, ma'am. A beef ranch not far from here." He nodded. "You had a bit of a drive if you came from Helena," he acknowledged.

"Not that bad. I'm at the north edge of the city." She shrugged. "I'll probably stop at Mom and Dad's on the way home. Helena's close enough for me to visit lots. It's a nice day for a drive."

So it was. Late spring was beautiful in Montana. Everything turned newly green and lush, with clear blue skies and rolling farmland and jagged mountains. Melly loved her job, but this time of year, she always found herself missing all the spring activity. Right now, her mom would be putting in the vegetable garden. There was something so satisfying about putting seeds into the earth and being rewarded by green plants that would then become food. The closest she got to that was a couple of planters on her balcony. With a sinking heart, she realized this was probably the last garden her mom would put in at the ranch. Their plan was to move to a smaller house, on a smaller lot, closer to town.

It was bad enough that Melly's life had fallen apart. Why did the things she relied on to always be there have to change too?

"Busy time of year for you too," she said, taking another sip of coffee, determined to change the subject. She didn't need to kill the vibe with her depressing attitude.

"It's always busy," he replied, but he smiled again. "Though, yeah, this time of year is particularly hectic, and fun. A few weeks from now will be insane. Vaccines, branding, all the other necessary things that happen to new calves. I'm sure you're familiar with that."

She perked up. "Of course I am. Though I have to admit, branding isn't my favorite job." She sighed. "And it's not something I've been a part of much since college. I kind of miss it."

"You don't go home to help out?"

He couldn't know how hard that question was to answer. "Not as often as I'd like. Teaching is a pretty demanding job. Though I do visit more in the summer when I'm off." She didn't add that James hadn't liked the ranch. He hadn't liked the dirt or the smells or anything about it. She'd rarely gone home when they were together. It was only in the last year or so, since the divorce, that she'd visited more frequently, put on her boots and gotten in the saddle again.

"It's probably the hardest time of the year," he admitted, "but I love it." He turned his coffee cup around in his hands. "Actually, I love just about every day on the ranch. I can't imagine doing anything else."

He looked up at her, and she could swear there was a defiant set to his jaw, as if daring her to challenge him. She wondered why. Wondered why he'd suddenly sounded a little defensive. If he expected her to disagree, he was going to be disappointed. To her mind, his life was pretty ideal. She was so done with the city, the cramped spaces and the traffic. Maybe it was true. You could take the girl out of the country, but it was a heck of a lot harder to take the country out of the girl.

"So," she said, a little nervous again, "you're divorced?"

"I am." He smiled grimly. "My ex-wife thought ranching sounded a lot more romantic than the reality."

Melly couldn't help it, she snorted. Brett's expression darkened.

She covered her mouth with a hand and tried to straighten her face. "I'm sorry," she offered, wanting to smooth the fretting wrinkle off his brow. "I didn't mean to do that. I shouldn't laugh."

"Yeah, well, I should have seen it coming. She never did really fit. I was just..."

"Dazzled?" Melly suggested, lifting an eyebrow.

His face relaxed a little and his eyes warmed, as if he appreciated the little bit of wit. "Yeah. Dazzled is one way of putting it. Thinking with the wrong head, if you'll pardon the crude expression."

She laughed again. And the wrinkle smoothed just a little bit more.

"Sounds like we both ended up with people a little flashier than our tastes," she observed. "Or maybe just a little too refined."

"Maybe," he conceded. "They might have done better with each other than the likes of us." He chuckled a little, and she got a tingly kind of feeling from him pairing them together, even in such a casual way.

Melly looked down at her cup. Her coffee was gone. She suspected Brett's was as well. As dates went, it had been different. And since the word dazzled had been brought up more than once, Melly had to admit she wasn't quite seeing stars and rainbows. But then there was the hint of a smile he'd shown her earlier, and his manners, and that interesting moment where something had connected between them.

Not love at first sight. But intriguing? Yes. His foot bumped hers under the table and a zing went up her calf. Oh, definitely intriguing.

"Melissa?"

She met his gaze. His clear blue eyes were settled on her, his brows pulled together slightly as if he were trying to figure out a puzzle.

"If you don't mind me asking, why did you decide to use a dating site? You're a beautiful woman, and I can't imagine you being desperate or having a hard time finding a guy. I don't get it."

She pushed her cup to the side and folded her hands on the table, determined not to fidget or let her nervousness show. "Well, to be honest, I know what I'm looking for in a partner. I'm not a city girl, and I'm not new to marriage. I've always enjoyed the outdoors, loved growing up on our ranch. So I figured I'd narrow the search by parameters. The website helped me do that. Kind of a made-to-order thing." She let a grin crawl up her cheek. "You know, like Meg Ryan in "When Harry Met Sally". She orders things just the way she wants them. No compromising."

"And then has that I'll-have-what-she's-having moment."

Ah, yes. The orgasm scene. Melly met Brett's gaze. Was he flirting? It was hard to tell. He seemed more of a still waters type than an open book. Still, it was a slightly suggestive comment to make at this point in the date, and she took it as a good sign. "You have to give the girl credit," Melly responded with a wink, flirting back. "She knew what satisfaction looked like."

The air hummed between them, and Melly lifted her chin a little, almost daring him to respond.

"Except she was faking." He raised an eyebrow and his eyes twinkled.

Game on. He was flirting with her. Melly felt a little more confidence slide through her and she leaned her elbows on the table, moving slightly more towards him, inviting him closer.

"Oh, she was just demonstrating a point. I've never seen the point in faking anything, have you?"

Two spots of color appeared on his cheeks. "Not really. I like a woman who knows how to speak her mind."

Was it getting warmer in here? It wasn't so much what they said, but the subtle undertones that seemed to raise her temperature. "Hey, there's nothing wrong with a little bit of mystery and surprise. As long as it's the right kind..."

The moment held, but then Brett suddenly leaned back a little, disengaging from the repartee. "Look, Melissa."

"Melly." She didn't like the sound of the way he said her name this time.

"Melly," he corrected. "Look, we're flirting a little here, and as nice as that is, I think I need to be honest with you, because I don't like to play games. You seem like a really nice woman. But you see...you're looking for something that I'm not. We don't want the same things, and I don't think it would be fair of me to let you think otherwise."

She appreciated his honesty at least. “Fair enough,” she replied, surprised at how disappointed she felt. Just when they seemed to be getting somewhere, he backed off. “But I hope you realize that I’m not looking at each date as a first step to the altar. You seem like a good guy. Perhaps a little jaded, but hey, failed marriages have that effect. I went with the dating site because it seemed a little less, I don’t know, meat-marketish than heading to the local honky-tonk for a few beers and some dance-floor flirting. That’s not my style. I’m more of a...” But she couldn’t come up with the right words. She was an English teacher, and she was coming up blank.

Brett’s smile blossomed. “More of an online shopper?”

She smiled back. “Wow, that doesn’t sound much better, does it?”

They shared a chuckle and then he spoke again. “So you’re actually thinking you might find love this way.”

“Well, yeah.” It was her turn to frown. “I want to get married again. Have a family. I figure meeting someone with common interests might be a good start, you know?” She looked up at him and decided that if he liked honesty, she might as well give him some. “That doesn’t mean I’m in a huge rush or that I’m taking inventory and trying to check boxes. I’m open to dating for the fun of it.” She blinked slowly. “Do you get what I’m saying?”

“I think I do.” His foot bumped hers under the table again.

“I’m glad neither of us chickened out today. Even if I do have your sister to thank for it.”

He grinned. “Busybody Manda? Yeah, I’m starting to forgive her for her interference. I’m sorry if I’m a bit rusty. I haven’t done this in a while, and I was nervous as hell.” Brett leaned forward on his arms, just a little, like he was preparing to share a secret. “I have to admit I was really relieved when I saw you.”

“You were?”

"You seemed normal. And pretty. And like someone I might have introduced myself to in a different situation. Then when your bag kept slipping—"

"I know. I'm so awkward." Such an idiot.

"No, that's not it. I just...I used to feel out of place with my ex. But when that happened, I don't know. It made me more comfortable. I wasn't so intimidated."

The confession softened her heart just a bit. "Aw. And it makes me laugh to think of someone finding me intimidating. Most of the time, I feel like a square peg in a round hole."

He shook his head. "No way." To her surprise, his face went a bit red. "You're very pretty, Melly."

He'd called her pretty twice now, and it gave her a lot more confidence. "You're not so bad yourself."

And there it was again. That jolt of excitement, of anticipation. Startling by its very presence, and delicious too.

Damn.

She held out her hand again, this time without the handbag flopping on her wrist. "Can we start over? Hi, Brett. I'm Melly. I'm twenty-nine, divorced, and I like skies full of stars, long walks, a cold beer on a hot day and wild roses."

He held her gaze as he fit his hand into hers. "Brett Harrison. I'm thirty-two, divorced, like the smell of fresh-cut hay, my mama's blueberry pie, watching the sunrise and—" he grinned, "—a cold beer on a hot day."

His hand was warm, firm, lingering.

Then he squeezed her fingers in his.

"Do you want to get out of here? Go for one of those walks maybe?"

So the date wasn't over. Melly got the feeling that it was actually just beginning.

"I'd like that," she replied. "I think I'd like that a lot."

Chapter Three

They left the coffee shop and stepped into the bright May sunlight. Melly wasn't familiar with Gibson, though the town was small and easily navigated. When Brett explained that there was a walking trail a block and a half south of Main that went along the river, Melly thought it sounded lovely. And public.

The trail wasn't paved, but it was leveled and covered with a thin layer of finely crushed rock. They turned right, walking so the river was on their left, darts of light sparkling off the surface in the early evening sun. It truly was pretty, and Melly let out a breath, relaxing a bit more. They weren't the only ones out on the trail, and she was delighted to see the odd bench or picnic table set up for people to rest or enjoy the view. She imagined people coming here to have their lunch, or packing a picnic and letting their kids run free on the grass. "This is really gorgeous," she commented as they strolled.

"I'm kind of surprised you said yes," Brett replied, his boots crunching against the gravel. "My sister, Manda—the one who set us up—thought you'd probably bring a friend as backup. You know, meeting a stranger and all."

Melly looked up at him. "I considered asking my friend, Leanne, to come along as backup. Honestly, I was glad you suggested coffee." She laughed a little. "Or rather, your sister did. Coffee is a low-maintenance date. Easy escape route." She smiled. "Just in case you were a troll or creepy or something."

"And yet here you are out walking with me. Harder to escape."

"You're neither a troll nor creepy, so I don't feel threatened. Should I?"

He stopped, looked down at her. "No."

That little zing of attraction zipped between them again. Could Brett be threatening? *Maybe to my willpower,* she thought, unable to look away from his gaze. Earlier, he'd asked why she'd used a dating site. She wanted to ask him the same thing, because from where she was standing there wasn't a thing wrong with him. And, yes, she knew he hadn't actually been the one to set up his profile, but how did a guy like this stay single?

She struggled to keep things light. Breezy. "I suppose if you were some stalkery predator type, you'd hardly answer yes to that question."

He laughed a little, then feigned a serious expression and rubbed his chin. "That's true. You're taking a lot on faith here."

She turned away and sighed, the spell broken by the very suggestion of having faith in anything—or anyone. "I usually do. It's what got me in this position in the first place."

"Pollyanna syndrome?"

She was starting to see he had a subtle sense of humor that she enjoyed. "Maybe a bit. I don't get that vibe from you though."

"I don't take a lot on faith," he admitted. "I like good solid evidence that I can see and touch."

Touch. Melly bit down on her lip as they resumed walking. She should not be thinking about him touching her, not this soon. They'd just met. But it wasn't difficult to let her imagination go there. He was a good-looking guy, rugged and capable and yet polite and funny. Then there was the shape of his lips that somehow begged to be kissed, the strong angle of his stubbled jaw that made her want to run her fingers along the side of his face. And he was just remote enough to make him a challenge. Not that she'd make the first move. Still, she'd have something to think about tonight when she was home alone.

"I understand that," she replied. "I find my optimistic outlook has a few more dark clouds than it used to."

"Divorce can do that," he agreed. "You know, it's not even so much the hurt anymore. I mean, I did love her. At least I thought I did, which at the time is the same thing. It's the damage left behind. It's the way you end up doubting yourself that really hangs on."

God, he was so right. She alternated between wondering how she could have been so blind to wondering how much of it was her fault. One minute she was strong and determined and had faith that there was love out there for her again, and the next she was terrified that she'd never be able to trust anyone, or take them at face value.

"Tell me about it," she answered. "I guess that's why I thought the site would be a good idea. I figured that if I dated anyone from there, they'd understand being gun-shy about the whole romance thing."

"But you said you wanted to get married again. That you believed in it." They skirted around a group of teens who crowded the walkway on their way towards town.

"Sure, in the grand scheme of things. Sometimes the practicality of it is quite different." She shrugged. "Maybe a few dates will at least, I don't know, get me out there again. Give me some confidence."

"Great. So I'm your guinea pig?"

His tone was teasing and she laughed. It felt really good. "How about...training wheels? I try to stay away from animal testing."

He laughed in return. "Training wheels. I don't know how to feel about that."

"Oh, don't worry. Hell, I haven't even..." She broke off, halting mid-sentence as her face flamed. Wow, had she gotten so comfortable that she'd been about to admit to her sexual dry spell too? That she hadn't had sex in nearly two years? Twenty-seven. She'd been twenty-seven when the truth had hit. They'd been married for eighteen months. God, she'd been divorced longer than she'd been married. Twenty-nine was feeling much, much older than the number suggested.

She could feel Brett's eyes on her and she struggled to breathe. "Well, that's embarrassing," she murmured, and she heard his soft laugh.

"If it makes you feel better, I haven't either. Not since Sherry left."

Sherry. That was her name. Then she absorbed what he was saying. They'd both been celibate since their splits. If anything did happen between them, they would be each other's firsts. She was kind of glad about that. Like she was at less of a disadvantage.

"Oh," she replied dumbly. The problem was, talking about the absence of sex in their lives had her picturing all sorts of things that she probably shouldn't be picturing on a first date.

They were getting farther away from the main part of town now, the path meandering along the river bank to where a bridge crossed over, marking the end of the business district. The path passed beneath the bridge, and it was cool and shaded in the shadows. And private, she realized. They hadn't met anyone on the trail since the teenagers, and the kids were long gone.

Her heart pounded a little harder simply from the knowledge that they were alone. Had he brought her here on purpose? She felt about sixteen years old, sneaking away with a boyfriend to find some secluded corner to make out. And God help her, she loved it. It was exciting. It made her feel vibrant and alive again. And maybe just a little bit adventurous since Brett was virtually a stranger.

"Melissa."

She didn't bother correcting him. Her name sounded different on his lips this time, like a caress, and his voice was dark and soft as it echoed off the concrete.

"Yes?" She turned to face him, and her heart leapt even more at the serious expression on his face.

He reached out and took her handbag from her shoulder and placed it on the ground by her feet. "Maybe we should just get this out of the way."

"M...my bag?"

He shook his head, stepped closer so that their bodies were nearly brushing and she could hardly breathe.

"Kissing," he said, the timbre of his voice deeply intimate.

She didn't want to stammer. Wanted to be flirty and confident and seductive, but that had never been her style. "Oh. Well, I suppose it would be a good litmus test, you know, to see if we're compatible and all and..."

She was babbling. And she stopped abruptly when he put a finger gently against her lips.

In the next moment, he was kissing her. Or almost kissing her. It was hard to tell, because she could barely feel his lips on hers. But they were there, fluttering, teasing, inviting rather than possessing. Their breath mingled and her eyes fluttered closed as she simply enjoyed the anticipation of what might come next. One thing for certain—Brett Harrison knew how to take his time and make a woman long for more. Because when he opened his lips and deepened the kiss, she forgot all about this being a first date and looped her arm around his neck, pulling him closer.

He was a good four or five inches taller than she was, and when his arm came around her, he pulled her up so that she was on her toes. His tongue swept in to taste hers. His tasted of rich coffee and man and dark desire. It exploded between them, and before she could sort out any kind of rational thought, he'd lifted her off her feet and cupped her buttocks as she instinctively wrapped her legs around him. A half a dozen steps and her back touched something cold and hard—the concrete of the buttress.

This was crazy. Insane. But there was no denying that the chemistry she'd sensed earlier was definitely there between them. His hips pressed against hers and she felt a carnal longing so intense it took her breath away. "Mmm," she murmured into his mouth, and when he slid his wide hand over the pebbled tip of her breast, the sound was replaced by a gasp of pleasure.

Brett let her down slowly, put his forehead against hers and shifted slightly, putting a little space between them. He was breathing hard and she matched him breath for breath.

"Holy shit," he said, inhaling deeply. "Holy shit."

Melly's voice was shaky. "Well. There was nothing awkward about that."

"Maybe we should have broken the ice that way. Saved ourselves a lot of time." She felt his face shift slightly as he smiled.

"It would have caused quite a scene on Main Street," she reminded him, her back still against the concrete, her body still humming from the stunning assault on her senses.

Brett stood back, and she knew she flushed again when he adjusted his jeans. "I didn't intend for all that to happen," he said, apology in his voice. "I thought I'd kiss you. Without an audience. See if there was any chemistry."

"Test the waters."

"Yeah. I didn't expect to... Well, I don't think chemistry is a problem." He let out a low, sexy chuckle.

Melly gathered up all the confidence she could muster. "I'm not sorry you did," she said plainly. "Bit sorry you stopped though."

His eyes held hers for a few moments, as if he was asking her to clarify what she'd meant. Would she have gone further? Would she have slept with him on a first date? Not here, not under a bridge like a horny teenager. But she wasn't sure she'd have stopped him from going further either. And if he asked her to follow him to a hotel right now, she'd be tempted. Mighty tempted. If the heat of that kiss was any indication, sex with Brett was guaranteed to be hot.

The problem with hot was that it was far too easy to get singed.

"I should probably walk you back to your car," he suggested, and she couldn't help feeling a little disappointed. Maybe he didn't want it to go further. Or maybe he was simply being a gentleman. What a novel idea.

"Okay," she answered dully.

"Mel..." He reached for her hand. "It's the first date. I don't want to rush things, that's all."

She felt a sliver of relief, knowing that he simply didn't want to move too fast. Back in the spring sunlight, they reverted to polite chat about Gibson, her job, the ranch. Nothing flirty, nothing suggestive. But Melly's lips still hummed from his kiss, and the little knot of tension low in her belly refused to go away.

Before long, she was pointing at which car was hers and their steps were slowing on the sidewalk.

"Well, here we are," she said lamely. She pasted on a smile and looked up at him, feeling increasingly awkward. Boy, it was hard getting back into the dating game again. Other than the few minutes when her hormones had taken over, she'd second-guessed just about everything today.

"Here we are," he echoed, his voice deliciously deep. Melly wanted to see him again. She knew that for sure. But she didn't want to be the one to ask. Despite putting herself on the website, she still liked the guy to make the first move.

"Thanks for the coffee," she said, then bit her lip. She'd bought the coffee. Man, he had her rattled. "I mean..."

"I know what you mean," he answered. Her bag was starting to slip again, and he reached out, adjusted the strap so it was on her shoulder, his fingers brushing her arm. Goosebumps rose up on her skin at the contact, and nerves tangled in her belly as he stepped closer.

"I had a nice time," he said softly, and then he dipped his head just a little and kissed her lightly. Just a soft, brief graze on the lips, but it was enough to nearly put her into meltdown.

"Me too," she said on a breath, blinking and looking up at him with dazed eyes.

"If you're interested, I'd like to see you again." Brett reached around her and opened her car door.

"I'm interested," Melly said quickly and then figured she looked overeager. She wondered if the day would come where she wouldn't feel like an idiot.

"Should I just message you through the site?" His blue eyes rested on her, and her nerves were so ramped up now that it felt like her whole body was on alert.

"Do you have a phone?"

He reached into his back pocket and took out his cell. She took it and quickly entered her number. "Here. Now you can text me. Or call. Or...whatever."

"I'll do that. Maybe we can go to dinner or something."

"That sounds good." She smiled. Wondered why on earth she thought grabbing him by the shirt collar and dragging him into her backseat sounded more preferable to a dinner date.

“I’ll be in touch then.” He smiled. “Thanks for the coffee, Melly.”

“Anytime,” she replied and got into her car while he was still holding the door. He shut it behind her and then moved to the sidewalk, lifting a hand in farewell as she pulled away from the curb.

“Well,” she breathed, looking at him in her rear view mirror. “I’ll be damned.

Chapter Four

Brett wasn't about to tell his sisters a thing about his date, other than she was nice and it went well. When Manda pressed him about whether or not he was going to see Melissa again, he merely shrugged and said he wasn't sure. But he placated his sister by asking her to give him the password for his profile, which she took as a good sign that he was on board.

And then he immediately changed the password so she couldn't get access anymore.

He texted Melly and asked her to dinner on Friday night, saying he'd drive into Helena this time. They agreed that she'd make reservations for eight o'clock since she knew the city restaurants better than he did, and she'd meet him there. Brett was nervous as hell. Melly was looking for love. He wasn't. She was open to dating for fun...that he could handle. Dinner was easy, but what about after?

There was no denying there was chemistry, but how far did he want things to go? What was, well, appropriate? Shit, he hated dating and rules and just...everything. He was still kind of reeling from the first date, if he were being honest. He'd gone to be polite and ended up beneath Memorial Bridge with her legs wrapped around him. Lord, she'd been sweet. Sweet and sultry.

At a meeting with his lawyer on Wednesday, he was so distracted that he barely registered that his latest offer on a property had been turned down. He finally turned to his buddy Austin for advice. Austin was married with a sweet wife and a little boy, but he was still good for a few beers and lots of laughs. Austin clapped him on the back, congratulated him on getting back out there again and handed him a box of condoms. Now, Brett was standing in his room, dressed in jeans, boots and a sport coat, hoping he looked okay. He stared at the box of condoms on the bed. It would be pretty presumptuous to think that they'd sleep together on the second date, wouldn't it? On the other hand, things had gotten pretty hot the other day. Wouldn't he be smarter to be prepared? She didn't need to know he had it with him. He wouldn't want her to think he was expecting anything...but if the opportunity did present itself...

Cursing, he opened the box, ripped one off the strip and tucked it into his wallet. Damn, just thinking about it had given him a hard-on. He ripped off another one and put it with the other. A guy just didn't know. He'd rather be safe than sorry.

They'd made arrangements to meet at the restaurant, and Brett used his phone to find the location and parked his truck in a nearby parking garage. He was surprised to find the restaurant was so small, but his mouth watered when he stepped inside. The smells were fantastic. It wasn't anything flashy or extravagant, but the warm colors in the decor and the candlelight made it cozy and welcoming. Sitting at a table for two was Melly, her dark hair falling over her shoulders and a glass of white wine in front of her. She looked up at him and suddenly her eyes lit up and she smiled.

"Do you have a reservation, sir?"

He dragged his gaze away from Melly and focused on the hostess. "My date's already here, thank you."

"Of course. Can we bring you a drink to start?"

He couldn't care less, but he nodded anyway. "I'll have whatever she's having," he suggested. Without waiting, he made his way past the other diners to reach their table.

Melly stood up as he approached and his eyes goggled at the sight of her. She was wearing a dress, and she had fantastic legs. The dress itself wasn't especially fancy, but the draped style highlighted her curves and made her look very feminine.

"Brett," she said, and her smile lit up her face.

The anxiety he'd suffered the whole drive to the city dissipated as he met her beside the table and kissed her cheek. "I'm sorry I'm late."

"You're not. I was a little early." Her cheeks colored prettily. "I don't know why, but while I was waiting, I was afraid you weren't going to show or something. I feel better now."

Their waitress brought a glass of wine and put it on the table in front of him. He started to laugh. "Excuse me, but could I have a whiskey, neat please?"

"You didn't order the wine?"

"I did. It's just..." He smiled at her, feeling a little bit foolish. "You can leave it too. Thanks."

As the perplexed waitress left, he looked at Melly, who was watching him with confusion. "It's your fault," he said. "I saw you sitting there and the hostess was asking if I wanted anything and all I could think of was, 'I'll have what she's having'."

When she laughed, the sound was enchanting. "Do you realize you've used that line in both of our dates?"

Right. The "When Harry Met Sally" thing. "I guess I have." He shrugged. "What can I say? You look beautiful, Melly."

"Thank you. You look pretty good yourself."

"I had help."

He probably shouldn't have admitted that, but it slipped out. After their coffee date, he'd also wondered what had compelled him to be so honest with someone he'd just met. God, he'd even talked about Sherry, which he never did. Maybe it was because Melly didn't seem to have an artificial bone in her body. She was incredibly genuine, or at least she appeared to be. And it prompted a comfort level that surprised him.

"You did? Your sister again?"

"Hardly. I'd rather keep her out of my business. A friend of mine. Who has a wife. I made sure she confirmed his advice for what to wear."

She laughed lightly. "They sound like nice friends."

"They are," he agreed. "The best." He and Austin had been in some good scrapes together. Brett had three sisters. Austin was the closest thing he had to a brother.

The waitress returned with his whiskey and menus, and for a few minutes, they pondered what to order.

"What's good?" he asked. "I'm guessing you've been here before?"

She nodded. "Only a few times. My favorite is the gnocchi, but you might want something more...meaty. I've had the thyme chicken. It's lovely."

He went with the chicken, because he had the sudden idea that eating anything with linguini or any type of long pasta could get messy. After they ordered, bread came, followed by a house salad. By the time the entrees were delivered, his whiskey was gone, Melly had accepted the second glass of wine and they were chatting easily about work.

It was easy. Almost too easy, Brett realized. In between bites, Melly told funny stories about her high school students and the pros and cons of teaching that particular age group, which led to sharing a few tales of their own teenage years. They ordered coffee and Melly suggested dessert to share, and they agreed upon the dark chocolate roulade. Her eyes had lit up when she saw the dessert menu, and the decadent choice didn't disappoint. Watching her put the spoon in her mouth and close her eyes with appreciation made his brain shift forward to the next part of the date...if there was, indeed, a next part.

He wanted there to be.

Brett put down his spoon, no longer hungry, and fixed his gaze on her face. There was something about her that drew him in. Maybe it was the way she smiled, or the softness in her eyes that put him at ease. And he was certain that she had no idea of the innate sexiness she possessed. There was a grace to the way she moved, a certain something that caught a man's eye and kept it.

"I'm so full," she announced, licking the last of the chocolate off the spoon. "I made a complete pig of myself and I can't find it in me to be sorry."

Several comments rushed through Brett's mind—about licking the spoon, about needing her energy for later—but he didn't say them. Instead, he reached across the table and took her hand in his, twining their fingers together.

She looked surprised, and then a little bit pleased as she held his gaze.

"What would you like to do now?" he asked, rubbing his thumb over the top of her hand.

"Oh. Well..." She hesitated and then smiled. "What would you like to do, Brett?"

He measured his words. He was quite good at self-editing when he put his mind to it. "For starters, I'd like to kiss you again."

Something flickered in her dark eyes. Desire? Awareness? Whatever it was, he liked it.

"Brett," she said, her voice low.

"You asked," he reminded her, smiling a little. "But whatever comes next is up to you. If you want me to take you home and call it a night, that's okay. It's been great spending the evening with you." In his head, he knew there was a benefit to taking things slowly. It didn't mean he necessarily wanted to.

"A drive home would be fine," she answered, and he tried to quell the disappointment he felt at the simple words. Maybe Manda had been right. Maybe he had been licking his wounds for too long. It was possible it was past time he got back into the dating world again.

Melly gripped her clutch purse tightly as they made their way out of the restaurant into the spring evening. Brett took her hand as they walked to the parking garage, and she thought about his last words. He wanted to kiss her again—for starters. What else did he have in mind? Did she want the same thing?

He opened the door to his truck and she hopped in, tucking her skirt around her legs and fastening her seatbelt. They were going back to her place. And she'd have to decide whether to leave him at the door or invite him in. She knew what she wanted. She just didn't know if it was the smart move.

Brett eased the truck out of the garage and back on to the street. With the radio playing softly in the background, she gave him directions, and soon they were heading north. It would only take a few minutes to reach her apartment. Minutes that seemed to go by so fast and yet so slowly.

"Take a left at the next set of lights," she instructed softly, her hands fidgeting in her lap. Brett was not interested in a serious relationship. She knew that. She was looking for something permanent...eventually. But maybe not yet. She'd done a crap load of thinking over the course of the week and she'd realized it wasn't fair to pin a prospective-husband tag on someone after a date, or even two. Why couldn't they just be in the moment and see where it led? Didn't that make more sense?

"Turn right, and it's the second building on the right," she advised. As he turned the truck into the small lot, she pointed at a few vacant spaces. "That's visitor parking."

He pulled into the spot and put the truck in park, then killed the engine. When she would have reached for the door handle, he put his hand on her left arm.

"Wait," he said, his voice a low rumble. "I'll get it."

With her stomach in knots, Melly waited as Brett hopped out and went around the hood of the truck to open her door. He held out his hand and she took it. She got out gingerly and reached back for her clutch.

"No big handbag tonight, huh?"

"Not tonight," she said, a little bit breathless as she faced forward again and found herself close to his broad chest.

They started walking to the door of the building, and Melly's nervousness ratcheted up several notches. Should she say goodnight at the door? Invite him in? If she did, would he make assumptions? Damn it, wasn't dating supposed to be fun? Instead, she felt as though she were walking through a field of landmines, afraid to take a step unless it was a mistake.

Brett stopped at the main door and waited. She was glad. He wasn't assuming anything and that helped. "Thank you for dinner," she murmured and then ran her tongue over her lips that suddenly seemed dry.

"It was nice," he replied and put his hand on her wrist, squeezing lightly. "And nice to spend time with you again."

She looked up. The tension sizzled between them, the elemental attraction that she simply couldn't deny existed. Was it so wrong to want to enjoy it? Maybe the whole narrow-down-the-search thing had been a good idea at the time, but right now she didn't want to think too far into the future. She wanted to enjoy the here and now. And right here, right now, Brett Harrison was standing in front of her, his fingers circling her wrist, his lips slightly parted and his eyes locked on hers, waiting for her to make the next move.

"Nice is an innocuous word," she said softly. "It was a good date, Brett. And I don't think I want it to be over yet. Do you want to come up for a nightcap?" He smiled a little and she winced on the inside. Could she have said anything more cliché? It sounded like something a woman would say on one of the soap operas she used to watch after school...

"I'm driving, so a nightcap might not be the best idea."

Disappointment and embarrassment rushed through her.

"But I'd like to come up anyway."

Whoosh. There went the embarrassment and back came the nerves. The excited thrill-of-the-unknown kind. "Right. Let me get my key."

She dug in her purse and got her key, and after she unlocked the door, Brett held it open, letting her through. They did the same at the inner security door and then she led the way to the stairs. "No elevator," she explained quietly. "But I'm only on the third floor."

Their shoes made scuffing noises on the industrial-grade carpet that covered the hall and stair steps. There wasn't another sound in the building as they made their way to her apartment door. Her hand shook as she put the key in the lock and the door swung open.

She reached for a light switch while Brett closed the door behind them.

"Nice place," he said quietly, and she took a deep, steadying breath.

"Thanks. Come on in." There, that sounded calm, didn't it? Her heels clicked on the ceramic tile of the entry as she put her purse down on a small table. "It's not very big, but there's just me."

She put on a smile and turned around. But the moment she did, the awareness seemed to overflow. Alone. Her apartment. Just the two of them. Before she could register a coherent thought, they each took a step towards each other. Brett's strong arms came around her and lifted her to her toes while she cupped his face with her hands and kissed him.

There was no easing into this one. It was pure, unadulterated desire that pulsed between them. "I waited all night to do that," she said on a soft breath, stepping back and gripping the lapels of his jacket. She pushed it off his shoulders and tossed it at a chair so that it draped there, lopsided. Her busy fingers fumbled at the buttons of his shirt while he simply pulled on the tie at the waist of her dress and it fell away, the wrap-style now gaping in the middle.

"I love that this is easy access," he replied, his voice rich and dark. She was still working on the buttons of his shirt when he put his hand over hers and stopped her progress.

"This is what you want?" he asked, his blue eyes piercing hers. "You're sure?"

There was a moment of uncertainty and she paused. "You don't?"

"Oh, I do," he confirmed. "But you need to be sure. We won't do anything you don't want to."

She could see the hollow of his throat, a V-shaped slice of skin visible where she'd unbuttoned his shirt. She wanted to taste it, to touch it. She wanted to feel strong and feminine and sexy and not awkward and unsure. For some reason, Brett was able to make her feel that way. He had from the moment of the first combustible kiss.

"I'm sure."

"Then, darlin', take that off for me." There was so much heat in his voice, she could swear her uterus contracted in simple anticipation.

"The dress?"

He nodded, slowly. "The dress. But you might want to leave those shoes on."

Melly swallowed. If that wasn't the sexiest thing she'd heard in a long, long time... She hoped her hands steadied as she found the fabric of her dress and eased it off her shoulders, letting the silky material puddle on the floor at her feet.

She was incredibly thankful that she'd had the foresight to wear good underwear. Her bikini panties were pale pink, with swatches of lace over the hips, and the bra matched, the plunge accentuating her cleavage. The look of bald admiration on Brett's face told her he approved.

"Your turn," she instructed.

Brett lifted first one foot and then the other, taking off his boots. Then he pulled the tails of his shirt out of his jeans and her mouth went dry as he undid the rest of the buttons, revealing a tantalizing glimpse of his chest and abs. God, he was sexy. Did he realize it? She didn't think so. There wasn't a trace of smugness on his face. Just longing—and intent.

"Come here," he said, and she took the few steps necessary to stand in front of him. She put her hands inside his shirt and touched the hard warmth of his skin, loving when a muscle ticked in his jaw. Daring, she kissed the center of his chest, then slid her mouth over to flick her tongue over a small nipple, smiling when he swore under his breath.

She put her hands at his waist, unbuckled his belt by feel alone and slid the button from the hole so that only the zip remained fastened. To her delight, Brett shrugged out of his shirt and hauled her close, the heat of his skin soft and warm against hers as they twined together.

They kissed right there at the spot where the tile entry met the soft carpet of her living room. A little squeak came from her mouth as he picked her up and carried her to the sofa. He put her down gently and then lowered himself on top of her, his strong arms braced on either side of her head and the stiff fabric of his jeans pressed against her panties. She wrapped her leg around his hip and arched up, rubbing against him as their kisses grew more fevered. He slid down a little and bit at her nipple through her bra, and she cried out as pleasure darted through her body.

Despite the urgency, Brett took his time until she was hot, pliant and so ready she thought she might lose her mind. He reached back into his pocket for his wallet and she saw him take out a foil packet before dropping the wallet on the floor.

She sat up a little, put out her hand when he would have returned to the sofa. "Not here," she said, her breath coming fast and hot. "Follow me."

She took his hand and led him to her room, stopping only to click on a bedside lamp, giving the room a soft, warm glow. It had been so long since she'd had sex, so long since she'd felt this carnal and beautiful. She wanted to see him. And she wanted him to see her. She helped him take off his jeans, stripped off her panties and then nudged him down on to the bed, taking the condom from his hand and putting it on him herself.

"Mel," he murmured.

When she lowered herself onto him, his head went back, his eyes closed, and she hesitated a moment to enjoy the sensation of him inside her. But soon the urge to move took over and she started a slow rocking that picked up pace as his hands gripped her hips.

"You feel so good." She sighed, bracing her hands on his pecs. "So good."

"God...you...too." His icy-blue gaze was on her, and he bit down on his lip when she gave her hips a sharp thrust. "God, woman..."

Crazy, that was what this was. Crazy and awesome, and she let all of her inhibitions go. She bent one knee up towards his ribs, straightened the other and levered her hips, feeling the orgasm building inside. Her hands were on the pillow on either side of his head, and as she moved he caught the tip of one breast in his mouth. That was all it took to light the fuse. Two thrusts later, her world came apart, her body shuddering over his as she cried out.

She was vaguely aware of hearing her name as Brett put one strong hand on her bottom and met her thrust for thrust.

They were a tangle of limbs and sweat and sex as they came down from their climaxes, their breath harsh and satisfied in the quiet of the bedroom.

Melly shifted, he slid out of her, and she collapsed beside him on the bed.

"Whoa," he said, a low sound of awe that made her feel sexy and accomplished and inordinately pleased with herself.

"Mmm," she replied. The cool air in the room caused little goose bumps to erupt on her damp skin.

"I need to...uh..."

She chuckled into the pillow. "Bathroom's the door on the right," she said. Funny how now that the moment was over, he was bashful. But then that was part of what she liked about him. He came across like this quiet guy, all manners and still waters, but then there was this intensity about him that hinted at the fire beneath the surface.

And so far, she'd touched the flame and hadn't been burned. She smiled to herself as he walked to the door, and she admired the rear view.

He was back moments later, his hair tousled, his skin flushed. Melly remained lying on her side on the bed, her elbow under her head, still catching her breath. Brett reached for his boxers and slipped them on before joining her on top of the bedspread.

He assumed a similar pose, propping up his head on his hand and he smiled at her. "Okay?" he asked.

"Very okay," she replied, moving her foot and sliding her toe along the side of his calf. "I don't know what it is with us. It's like we touch each other and...well, it's like lighting a match."

"I know. I hope you're not asking me to be sorry. I still feel like I'm having a slight out-of-body experience."

She laughed. "Me too. That was good, Brett. Really good."

"I don't usually move this fast. I mean, second date and all. Pretty sure my mama would flay me alive."

"You're a bit old to be worried about your mama," Melly laughed.

"Are you kidding? Obviously you haven't met mine." But he was grinning. "Seriously though. I'd be given a lecture on respecting a woman and taking my time." He frowned. "I'm not sure what I'm trying to say here, except this kind of thing isn't something I make a habit of."

Clearly, if it was true that he hadn't been with anyone since his divorce. Her heart melted a little bit at his consideration.

"I wasn't exactly taking my time either, cowboy." She ran her fingers over his ribs. "I knew the first time you kissed me that if it came to this, it would be good. Thanks for more than living up to the expectation."

His eyes glowed at her. "Damn, I like you."

"I like you too."

There was another decision to be made, and that was where to go from here. Invite him to stay? The idea of waking up with him was enticing, but it might also be too soon. So far, it had been two dates and one major release of pent-up sexual energy. Yet she didn't want him to just get up and get dressed and leave.

"You want to stay a while? We could, you know, talk or something."

"Or something?"

"Don't you need recovery time?"

He laughed then, a big, full laugh that warmed her down to her toes. She couldn't help but join in. Damn, this whole thing was surreal. Just a week ago, she'd been scared he'd be a no-show at the coffee shop. It had been slightly awkward, until he'd kissed her. That had been different. That had felt right from the start. Just like tonight.

Maybe their relationship was going to be based on sex. If that were the case, it would burn out soon enough. The idea was slightly depressing, and her laugh drifted away.

"What do you want to talk about?" he asked. And then he rolled to his back and stretched out his arm, inviting her to curl into his side.

Melly got off the bed, went to a chest at the foot and took out a soft blanket. She spread it out and then got under it and covered them both as she cuddled into his body. Mercy, he felt good. All heat and muscle and lean strength.

"How about you tell me what you've been up to?"

"Just the regular ranch work. It's not that interesting. Besides, you probably have some school stories that are more entertaining."

"A few that would curl your hair." She chuckled. "You know, I love teaching literature. And this can be such a great age. But oh my God, the hormones. The drama."

He chuckled. "I remember my sisters at that age."

"Oh, it's not just the girls." She turned her head and looked up at him. "Boys are almost as bad." She grinned. "Almost."

She sighed. "But you know, sometimes I envy them. At that age, the world is your oyster. There are no limits, only ambitions and dreams."

"And you've given up on dreams?"

"I don't know." She pursed her lips, considering. "It's not even that. It's more...I don't know. The world changes. Things that you count on that disappear."

He shifted his weight a little. "You mean your marriage?"

She supposed she did, in a way. But lately, she'd been thinking more and more about her mom and dad. They'd been her one constant through everything. Home was always home. The idea of the ranch not being a place to go home to anymore...

If only her cousin Dustin could get approval from the bank, at least it would stay in the family. But this week her mom had confessed that they'd had an offer and they were tempted.

"Mel?"

She liked how he called her Mel, not Melissa or Melly. It was like the shortened version of her name was only for him. Once more, she sighed, feeling weary. "It's my mom and dad's place. Dad's heart won't let him work it anymore, and to be honest, they can't afford to keep it. It's up for sale. And I know they've had an offer and it makes me sad."

"Of course it does. It's your home."

"Yeah. It's kind of...well, it's not just a house. It's a whole way of life, constant and secure. Only it's not. That freak storm last year? It cost Dad a quarter of the herd. Between that and his illness... But I thought it would always be there for me to go home to."

She was mortified to find her eyes had watered and her voice wobbled.

"I'm sorry."

"No, I'm sorry. I didn't mean to get emotional on you." She lifted her hand and scrubbed her eyes. "Honestly, I'm kind of mad. I don't even know who at. Circumstance, maybe. Shit, Melly Carmichael is supposed to be tougher than this."

Brett's hand had been stroking her arm, but suddenly he stilled. "Did you say Carmichael? I thought your last name was Walker."

"Walker's my married name. I never changed it back."

"And your parents live where again?"

A little bit of unease trickled through her. "Just east of Lincoln."

"Christ." Brett shifted, sat up a bit. "Not Jim and Becky Carmichael?"

She pushed herself up on the bed, clutching the edge of the blanket to her chest. "Wait. You know my parents?"

"We've met. Mel, I'm the one who put in a bid on the ranch."

She stared at him. "You? But..." God. Little things started racing through her brain. Was it all a coincidence? That out of all the girls on the dating site, he'd picked her? That he'd just happened to mention a purchase over coffee last week? She knew for a fact that her parents had turned down his offers. Three of them, to be exact, but they were weakening. He wanted the property, and he wanted it badly. The question was how far was he willing to go to get it?

Enough to use her? She scrambled off the bed, snatching the blanket and wrapping it around herself, leaving him exposed. "You need to go."

"Mel." He had the audacity to look surprised. "Look, I had no idea..."

"Really? You really didn't?" She lifted her eyebrow in a cynical arch. "Was this all part of your plan? What was the idea, get me talking and find out if my parents were softening or what it would take to get them to say yes? I'll answer that right now. Never. You are *never* going to buy our ranch."

Forget the nerve to be surprised, he was actually angry if the thin slash of his lips and furrowed brow were anything to go by.

"What exactly are you accusing me of? Sleeping with you to...what? I didn't even know who you were."

"So you say." She was naked under the blanket. *Naked.* She thought she might actually be sick. "My *sister* set up my profile. My *sister* contacted you first." She shook her head as she mimicked him. "You really expect me to believe that?"

"It's the truth. A dating site is not my speed at all. And I only agreed to meet to be polite."

Ouch. Why that actually hurt her feelings was a mystery. "Well, what a gentleman you are. You wine and dine me and get me in bed with you and during the day you're working to destroy the one thing that still matters to me."

Brett reached for his jeans and pulled them on. He shoved the rivet through the hole and glared at her. "This had nothing to do with you. It's business. I want to expand our operations and the ranch is perfect for us. I didn't even know you existed. I'm not trying to take advantage of anyone here." He rammed his shirt tails into his jeans and zipped them up. "Least of all your parents. The price I offered your folks was more than fair. More than."

"Well, aren't you just a paragon of virtue."

"You're angry," he said, straightening his shoulders. "I get it. You don't want them to sell the place. But they are going to sell it, Melly. So maybe you should take some time to decide who you're angry with. Because I don't think it's me. It's them. Or yourself. Or whatever."

She couldn't think of a single thing to say.

"I'll see myself out."

He left her standing there in the bedroom, and she heard the door shut behind him.

Chapter Five

Brett was still angry days later. Even the grueling branding weekend hadn't eased the knot in his chest.

He ran the brush over Charley's hide, putting lots of energy into it. The old horse loved every stroke, closed his eyes lazily, his skin shuddering from time to time. Brett sighed and dropped his forehead to Charley's smooth neck, just for a moment.

"Women," he breathed, then straightened and rolled his shoulders. "You're smart to steer clear, Chuck." Charley's eyes stayed closed, but he flickered his ears at the sound of Brett's voice. "I didn't even want to go on that date. And then I ended up liking her. Damn, I liked her a lot. And then she hit me right in my pride."

Charley's lashes fluttered. Brett gave another long stroke of the brush.

"I mean, I understand her being surprised. And even upset. But she insulted my character. My ethics. My manhood."

"What about your manhood?"

Manda was standing at the stall door, one shoulder resting on the frame.

His sister was not the person he wanted to see right now. "This is all your fault," he said, pointing the brush at her. "So don't bat your eyes like you're innocent and give me that wounded-girl look. That hasn't worked since we were kids."

No batting of eyes. She raised one eyebrow. "What the hell did I do now?"

"You set me up on that website, that's what." He tossed the brush into a bucket. "Of all the gin joints in all the towns in all the world..."

"What are you muttering about?"

"Melissa, that's what." He gave Charley an absent pat, picked up the bucket and headed out of the stall, passing his pregnant sister with as much indignation as he could muster. He hated that he had a soft spot where she was concerned. "Shut the door."

"What about Melissa? I thought you went out again."

He wheeled on her as she was latching the door. "The ranch I bid on? Turns out it's her parents'. And she's pissed."

Manda's eyes widened. "That's a crazy coincidence."

"Yeah. Except she doesn't think it is a coincidence. She thinks I engineered the whole thing."

"That hardly seems likely." Manda frowned.

"That's what I said." And he realized that Melissa had spoken in the heat of the moment. But it had been over a week now, and there hadn't been one single text, let alone a phone call.

It wasn't just the accusation he couldn't forget. It was the hurt look in her eyes. That he even had the power to hurt her was surprising. They hadn't known each other that long. Long enough to sleep together, he reminded himself.

"So what's the status on the bid now?" Manda's question brought him back to the present.

"There was a counter offer. I'm upping my bid."

"How long before you top out?"

His smile felt grim. "I can't go any higher," he said. "I've thought about just letting it go. But that's hardly logical, is it? I mean, someone's going to buy the place if I don't. And it's perfect for what I want."

Manda came over and put her hand on his arm. "I'm sorry, Brett. If you don't get it, there'll be another place to go up for sale that's nearby."

"I know. It's just a pretty piece of land. And with Mom and Dad and you guys sticking around here..."

"I know. You want your own place. To make your own mark."

"To expand Lazy H. There's a difference."

"Maybe your loyalty to this place is how Melissa feels about her folks' place too."

"I've thought of that. I'm not blind or stupid. But I didn't date her with an ulterior motive. Hell, you're the one who set us up."

"And if I'd known who she was, I never would have suggested it."

For all Manda's manipulations, he believed her. Because he had faith in her. Something that had been completely lacking between himself and Mel.

Then again, they'd gone on exactly two dates. How was she supposed to have faith in someone she barely knew? Chemistry, desire...that was one thing. But trust was something entirely different.

"Brett, maybe you need to talk to her again. If you argued, you both probably needed time to cool off."

"If she's cooled off and hasn't been in touch, doesn't that mean she still thinks I used her?"

Manda let out a huge sigh. "Maybe she's waiting for you to cool off and deny it. Maybe she thinks your silence indicates guilt. Until this misunderstanding, did you like each other?"

Heat crept up his neck and he turned away and walked towards the feed room to get Charley a scoop of oats. "We got along okay."

Okay, hell. Maybe he'd be less offended if he could get the picture of her on top of him out of his head for five minutes.

"Then maybe you shouldn't give up so quick."

"Manda, two dates isn't really a huge emotional investment. I'll get over it."

"Great. Then we should browse the site again—"

"No." He held up his hand. "Just no." He scooped up some oats and started back to the stall. Anything to keep his hands busy. Keep moving. Because if Manda took one look at his face, she'd figure a whole lot of stuff out. She'd always been able to read him like a book, and it drove him crazy. Having a twin was sometimes awesome but sometimes a big ol' pain in his ass.

"Well, you've turned into Crabby McCrabby Pants. Maybe you should just talk to her, instead of leaving things the way they are."

"She has my number."

Manda smacked herself in the forehead. "Will you forget your pride for two seconds? Men."

"Women," he responded. But then he couldn't help it. He smirked. And she smirked back. "All right. I'll call her or something. At least clear the air. Calmly."

"And what about the ranch?"

He shrugged. "It's exactly what I'm looking for to complement our operation, but my budget isn't limitless. I've got one more chance, but if the other party counters, I'm out."

And wouldn't that make Melissa happy. Except someone else would still be buying the property. She had to realize that the problem wouldn't go away even if he were out of the picture.

It took him two more days to work up the nerve to send her a simple text that said *"Can we talk?"* And a day after that for her to reply with a blunt, *"About what?"*

He waited until work was done for the day and his parents were inside watching the evening news. Part of the reason he was excited about the prospect of expansion was the chance to get out on his own again. Since the divorce, he'd stayed at his childhood home while his house had sold and the proceeds split between himself and Sherry. It was time. A man his age had no place worrying about a phone conversation being interrupted by his parents.

The June evening was mild, and he sat on the back porch, overlooking a hayfield that would be ready for cutting in another week or two. He dialed her number and waited. By the third ring, he assumed it was just going to go to voice mail. Instead, there was a click and her breathless voice said, "Hello?"

"Mel? It's Brett."

A beat of silence. "Hi."

She was breathing hard and he felt compelled to ask, "Is this a bad time?"

"I was out for a run."

He pictured her in short shorts and a T-shirt with her hair in a ponytail and thought she probably looked both adorable and formidable. "I can call back."

"No, it's fine." Her tone said anything but, but he hadn't expected a warm greeting.

"Listen, I just want to talk. About what happened, about what you think happened. I don't like how we left things, you know?"

She'd still been naked and wrapped in a blanket when he'd walked out of her apartment.

"You're the one who left."

"I was offended. And...hurt, to be honest. And unless I was reading things wrong, you were really upset. I'm not sure staying would have helped to clear the air much."

She sighed. "Yeah, you're probably right."

It was a start.

"Maybe we can meet up this weekend. Sunday afternoon or something," he suggested.

"I've got plans on Sunday."

She was not making this easy. And damn it, he hadn't even done anything wrong. He ran his hand over his hair, wondering what to say next, when she spoke again.

"I could stop by on Saturday. I'm driving up to Great Falls for a baby shower Saturday night."

"Saturday afternoon would be fine." He swallowed, inexplicably nervous again. What was it about this woman that got under his skin so easily? "Do you want to meet for coffee again somewhere? Or you could come here. That way you're not locked in to a specific time. I'll be here all day."

"You mean come to the Lazy H?"

"Only if you want to."

There was another long pause. "Let me think about it, okay?"

"Of course."

His excited mood deflated. Thinking about it would probably mean waiting a day or two and then cancelling, saying something had come up. But he'd tried. And he did feel better knowing he'd at least reached out to her.

"Mel?"

"What?"

"I swear I didn't know who you were. Please believe me."

"I'll be in touch," she replied, her voice tight. "Bye, Brett."

The connection clicked off in his ear and he frowned, dropping the phone into his lap as he stared out over the fields.

Two dates. It really shouldn't matter what she thought. But it did. More than he cared to admit. If nothing else happened between them, he'd at least convince her that he wasn't guilty of using her.

Mel figured she had to be ten kinds of crazy to be visiting the Lazy H after all that had happened. But she was curious. How prosperous was the ranch anyway, that he could afford to beat every offer her cousin had been able to scrounge together? Dustin had offered ten thousand more than Brett's last—her parents had told her that yesterday. And Brett hadn't countered. Maybe he was finally letting it go.

That encouraging thought was the only reason she was driving up the dirt lane leading to Brett's house. Maybe there was some hope for them after all. He'd been the one to call her. He'd invited her here. Maybe, just maybe, he'd reconsidered and was going to tell her to her face.

The Lazy H spread was huge. As Mel drove closer to the house, she saw several barns and outbuildings, long lines of fencing sectioning the rolling hills, and a big, rambling ranch house with a front porch that looked welcoming and a bit worn, in need of a fresh coat of paint. She could tell it was a much bigger operation than her family's. A couple of trucks were parked next to a long building, and she recognized Brett's as one of them.

She pulled up close to the house, next to a silver sedan that looked out of place among all the pickups, and took a breath. He said he'd be home. She'd texted for directions, but that was it. They hadn't actually spoken. Now she was nervous as hell.

The last time she'd seen him, they'd had sex. Mind-numbing, fantastic, amazing sex. And then they'd argued.

What on earth was she going to say?

She cut the engine and took a deep breath, only to have it come out in a whoosh as a woman appeared on the porch. A pregnant woman, she noticed, and one who looked a lot like Brett. Her hair was darker, but the face shape was the same, and so was the mouth. Was this his twin sister, Manda? The one he claimed had set them up?

Maybe this was her chance to go directly to the source for the truth.

Melly pasted on her best meet-the-parents smile and got out of the car. "Hi there," she called, keeping her tone light and pleasant. "I'm Melissa. I'm looking for Brett?"

The woman came down the steps, matching Melly's polite smile with one of her own—but Melly saw that it didn't reach the woman's eyes.

"I'm Manda, Brett's twin sister."

Melly fought back the butterflies in her stomach. "I thought so. You look a lot alike." She would be friendly. It was hardly her first awkward conversation.

"Brett's down in the barn. I can let him know you're here or take you there."

"Whatever's most convenient," Melly replied.

"The barn it is," Manda said, and started to walk across the grass towards the outbuildings.

Melly moved to catch up. "Listen, Manda—"

Manda shrugged. "If you're going to ask, the answer is yes. Yes, I set up his profile and answered your emails. Brett didn't *target* you because of your folks' ranch. He's mighty put out that you thought he'd do something like that."

Wow, talk about not pulling any punches. Forget polite chit chat then. "Did you?" She asked the question bluntly.

"Did I what?" Manda stopped and faced her, her eyebrows pulled together in what appeared to be confusion.

"Did you know?"

Manda stared at her for several seconds, but Melly held the gaze steadily even though her insides were quaking.

"No," Manda said finally. "Melissa, you need to remember there aren't even any last names on the site, so how would I go about doing that anyway?" Her frown deepened. "He could ask the same of you, you know."

"What do you mean?"

"I mean, it's just as plausible that you knew he was trying to buy your folks' place and you hooked up with him to change his mind."

A mix of fury and embarrassment flooded through her. She wanted to ask how dare Manda suggest such a thing but couldn't, because it was exactly what she'd accused Brett of. Her cheeks flamed hot and she looked away for a moment.

"You're right. I never thought of it that way. It's just...it seemed like too much of a coincidence."

"Hey, I don't know you, so I'm going to go out on a limb here and say I'm guessing that someone, at some point, gave you a reason to be cynical. I know my brother, Melissa. He's a standup guy who would never do anything sly or underhanded. He honestly didn't know."

Melly looked back at Manda and sighed. "I want to believe you. I do. That's why I'm here."

"Give him a chance." Manda looked like she was going to say something else, but at that moment Melly's attention was diverted over Manda's shoulder as Brett stepped out of the barn. Her heart gave a solid thump in response to his appearance. He looked good. Better than good even in a work shirt and jeans and boots. And when he saw her, he halted. The same current that had run between them that first day at the café zinged to life.

Manda followed Melly's gaze and sighed.

"So that's how it is. The two of you are idiots, you know." But there was warmth in the words that had been absent before.

"Sorry?" Melly asked, dragging her gaze away.

"Nothing." Manda started back toward the house. "See you around, Melly."

Brett started walking in her direction, each step strong and deliberate. There was no denying the physical attraction, and between that and Manda's claim of innocence about the situation, Melly was a mess of emotion. She wanted to believe him. And she was terrified it made her weak—and a fool.

"You came," he said, stopping several feet away. "I wasn't sure you would."

"I wasn't either. Not until I actually turned up the lane." She tried a smile. "I met your sister."

"And survived." He grinned at her and a little of the awkwardness dissipated.

"She came to your defense in no uncertain terms," Melly admitted. "And said something that made me think. It's hard for me to believe in coincidences, Brett. It makes me feel naïve and gullible."

"And after your ex, you don't want to feel that way again."

"Yes." She let out a huge breath. He got it. He understood without her having to explain in depth. This was why things had clicked so easily before. And yet there was a little part of her that simply didn't trust it. Or him.

"But you believe me now? That I honestly didn't know of the connection?"

She nodded. "Yes." Their eyes met. "Brett, I think I knew deep down the moment you went out the door. It was just easier than admitting the real truth to myself."

"The real truth?"

"It was easier to blame you than to admit that I reacted as I did because I'm probably not ready to be seeing anyone. I wanted to think I'd moved on. Moved past my anger and my...well, disillusionment is probably as good a word as any."

Brett's smile softened. "Looking in the mirror isn't easy on the best of days. You're here now. That's what matters."

There was a quiet pause as they let everything settle. Then Brett smiled at her and said, "So what do you say? Would you like the nickel tour? We could saddle up a couple of the horses and go for a ride."

It sounded lovely. A warm breeze was ruffling the leaves on the trees and she had a couple of hours to spare. "I haven't gone riding in a while. That sounds fun."

"Perfect. Come with me. I have the perfect horse for you. His name is Charley and he has a soft spot for pretty girls."

Chapter Six

She'd really come.

Brett glanced beside him, admiring her straight and tall form in the saddle. She'd taken to Charley right away, but then the old gelding had always been a charmer. Brett had watched her hands as they rubbed Charley's neck, heard the soothing sound of her voice as she spoke to the horse while she slipped the bridle over his ears and the bit into his mouth. Despite Brett's best intentions, he hadn't been able to stop himself from comparing her to Sherry. To his recollection, Sherry had never saddled a horse in her life. She'd gone riding now and again when Brett pressed her to do so, but he'd always had to tack the horses so that all she had to do was hop into the saddle.

Melly did it all like she'd been doing it for her whole life...which she probably had.

They rode silently for several minutes. Brett liked that he didn't feel the need to make conversation. There didn't seem to be any awkwardness in the quiet. It wasn't until they were out of sight of the yard and starting an incline that Melly nudged Charlie closer and started speaking.

"This is really beautiful," Melly commented. "But Lazy H is bigger than I expected. You downplayed it a little when we met."

"There are a lot bigger ranches in the area," he replied modestly. "Between my sisters and their spouses, and my mom and dad...well, I've wanted to strike out on my own for a while now."

"Leave Lazy H behind?"

"Naw." He smiled, took a deep breath of air scented with grass and sunshine. "I still want to be part of Lazy H. Mine will be more of a satellite ranch. I think it'll work really well for everyone involved."

"Won't you miss it here?"

He nodded. "Of course. I grew up here." The horses plodded along, following a path that climbed a rise. "Melly, I understand your attachment to your ranch. I really do. It's why I suggested riding today. I want to show you something."

"You do?"

"Just over this knoll." He pointed with his left hand. "Come on."

He nudged his horse into a trot and heard Charley's hooves following close behind. In no time, he'd reached the crest. The valley spread wide below him, a palette of greens and golden browns of pasture and grain fields, stretching out for miles. A few other ranches could be seen, their buildings dotted in groups in the distance.

Melly came up beside him and reined in, patting Charley on the neck. "Wow. Look at it up here. What a view."

"It's my favorite spot on the ranch," Brett admitted. "Whenever I was troubled or needed to get some perspective, I'd come up here for some peace and quiet. It always made me feel a bit better. Like I was part of something bigger than myself. Like I was connected to something even when I felt alone."

He felt a little silly admitting that to her, but this might be his only chance. She believed he hadn't had an ulterior motive, but that was a far cry from making things right. Starting over. And he wanted to, he discovered. Yeah, he'd been angry at what she'd said. But if he'd been in her shoes, he might have thought the same thing.

He watched her dismount and hold Charley's reins as she walked along the narrow dirt trail, worn from years of travel. Lord, she was beautiful. The way she was looking at the valley right now did something to his heart he hadn't expected. It was healing, he realized. Realizing that someone else could have the same attachment and love for his way of life rather than disparaging it. It was very different having someone care for him because of it rather than despite it.

He also dismounted, and together they walked along the ridge, the warm breeze ruffling his hair and the sun soaking into his face.

How would he feel if someone wanted to take this away from him? Angry. Sad. Helpless.

"Mel?"

She turned her head to look at him. Their steps had grown lazy, and he fought the urge to simply pull her into a hug. There was something in her expression that bothered him. She looked like she appreciated this place, but there was sadness, or maybe resignation too, that dulled her eyes and kept her lips from curving up as he liked.

"I'm sorry," he said quietly.

"For what?" She raised one eyebrow, then broke eye contact and dropped her gaze to the path at her feet.

He reached out and put his hand on her arm. "For circumstances. That your dad isn't up to running the ranch. That you feel like you're going to lose the special places close to your heart."

"I wouldn't if you'd let my cousin buy it instead. It would stay in the family."

He sighed. "Mel, it's not that simple. This is something I've wanted for a long time. I've dreamed of having my own place for as long as I can remember. I know why you're asking it, but you have to realize that for me...you're asking me to give up my dream. It's not an easy thing to do."

"Particularly because we've only been on a couple of dates?" She moved her arm away from his hand. "If you'd never met me..."

"I'd be pretty focused on closing the deal." He let out a breath of frustration. "It's business."

"It's never just business. Not to people like you and me, Brett." Her voice was sharp. "There's a connection that goes from your boots to the earth. You know that."

It burned that she was right. And the one thing he really, really liked about her—that understanding of his way of life—was the one thing that made this whole mess worse.

"After my divorce, I swore if I ever got involved with a woman, it would be with someone who was Sherry's opposite. And now here you are and it's more complicated than ever."

"Would you call us involved?"

"Hell, yes." The question irritated, and he reached out and grabbed Charley's reins, tucking them into his palm alongside the other set. Melly faced him and he saw the defiant set to her mouth, recognized it. Even though he'd known her such a short time, he knew it was the I-must-stand-my-ground expression—but it also meant that she needed to remind herself to hold steady. And he did like a challenge. "Wouldn't you say sleeping together constitutes involved?"

She blushed.

"Mel," he said, his voice slightly lower. He let go of the reins, let them drop to the ground. The horses wouldn't go anywhere, and he wanted both his hands free. He took a step closer to her, saw her pupils widen and her lips drop open just the tiniest bit in surprise, in invitation.

He reached out and gripped her upper arms in his hands. "Doesn't making love mean we're involved?"

Her lips closed. She swallowed, met his gaze and lifted her chin. "Only if it meant something."

Minx. “If it meant nothing, you wouldn’t have been so upset afterwards,” he replied. And he pulled her closer and kissed her.

She was as sweet as he remembered, sweet and sultry as her mouth opened beneath his. There was no denying the chemistry between them as he let go of one of her arms and moved his hand to her neck, losing it in the thick mass of her soft hair.

She wrapped her arms around his ribs, holding him close, and she made a soft sound in her throat as the kiss took on a life of its own, as wild and free as the waves of grass around them.

He thought briefly about laying her down and making love to her then and there, with the sun warming their skin and the verdant scent of grass and earth surrounding them, but he wasn’t prepared. Neither did he want it to be rushed. He wanted to take his time, let them savor each other, maybe on a soft bed with the whole night ahead of them. He gentled the kiss even though his body was raging. “Do you have to go to Great Falls?” he asked hoarsely. “Stay here. Spend the weekend with me.”

“With your parents? Really?” She laughed, a breathy, sexy sound that went straight to his groin.

“We’ll take off for the night. Get a hotel room. Take a bath with bubbles, make love all night long. It was so good the first time, Mel. I want to try again.”

“As enticing as that is, I need to go.” She stayed in the circle of his arms though, which he took as a good sign. “It’s a shower for a good friend. I can’t miss it.”

“Well, damn.” He trailed his lips down her cheek. “Are you sure?”

“It’s tempting, Brett.” She turned her head a little and her lips touched his again. This time, the kiss was less heated but no less devastating. Long, deep, lingering.

Melly pulled away, but he got the sense she was doing so reluctantly as she nibbled on her lower lip and looked up at him, her eyes dazed. "There's no denying we do that well, is there?"

"None."

"I wish we didn't. How can I want to be with you so much and be angry with you at the same time?" Her eyes were clouded with confusion. "You're still the man who's going to take away the one thing that means the world to my family."

"And you feel like a traitor?" He kept a firm grip on his irritation. He didn't want to lose his cool like he had back at her apartment. But he did want her to understand that he wasn't trying to destroy anything.

"I feel like a hypocrite, that's for sure." She turned away and reached for Charley's reins. "I can't get past it, Brett. If you'd just leave things be, Dustin could buy it and it'd stay in the family."

"And could the Almighty Dustin manage it was well as I can? Will he build on what's there? How do you know it'll be in better hands than mine?"

She scowled at his cocky words. Damn, he'd spoken without completely thinking it through again, and sounded so arrogant in the process. Still, he wasn't doing a thing wrong, and he was sorry he'd told her his plans. All she'd done was ride his ass about it. Maybe this wasn't worth it after all. He'd enjoyed himself with her, but it was just like he'd told Manda. Women were not worth the headache, no matter how sweet and alluring.

"How do I know?" she asked, her words clipped. "Because he's family."

"And that is a loyal but naïve answer," he replied.

"You know, a few minutes ago, I was hoping we could work something out, but I guess not." She put her hand on the saddle horn and swung herself into the saddle. "I've already been with someone whose arrogance and pride came before our relationship. I won't do that again."

"You think this is arrogance and pride? Which one of us is being arrogant here?" He snatched the reins left trailing on the ground and mounted his horse with a creak of saddle leather. "You've insulted me, judged me, asked me to give up, and the only thing I've expected is, well, some understanding of my position. Newsflash, Mel. You can't stop change from happening. If you're that attached to the place, maybe you should have stuck around and worked it yourself."

He dug his heels into the horse and shot forward, cantering back down the path they'd come. She could find her own way behind him for all he cared. Charley would get her home. His teeth were clenched together and posture ram-rod straight as the benevolent sun warmed his back. They had chemistry. He was in no doubt of that. And they had some things in common too. But Brett was starting to realize that there were things missing. Like basic respect, for one.

She'd said she wouldn't repeat past mistakes again. Well, neither would he. The first time he'd chosen wrong, he'd nearly lost Lazy H. He'd be damned if he'd risk this deal, too.

Melly blinked against the stinging in her eyes. Her mouth still hung open from the shock of his last comment. He couldn't have aimed that stab to her heart any better.

She gave Charley a half-hearted nudge and he began to plod his way back down the hill. Melly could see Brett in the distance, his horse taking him farther away with each long, smooth stride.

How many times had she regretted the path she'd taken? She might have stayed home and taken over the ranch as any son would have. But at eighteen, she'd rebelled. She'd wanted to get away. Get her education, be something different. In hindsight, she'd taken her home for granted, thinking it would always be there.

At twenty-one, she'd considered it again. But then she'd met James and everything had changed. She liked her job too. It wasn't that. But there were times she wished she'd done things differently. That she hadn't been so determined to be something or someone she wasn't.

She let Charley walk, plodding his way through the waving grass. Something else was bothering her too. As much as she liked her cousin Dustin, he was the kind of guy to keep things at the status quo rather than innovate. Under his ownership, the ranch would likely prosper, but it probably wouldn't flourish or live up to its true potential. If Lazy H was anything to go by, Brett could do great things with her family's property. It burned her ass to admit it, but it was true.

She had been arrogant. And prideful. It smarted that he knew it.

When she got back to the barn, Brett was waiting to take Charley. She was surprised at that. She'd figured he'd be nowhere to be seen. But of course, despite his outburst and riding away, Brett had manners. He was a gentleman. Both times when she'd been rude and judgmental, he'd been the first one to reach out.

This time though, his face was a mask of cold politeness as he held Charley's bridle and waited for her to dismount. She hopped down and gave Charley's neck a pat. The earlier silence had been comfortable, but now it was awkward as anything.

"I'd better get going. I still have to drive to Great Falls and get cleaned up before the shower."

"I'll put Charley up. Thanks for coming, Mel."

But his words held little warmth. They were a show of manners, nothing more. It was getting clearer by the second that he'd wanted to bring her around to his way of thinking...and she'd been trying to do the same and they were simply at an impasse.

Any romance was doomed from the start. It was time they faced facts. Some raging libido couldn't make up for all the other problems. They were bound to be on different sides.

"Thanks for showing me around," she replied, suddenly dreading driving away. He wouldn't be calling her again. She knew that as sure as she knew the sky was blue.

She might have said something more, but he was already walking away, leading Charley to the barn. She watched for a few seconds, the way the back pockets of his jeans shifted as he walked away, the straight line of his strong back.

He didn't look back.

Melly sighed and then made her way across the yard to her car. When she drove away, she kept looking in the rearview mirror to see if he was watching. He wasn't. Today's conversation had completely killed any chance they might have had. He wasn't *the one*. Even though at times she'd thought he could be. It just went to show that ticking all the right boxes didn't mean a damn thing.

Not a damn thing at all.

Chapter Seven

Melly's hand shook as she put down the phone.

It was done then. Brett had outbid Dustin, who'd maxed out his approved financing on his last bid. Before the end of the summer, Brett would take possession of their ranch. Angry tears streaked down her cheeks now that the conversation was over. Not just angry at Brett, but at her parents too. They could have accepted a lower offer and kept it in the family, and they'd chosen not to.

At the bridal shower, her friends had laughingly come up with a solution to all her problems. If she married Brett, she'd get to keep the ranch anyway. So what was the problem? He was good looking and they had chemistry...there were worse things.

But she'd already been in a marriage based on a lie. There was no way she could do that again. And she hardly knew Brett well enough to know if she could ever love him. She wasn't so gullible as to believe that lust and love were the same thing.

She flopped down on her bed and stared at the ceiling. It wasn't fair. If this were a book or a movie, the ranch would be saved and the girl would get the guy and it would all work out. Instead, neither of those things had happened. And she was right back where she started. Alone.

Disgusted, she got up from the bed and went to the kitchen, where her laptop sat on the counter. In moments, she'd booted up and logged on to NotMy1stRodeo.com. Two new hat tips waited for her acknowledgment. Instead, she went to her dashboard and looked at her messages. There was Brett's picture, so handsome and yet a pale likeness to the man she'd met. The photo didn't capture the power of his smile or the heat of his touch. Neither did it touch on the spark of anger in his eyes when he was wronged. And in some ways, she had wronged him. The kicker was she admired him for his perseverance to his goals, the strength of his resolve. She wished her ex-husband had demonstrated more of that strength rather than weakness. And she wished Brett's resolve could have been aimed somewhere other than at her parents' ranch. It was like he said. They both thought they knew what they needed from a partner, but when they got what they wanted, things were more complicated than ever.

Her heart was heavy and there was a lump in her throat as she hit a button that said *delete profile*. When it asked for confirmation, she gave it...and then she was gone. Gone from the site. Enough of online dating for her.

It was time she moved on. From everything and got a fresh start.

Brett hopped out of the truck and smiled at the couple waiting at the bottom of the steps. "Jim. Becky."

"Hello, Brett."

Jim held out a hand and Brett shook it. Over the past month, he'd gotten to know the Carmichaels better, and he liked them. A lot. Having new surveys done and changing the purchase agreement had taken the lawyers some time, but it was all settled now the way they wanted it. Brett was more than satisfied with how it had turned out, and he had Manda to thank once again. It had been her idea to separate the house from the rest of the ranch, enabling Jim and Becky to remain in their home. So Brett had given them the option, knowing that it might be too difficult for them to watch someone else ranch the land.

But they'd accepted, gratefully.

"Coffee's on," Becky said, smiling up at him. "Why don't you come in?"

"Just for a minute," he answered. "I really just came by to pick up the keys to the buildings and barns."

He followed them up the steps while Jim lamented the old days. "Used to be we didn't have to lock our doors around here."

"I know," Brett replied. "For a long time, you just needed a good guard dog. Now it's locks and security cameras."

He sat down at the kitchen table while Becky got coffee from a pot. The house was comfortable and plain, a regular farmhouse much like the one he'd grown up in. The coffee was joined by a plate of cookies and they all sat around the oak table.

"I just wanted to let you know that starting tomorrow, the construction crews will be at the building site." Brett took a sip of coffee. "Hopefully, they won't cause too big of a disturbance."

"It's your place now, Brett. I think you chose a good spot for the house." Jim reached for a cookie.

"Well, it just made sense. I want my own home, and it didn't make sense for you to have to leave if you wanted to stay. It'd be a hard thing to say goodbye to, I think."

"Our daughter certainly thinks so." Jim's face fell a little. "She's very angry with us for selling to you."

"Because you could have sold to Dustin?"

Jim's gaze snapped to Brett's. "You knew about Dustin?"

"I knew more than that, sir." Nerves tangled in his stomach. It wasn't about the deal. They'd agreed to that ages ago. It was Mel. Always Mel. After several weeks, he should be able to leave her behind, but he somehow couldn't.

He put down his cup. "Mel didn't tell you, did she?"

"Melly? What does she have to do with this?"

Wow. Brett had actually been surprised when the Carmichaels had accepted his offer. He figured Mel would have gone to them and pleaded her case, told them everything in an effort to change their minds.

"We met back in May, but I didn't know who she was. She still goes by Walker—"

"Yes, we know," Becky said a little sharply. Brett wasn't sure if that was aimed at him, or due to dislike of the ex.

"It wasn't until we'd seen each other a few times that the pieces came together and she realized it was me who was trying to buy the ranch. She was really mad at me for that, but we'd only been seeing each other briefly and, well..." Brett's face heated. "Truth is, I'm also divorced. This was a big decision, and not one I was willing to let be influenced by a relationship that was so new and uncertain."

"I see."

Brett met Jim's gaze full-on. "Sir, I made it clear to Mel that I didn't know who she was before we went out, and I think she believes that now. But she's still put out that I didn't step aside."

"Is that why you suggested splitting the property?" Becky asked softly.

"Only partly." More than he wanted to admit, if truth be told. He couldn't deny he'd felt better knowing that Mel would still have a place to come home to like she wanted. "I really do want to build my own house," he continued. "But Mel made me think. There is a special connection between a rancher and the land. I know this place means a lot to you, and to her, and so I offered the split if you wanted it. I promise you the operation is in good hands. This way we all get what we want in the end, right?"

There was quiet in the kitchen for a moment. "She doesn't know about the split." Becky's words came out on a sigh. "We were going to tell her, but she decided to go away for a while over her summer break. She's always wanted to go to California and drive up the coast, and I think she chose this summer because she didn't want to be here to see the ranch change hands."

"She probably didn't want to see me either," Brett admitted. "She wasn't very happy with me the last time we saw each other."

"She doesn't know you did this for her, then."

"Did what for me?"

Mel's voice broke through the conversation and the three of them swiveled in their chairs to face her.

"I didn't hear you come in, dear," Becky said, but Mel's gaze was glued to Brett's.

She was so pretty. Her hair was back in a ponytail and her face was tanned, highlighting a few freckles on the bridge of her nose. She was dressed for the heat, in denim shorts and a blue T-shirt and sandals. It made her look about twenty years old.

"Melissa," he said, embarrassed when her full name came out on a croak. She could still make him so nervous.

"Brett."

The word was so cold he was surprised it didn't freeze midair, despite the summer heat.

"Brett's taking possession today," Jim said quietly. "We were just talking things over."

"How long has he given you to pack and get out? Do you know where you're going to live?"

"You might have known these things if you'd stuck around," Becky reminded her, a sharpness to her voice that said she wasn't happy with Melissa's tone.

"It's why I came back."

"No one is going anywhere," Brett announced, impatient. "And I'll explain why, if you'll sit down."

"Another explanation? Each time you give me one of those, Brett, the results are the same. You on our ranch."

"My ranch," he corrected calmly. "Melissa, sit down."

"I don't think—"

"Sit down," he repeated firmly.

A mutinous set to her lips, she pulled out a chair and sat.

He focused on her. Not on her father or her mother, just her. He wasn't sure he wanted an audience right now, but things needed to be said and he was going to say them. It might be the only time she'd listen.

"I did some thinking after we last saw each other," he began. "And I talked to Manda too. She knows me best out of all my family. I think it's a twin thing." He smiled a little. Sometimes having a twin was a pain in the ass, but sometimes it was handy. "She knows better than anyone what I went through when my marriage ended. I was left feeling like I was nothing more than a hick with a pitchfork. Sherry had...I don't know, some image of how glamorous life as a rancher would be. Like all the dirty work would be done by the hands and I'd strut around in clean boots and big belt buckles with her on my arm. When she left, in my head I knew she'd simply not been prepared for life on a ranch. I knew that she hadn't really loved the person I was, just the person she wanted me to be. But I think you know as well as I do that the heart can be harder to convince. I felt like less of a man, and it's taken me a long time to want to put myself in that position again."

"Believe me, your manhood has never been an issue."

Brett's face heated a little and he wondered if the blush was noticeable.

Mel's expression had softened a little. "Look, I know I haven't always been fair. It's got a lot more to do with me than it does with you, and in the end it still hurts that the ranch has been sold. Family should come first." Her gaze flitted over her parents. "I would have thought you'd feel the same way. We could have kept it in the family—"

"I like Dustin," Jim spoke up. "He's a good kid. But I'm not sure he's ready to take this on. Both from a work perspective, and from the financial burden. He's got a wife and kids to think about."

Brett leaned over and put his hand over her fingers. "Mel, I always had the best of intentions. I did think about walking away from the deal, you know. But I'd worked for this for so long, and I don't trust easily. How could I logically walk away from it because we'd been out on a few dates?"

"I had started to feel it was more than that," she admitted softly.

"Me too," he agreed, his voice quiet. "But I didn't trust what was between us. It just kept snowballing into a bigger mess. And then, when you walked away, I came up with a compromise."

Her gaze met his, and he could see a little bit of hope there. Just a brief moment, but there was a flash of uncertainty that encouraged him.

"You want to be able to come home," he said, squeezing her fingers. "I understand completely. You want to know that one thing in your life is a constant. I wanted to buy the ranch, but not your life. Not your parents' lives either. So we had everything re-surveyed and another purchase agreement drawn up. The house and two acres around it still belong to your mom and dad. They can live here as long as they like. And your dad has agreed that if they ever want to sell and move somewhere smaller, you get first crack at the property. I get the second."

Her eyes grew round. "But...where will you live?"

"I'm building my own house south of here. I'm not the enemy, Mel. I promise you, I'm not."

She pulled her hand away and her eyes filled with tears. "I don't know what to say."

"Sweetheart," Becky jumped into the conversation. "We know how hard the last few years have been for you. This wasn't an easy decision for any of us, and we never wanted you to feel like you were, well, displaced. No matter where we are, you can still come home, okay?"

Mel nodded. "I'm still sad. I hate that things have to change."

Brett laughed a little, but it was thick with emotion. "Oh, I know. But sometimes change can be a good thing. Sometimes a person can resist it all they want, and then they get a boot in their ass and end up going for coffee."

Jim and Becky looked confused, but he knew Mel understood, and her lower lip wobbled just a bit. "You should hate me for being such a spoiled brat," she murmured, looking down at her lap.

"Not spoiled. Just scared. And I could never hate you."

The kitchen was silent. He wished they were alone but he was also glad somehow that the four of them had sat in a room together and talked. Still, there were things he wanted to say without an audience. Things that had little to do with the ranch.

"Mel, let's take a walk."

Mel looked up at him then, and the old chemistry was there, simmering behind her eyes, heavy in the air between them.

Maybe what was between them couldn't be fixed.

But he'd like to have a chance to try. And if it was really over, they could leave it in a better place, without anger and resentment.

Chapter Eight

Melly didn't know what to say. She'd agreed to take a walk, partly because she wanted to hear what he had to say and partly because she really needed a few minutes to get her head in the right space.

The past month, as she and Leanne had traveled the coast, she'd done a lot of thinking. She'd thought about the ranch, about her family, about Brett, and about letting go. She'd come to terms with it for herself, but the idea of her parents leaving the place they'd lived for over thirty years broke her heart. They'd invested so much time and energy and love into the place to just up and leave.

Walking in and seeing Brett sitting at the kitchen table? Her reaction had been so instantaneous, so unexpected that she'd immediately thrown up barriers in the form of hostility. But it wasn't her anger at Brett that had resurfaced. She might have been able to deal with that. It was something else. It was attraction and longing that had slammed into her like a freight train, stealing her breath. After everything, he still had the power to turn her to mush—and all without saying a word.

Finding out he'd made provisions for her parents to stay meant more than she could say. But she had to try. She already owed him an apology. Knowing he'd taken this step simply blew her mind.

Melly knew where she needed to take him. They followed a path behind the house, through the grove of trees to a meadow, and then through more woods until they came to a narrow creek burbling over the rocks and stones.

"It's peaceful in here," Brett commented, letting out a big breath. "I've seen the whole ranch, but I never knew this was here."

"I kept it a secret," she said softly, picking her way down over the bank to the water. There was a spot part way down where the dirt had eroded away from a thick tree root, and it formed a natural seat about four feet wide. Melly eased herself into it and patted the hard earth beside her. "Come sit on my sofa," she invited.

He did, stretching out his long legs. The air was cool in the shade of the trees and the sound of the trickling water was soothing.

"You know your big view back at the Lazy H? This is that place for me." She turned her head and looked at his profile. "I used to come here to ease my tension and stress. It was a busy spot during my teenage years."

He chuckled, the sound low and warm.

"Brett, I'm sorry. What you're doing for my parents...well, I'm not sure Dustin would have done the same." It pained her to admit it, but it was true. Dustin had a family. He would have moved into the house and not thought twice about it. Which would have been his right. Maybe that was what made Brett's compromise that much more amazing.

"It was Manda's idea," he replied, staring at the stream. "Turns out she has some good ones now and again."

"That's generous of you to say. I mean, our first few dates were good up until...well, you know. Until it all blew up. I did a lot of thinking this summer, and I realized my whole perspective was clouded by fear and emotion. It was unfair of me to blame you for everything, or to expect you to change your plans. It had far more to do with feelings I hadn't dealt with yet."

"About James."

"Yeah." She sighed. "I thought I had, but having feelings for someone again, and then finding out you were the one trying to buy the ranch...I thought it was you I didn't trust. Turns out it was my own judgment."

He turned a little, though the seat afforded minimal room. His knee bumped against hers as he looked into her eyes. "You weren't the only one who was stubborn. I considered withdrawing my offer. The fact that it even crossed my mind scared the hell out of me. I felt like you wanted me to change who I was, and I'd already had to do that before, only it failed miserably. Maybe neither of us was ready to enter the dating game again."

Did that mean he wasn't interested now? Not that she deserved another chance after all she'd said.

"The thing is..." Her tongue felt thick in her mouth as she fumbled around for words. "The whole time I was gone, I couldn't stop thinking about you. I thought I'd go away and shake this whole thing off, come back, make a fresh start. Instead, I found you at my parents' kitchen table and everything came rushing back and..." She looked away, embarrassed. "Well."

"What are you saying?" he asked.

She took a deep breath. "Not that I'd deserve it, but I'd like to give us another chance."

That little sideways smile teased his lips. She'd missed that.

"Like go out on a date?"

"Maybe." She looked into his eyes, found warmth and invitation there. "Maybe just take things one day at a time and see where it goes."

He lifted his hand and placed it on the side of her cheek. "You keep saying you don't deserve a second chance. But, Mel, one of the things I did after you left was try to put myself in your shoes. I get it. All of our actions are colored by our past experiences." He smiled, bigger now. "Hey, just because you were wrong about me doesn't mean I don't understand where you were coming from."

She rolled her eyes, amazed that they were actually teasing about this. "I see your ego didn't suffer any permanent damage." She put her hand over his. "Aw, hell, you have to know I'm kidding. You probably have the least ego of anyone I've ever met."

He moved his thumb, rubbing against the tender skin of her cheek, the teasing expression gone from his face. Just tenderness remained, and her heart did a crazy weird thump thing. The sun created dappled shadows around them, the birds in the trees and the rushing stream their background music. And when Brett leaned forward and kissed her this time, she met him halfway, curling her hand around his neck and drawing him closer.

This kiss was different, Melly realized. Better. One hundred times better. There was still sweetness and passion, but now there was something more. Trust. Acceptance. Possibility. All the things she'd wanted and had been searching for.

And when he pulled her into his embrace and wrapped his arms around her, she figured that maybe she'd been right after all. Maybe there really was nothing like a cowboy.

Chapter Nine

The leaves on the poplars and birches were like millions of gold coins, glowing against the blue sky and creating a gilded carpet on the forest floor.

Brett held Mel's cold hand in his as they ambled through the grove, something they often did on Sunday afternoons when she came out to the ranch. Her favorite spot had now become his too. They often sat on the creek bank and cuddled together, isolated from the outside world. The last time they'd come out here, they'd made love under the canopy of the trees. It had been the first time since they'd decided to start over. For Brett, it had been something particularly precious. It hadn't been the rushed and fevered joining that they'd experienced at the beginning of their relationship. It had been slow and profound. It had stirred something inside him that he welcomed and yet scared him too. He'd fallen in love with her, heart and soul.

"What are you thinking?" Mel asked, nudging his shoulder as they walked. "You're awfully quiet."

"I was thinking about the last time we walked out here," he replied, squeezing her hand.

"Oh, right." She looked up at him and her eyes twinkled at him. "Listen, cowboy, it's getting a little chilly to be sneaking off to have sex in the great outdoors."

"I can think of ways to keep you warm."

"I just bet you can."

He could hear the trickle of the creek ahead, but he slowed his steps, nervous but in a good sort of way. Today was the right time. He wanted to take things to the next step.

So he tugged on her hand, pulling her off the dirt path. The light in her eyes told him that sneaking kisses would be a welcome pastime, so he indulged her by pressing her against a smooth birch trunk and tasting her lips, slowly and thoroughly. As always, her gentle touch made his body spring to life, and before long they were both breathless.

"You're very good at that," Mel whispered, snuggling close against his jacket. "I missed you this week."

"I missed you too." He'd rented a room with a kitchenette at a local motel while the house was being built, and it was damned lonely at night. "Our phone calls just aren't the same as seeing you in person."

"Hey, I showed you how to chat on your laptop."

"Didn't the dating site thing convince you I'm a techno-idiot?"

She laughed. "Maybe you just need to be properly motivated. I'll have to make the view...interesting."

"Tease."

But he loved it. Ever since they'd cleared the air, she'd been so open, so amazing. It wasn't perfect; nothing ever was, and they both knew it. It was, however, a real revelation to be so compatible with someone. They liked and appreciated so many of the same things. She embraced his way of life because she'd lived it and loved it herself, and he'd never experienced that sort of acceptance before. In return, he loved that she preferred these afternoon walks to other more sophisticated activities, where he felt out of place. He was learning that as a teacher she was big on organization, and he was more of a go-with-the-flow kind of guy. But Brett figured that just balanced them out a bit and kept things from being boring.

"Mel?"

"Yes?" She'd stuck her hands in his jacket pockets and was grinning up at him cheekily.

"I love you."

The smile slid from her face, replaced by a look of surprise and what he hoped was wonderment. "Brett," she whispered. "I...wow." Her dark eyes were wide and luminous as she looked up at him. "You...when did this happen? How?"

It wasn't quite the response he was hoping for, but he pressed on anyway. "It snuck up on me, I guess. But last weekend, I knew. When we were together it was...different. Suddenly, it wasn't just me and you anymore, but us."

He cradled her face in his hands. "I don't know how to explain it, other than to say that when I was inside you, something clicked. Fell into place. Like turning on a light in a dark room, you know? It had been coming for a while, but that was the moment that I knew without a doubt that I was in love with you."

She swallowed and her eyes glistened with emotion. "I love you too."

He let out a breath. "Thank God."

Their soft laughter floated away on the air. "When did you know?" he asked.

She stood on tiptoe and kissed his cheek. "So remember the Friday night I showed up and you had the bouquet of daisies that you'd picked? That was the clincher for me. No one has ever picked me flowers before. I remember thinking that this was the sort of man I should have been with all along. If I'd had any hesitation, it was gone after that moment."

"And you didn't say anything?" He'd been tormenting himself all week and she'd already been there?

"I didn't want to be the one to say it first," she admitted, blinking, her lips curving in a sweet smile. "Besides, I thought all you cowboys liked to take the initiative."

He tilted her chin, gazed into her eyes. "Not about everything, minx."

"Hey, guess what?"

"What?"

"I love you."

He couldn't stop smiling. Manda was near impossible these days, crowing about her success as a matchmaker, but he let her because he was happy. For the first time in as long as he could remember, he was perfectly content. He was working his own place, had a woman he loved, and the future was looking at lot brighter than it had a few short months ago.

"I can't wait for the house to be finished," he said, sliding his hands down to her shoulders. "When it is, I'm going to carry you up to the bedroom and make love to you all weekend."

"Mmm. Sounds lovely. Any ETA on that?"

"Contractor says three, maybe four weeks."

"That's a long time."

"Tell me about it."

They started walking back towards the path, their boots making shushing sounds in the leaves.

"Mel?"

"Yes?"

He took a breath and said the other thing that had been on his mind for a while now. "I wish you didn't live so far away."

She laughed. "It's only an hour."

"I know. I miss you during the week, that's all. I know that you have work and then prep and marking and all."

This time she was the one to tug on his hand, halting their progress. "Well, I've been doing some thinking about that myself."

"You have?"

She nodded. Her cheeks were pink from the autumn air, and he was certain that even without any makeup she was the most beautiful woman he'd ever met. Lord, was he getting sappy or what?

"I was thinking about looking for a teaching position a little closer for next year. I mean, I don't want to assume anything, but...well, I'd be closer to my mom and dad. And as far as you and me..."

She touched a finger to his nose. "I'm done with sabotaging the best thing to happen to me by letting doubts creep in. I love you. You love me. And today that's enough. It doesn't get any better than that."

But oh, she was wrong, Brett thought. His heart was full as he gazed into her eyes and caught a fleeting glimpse of forever.

"It gets better all right," he promised. "You just wait and see."

About the Author

A busy wife and mother, Donna Alward believes hers is the best job in the world: a combination of stay-at-home mom and romance novelist.

An avid reader since childhood, Donna always made up her own stories. She completed her Arts Degree in English Literature in 1994, but it wasn't until 2001 that she penned her first full-length novel, and found herself hooked on writing romance. In 2006 she sold her first manuscript.

Donna loves being back on the East Coast of Canada after nearly twelve years in Alberta where her Harlequin career began, writing about cowboys and the west. Donna's debut Harlequin Romance, *Hired by the Cowboy*, was awarded the Booksellers' Best Award in 2008 for Best Traditional Romance.

Donna loves to hear from readers; you can contact her through her website at www.donnaalward.com, visit her Facebook page, find her on Twitter at @DonnaAlward or through her publishers.

Look for these titles by
Donna Alward

Now Available:

Almost a Family
Sold To The Highest Bidder
Breathe

First Responders
Off the Clock
In the Line of Duty
Into the Fire
Beneath the Badge

Print Collections
First Responders, Volume 1
First Responders, Volume 2

Something About a Cowboy

Sarah M. Anderson

Dedication

To Donna Alward and Jenna Bayley-Burke, for roping me into this! It's been a blast, ladies!

Chapter One

It wasn't supposed to be like this.

Mack Tucker stood just inside the hotel bar, scanning the sparse crowd in front of him. Even though this was one of the fancier hotels in the area, complete with an indoor water park, the place was not crowded. But then Tuesday nights in the middle of January in Billings, Montana, weren't exactly peak tourist season.

He wasn't supposed to be here, not alone. Not looking for a blind date with a woman he'd met on a website named NotMy1stRodeo.com, of all ridiculous things.

If he was in a hotel looking for a woman, it should've been his wife, Sue. God rest her soul. He was married. Or at least he had been, back before the cancer had taken her.

But Sue had been gone for six years, and Mack's three boys kept insisting it was time for him to get out there again, as his youngest, Tommy, kept saying.

It'd been Tommy who, unbeknownst to Mack, had put up a profile on NotMy1stRodeo.com. Tommy, who'd been screening likes and flirts and messages and God only knew what else people did on online dating sites.

And it'd been Tommy who'd given Mack's email and home phone number to a woman.

The woman Mack was supposed to be meeting tonight.

He could still bail. It didn't matter that he'd driven almost three hours in the dead of winter to get to this fancy hotel. It didn't matter that the woman, by the name of Karen Thompson, had the kind of voice that had made him sit up and pay attention when she'd called. It had absolutely no bearing on the situation that, at least in her online pictures, she was beautiful—delicate and refined but with a mischievous glint in her eyes.

He was not now, nor had he ever been, the kind of man who met a woman he didn't know and do *anything* with her, much less have sex with her. He was forty-six and far too old for this kind of shit.

Then he saw her. Well, he didn't know if it was *her* her, but he saw a woman sitting at the bar in a dress that wasn't all there. He only caught glimpses of red fabric low on her hips and high around her neck. The rest was bare skin, smooth and creamy and begging to be touched. Her mass of dark brown hair was twisted up and off her neck with a red rose pinned behind her ear, making her look elegant and sophisticated and absolutely *not* the kind of woman who would be interested in a working rancher who got cow shit on his boots every single day.

Maybe he'd get lucky—lucky enough—and that wouldn't be his date. That'd she'd be a happily married woman waiting on her happily married husband and Mack could go on with his life, none the worse for his small temptation into sin. Absentmindedly, he spun his wedding ring on his right hand.

His phone chimed—Tommy's chime. *"You can do it! Have fun, Dad!"* the message read.

He sighed at the text. Out of all his three boys, Tommy was the one who was pushing him the hardest to move on. Whether he liked it or not, Mack was going to be dragged into this decade kicking and screaming by a young man who wasn't technically old enough to even drink.

"Excuse me," said a voice heavy with irritation. "You're blocking the door."

Mack startled back to himself. How long had he been standing here? He didn't know. He stepped all the way into the bar and let the man—a business traveller by the look of his suit—pass.

Then he looked back up to where the woman in the red dress was sitting. She'd pivoted on her stool, no doubt to see what all the commotion was about.

Her gaze met his and she smiled.

Oh, *hell.* It was her. Karen.

There was no turning back. Aw, who was he kidding? There'd been no turning back the moment he'd agreed to meet her. He tried to return her grin, but it didn't feel right, so he gave up the effort and settled for walking toward her. As he did, he kept looking at her.

She was, if possible, even better looking in the flesh than she'd been in her NotMy1stRodeo.com photos. There, she'd been grinning goofily at the camera, holding up a small dog—the yippy kind—and generally being unselfconscious about her appearance.

But now? As he closed the distance between them, she stood, and Mack got the full magnitude of that red dress. In addition to being backless, it had a deep V that cut close to firm, high breasts and a slit that went most of the way up her leg. The whole thing skimmed over her curves, leaving just enough to the imagination. She had a lush, full body—hourglass shaped and perfect in proportion.

For six long, dark years, he'd not allowed himself to think, much less look at another woman. Suddenly, one siren in a red dress had him thinking about what it'd be like to undo the tie on her neck and let those breasts, those hips free from that dress.

Desire hit him low in the gut. He was really doing this. This was really happening.

"Mack?" she said, her eyes lighting up.

He nodded. “Karen?” Then, because he wasn’t sure what he was supposed to do next in this situation, he stuck out his hand. It seemed the safest bet.

Except it wasn’t. She grabbed his hand and pulled him into her arms. She wore a scent that was light and sweet, almost like vanilla and roses. Unconsciously, he closed his eyes and inhaled deeply. As he did, her breasts pressed against his Sunday-best blue dress shirt and his only suit jacket, the heather-gray one that Sue had picked out for him to wear to her funeral.

It was damned hard to think of Sue and have Karen hold him like this, her arms tight around his chest, murmuring the words, “It’s *so* good to meet you in person.” So he tried to stop. Sue was gone and she’d wanted him to go on with his life. She’d made him promise he would, because that was the kind of woman she’d been.

So this was Mack trying to go on with his life. “It’s, uh, it’s good to meet you too.”

He didn’t know what he was supposed to do with his hands. If he hugged her back, he’d be touching her bare skin or—worse—if he wasn’t doing that, he’d have his hands on her ass. It really didn’t matter how nice her ass was—he glanced down. Whoa. It was a *nice* ass.

He began to get hard and then he immediately started to panic. This was too much, too soon. He was still married, for God’s sake. Sort of. In the eyes of the Lord. Probably.

Thankfully, she let go of him and stepped back, which helped a lot in the sense that she wasn’t pressing her body against his and wouldn’t be able to feel his erection. But it didn’t help that he now had an up-close-and-personal view of her in that dress. It left *very* little to the imagination. He was sure that if he looked at her just right, he’d be able to make out the details of her nipples through the thin red fabric.

He kept his gaze locked on her face.

"I'm glad you came out tonight," she said, and the next thing he knew, she'd leaned up on her tiptoes and planted a kiss on his cheek. She still had a grip on his hand. He couldn't go anywhere. "I was hoping you would."

"We made a date," he heard himself say. "I keep my word."

Which was pretty much the only reason he was here, looking at temptation in the form of a divorced florist named Karen Thompson instead of sitting in his living room, a beer in one hand and the remote in the other, just like he'd done every other night for the last six years.

She lifted one of her eyebrows as she beamed at him. "I am very glad to hear it. Do you want to eat dinner or..." Her voice trailed off and Mack had to lean forward to try and catch the last part of the sentence. *Or what*? "Well, dinner," she finished. "We can talk."

Talking. Not one of his stronger suits, not anymore. "Sure," he forced himself to say. "That sounds great."

"This way." She turned and, without releasing his hand, led him across the lobby to the restaurant. Mack followed. What choice did he have?

The restaurant, much like the rest of the hotel, was nearly deserted. Not much tourism in Montana in January, apparently. The waitress lead them back to a small table for two tucked behind a screen of heavy damask draperies that muffled the noise from the restaurant. Mack held Karen's chair for her and then put his hat on the table behind them.

He didn't know what to say, so he waited for her to take the lead. Instead of making small talk, she took her time looking him over.

It made him nervous, which was not an emotion he enjoyed. Some of the women at church looked at him like that every single Sunday. Mack had trained himself to ignore them because, as nice as some of those ladies were, he was not interested in getting married again. He'd been married once and once was it.

And yet here he was, sitting in a restaurant far away from the prying eyes of home with a woman wearing very little clothing. This was not a meeting that would lead to marriage and more kids, that he knew.

But it might lead to sex.

He still wasn't so sure about that. Then he noticed the two tight points poking through her dress. Okay, part of him was positive that all roads tonight led to sex. Wasn't that why he'd come? Wasn't that why he'd swallowed his pride and stopped at a drugstore here in Billings—where no one would recognize him—and bought some condoms? Because he was still a man and a man had needs and those needs were best met by someone he did *not* have to sit across the aisle from in church as they listened to the preacher go on about resisting temptation and avoiding sin.

Could he do that? Sleep with a woman he barely knew? Even a woman as beautiful and sensual as Karen Thompson?

She just kept on looking. Finally, he couldn't take it anymore. "Yes?"

"I was just wondering," she began, trying to turn her attention to the menu, "what time you got up this morning?"

He began to spin his wedding band. "Five. Well," he said and honest-to-God blushed. "Five fifteen. I did hit snooze once." It was a bad habit he got into during the winter months. But it was damned hard to get up when it was below zero outside.

"You say that like it's a crime or something, to lay in bed for an extra fifteen minutes at what a reasonable person would still consider to be the middle of the night."

His face got even hotter. When was the last time he blushed? "I'm not much of a night owl. I get up at four during the summer. Better to get all the work done before the afternoon when it's just too danged hot."

She smiled at him as she leaned forward. "Danged, huh?"

If his face got much hotter, he was going to burst into flames. "I'm in the presence of a lady."

Something in her eyes...deepened, like that was the answer she'd been waiting all day to hear. "I won't keep you up too late then."

He nodded his head in appreciation of this simple observation, but the truth was he had made plans. Emergency plans, just in case. In case he didn't make it home tonight. After all, he was a long way from home in the middle of winter. The roads could ice. A freak blizzard could hit.

Or he could spend the night with Karen Thompson.

Thankfully, the waiter came. Without even looking at the menu, Mack ordered a beer, the T-bone—bloody rare—and the baked potato. Karen got the chicken with a side salad and a glass of chardonnay.

Then they were alone. He was spinning his ring again, but he was powerless to stop. How long would it take to get his beer? Because he could use a drink. Maybe he should have ordered whiskey.

"How far did you drive?"

"It's about three hours from my side of Butte to Billings." He desperately wanted to say something else—something witty or funny or charming even. Something that one of his sons might say. But he had nothing. He had no idea how to talk to a woman.

"Are you headed back tonight?"

Mack swallowed down his nerves. He needed to suck it up here and fast. So what if Karen was looking at him like he was a puzzle she was trying to work? He'd made his bed. He had to lie in it. "I made contingency plans, in case the weather turns or something."

Something that involved nudity.

His phone chimed. "Sorry about that," he said as he glanced at the text—another one from Tommy. *"Ask her about her store!"* it said.

"Shutting down, kid," he texted back and turned his phone off.

Karen had a bemused look on her face. "That was my boy, my youngest. He likes to text," Mack tried to explain.

"Tommy, right?"

Mack nodded again. "Listen, I don't know exactly what happened, him setting me up on that website like he did. If he crossed a line or misled you in any way about..." he swallowed "...about me, I apologize. I don't like the thought of you being here under false pretenses."

One of her eyebrows notched up and she leaned forward. "False pretenses? And what might those be?"

"I'm not looking to get married."

For some reason, that made her laugh. She leaned back and a carefree laugh broke free from that righteous chest of hers. "Oh, Mack. I'm not looking to get married either. I tried that once and it didn't work out so well."

Mack's face got hotter. Much more of this and he was going to start sweating. "Is that why you were on NotMy1stRodeo? If you don't mind me asking. I'm going to be honest, I'm not real sure what I'm supposed to be doing here."

She laughed. "Trust me, that's not an offensive question."

He managed to crack something that was almost a smile. "Glad to hear it."

"I was...curious," she explained. "I was married right out of college to a man who was supposed to be this amazing catch. Roger." She made a face, as if the name left a bad taste in her mouth. "It was supposed to be perfect. He had a great job with his dad's law firm, good looks. We were going to start a family and live happily ever after, the true American dream."

The drinks came, thank God. Mack took a long pull of his beer. "Happily ever after is a long time," he said without looking at her.

"It is. Looking back now, I'm not sure he was ever faithful to me, but I didn't catch on for a couple of years. We went through a few years of counseling but..."

She paused. Staring at her wine, she gently spun the glass in her hands.

Mack felt a surge of anger. "He didn't deserve you," he announced. "He was an idiot. When a man promises to love and honor a woman, he should stand by that promise."

Karen held his gaze. He might have been imagining things, but he thought he saw her sigh in satisfaction "Yes, that's exactly why I was on a website called NotMy1stRodeo.com."

"What is?"

"That sense of honor." She leaned forward. "I understand that this is not exactly comfortable for you, but you made me a promise and you kept it. I grew up in the Chicago suburbs, which was a great place, but there wasn't that sense of obligation. People gamed the system, the buck stopped somewhere else and people judged you on every single thing you did."

"I've heard the big cities can be rough," he agreed. "I've never been anyplace bigger than Billings, except for Cheyenne, Wyoming." That was where he'd spent his honeymoon, because that was as far as they'd gotten before they run out of gas.

He felt a little stupid, because that statement made him sound like some yokel from the sticks. He knew that Cheyenne and Billings combined wouldn't even come close to Chicago. Dammit, he was not making the best of impressions here.

But Karen just smiled encouragingly at him. "My dad always liked watching old Gunsmoke and Maverick reruns, where a man's word was his bond." She looked up at him through thick lashes. "I guess I was curious...to see if cowboys really were like that—truth, justice, the American Way—all of it."

She reached over and rested her hand on top of his right one—the one that was still spinning his wedding ring. Mack forced himself to be still. Her palm was warm and light against his skin. "I'm not looking to get married either. I just want to know if...if there are men still worth believing in."

In that moment, Mack forgot about his nerves. He forgot about being too old or being out of practice. Even Sue's death—well, it's not like he could forget that. But the sting of it seemed to fade to the background.

Maybe he was old-fashioned, and maybe he was stretching here, but there was something in her tone that made him want to shelter her from the rest of the world full of weaselly ex-husbands and people who game the system. He wanted to prove to her that he, at least, was someone she *could* believe in.

He flipped his hand underneath her palm and curled his calloused fingers around hers. It was a small touch, but he felt a connection between them—a heat that went beyond a handshake.

"Karen," he said, rubbing his thumb over the back of her hand, "you have my word, when I make you a promise, I *will* keep it."

Chapter Two

"Oh." Karen exhaled as every single thing about her responded to Mack Tucker. Her nipples tightened—hell, her clit tightened—as his rough hands stroked hers and his words reverberated through her. This strong, silent cowboy was *exactly* what she'd wanted when she'd joined that ridiculous dating site. "That's...that's good to know."

At her breathy response, something changed in his face. The worry lines that creased his forehead softened at the same time his eyes deepened. Suddenly, Mack looked less like a man being audited and more like a man who might like to go up with her to the king suite she'd gotten for the night and spend the next several hours proving all the different ways he'd keep his promises.

"So," Mack went on, "tell me about you." He moved his thumb over her skin again, strong and sure. "Tell me about your store."

God, she wanted to swoon right here. But she'd just gotten him to open up a little bit and she didn't want to scare him off. There was still a difference between keeping the promise for dinner because of a sense of honor and a night in this cowboy's arms. So she forced herself to pull it together. "After my divorce, I decided I wanted to get away from Chicago. I needed a fresh start someplace new. I'd been working at my husband's law firm, and I didn't want to do that anymore. I wanted..." She sighed. "I know this sounds silly, but I wanted to make something with my hands. I wanted to make people feel like there was still hope in the world."

He gave her a confused look. "So you became a *florist?*"

"Well, yeah." She laughed. "I looked back at my marriage, my life, trying to find the thing that would make me happy. And the thing that kept coming back to me was when I got flowers. I think that's why I fell for Roger. I remember him sending me a dozen roses after that first date and feeling..."

"Hope," Mack said, nodding. "I get that. Even before Sue died, people were sending flowers so she could see them. It was..." He lowered his head, like he couldn't bring himself to look at her. "It was like this little bit of life that went on, a little bit of beauty and grace in a dark time."

She squeezed his hand. "I couldn't have said it better myself." They sat there for a moment, their hands linked.

This wasn't exactly how she'd thought this date would go. She knew Mack was a widower—his profile had said so. But on the other dates Karen had been on since she'd moved to Billings, they'd studiously avoided discussing past relationships as if they were Kryptonite. Apparently, one simply did not acknowledge one's past on a first date, which had always felt a little dishonest to her. It wasn't as if she wanted to rehash all the myriad ways Roger had done her wrong with someone who was essentially a stranger, but she had trouble pretending that part of her hadn't happened. Being divorced was a central part of her identity now, just as Mack being a widower was part of his. There wasn't any way to ignore the facts.

Their food arrived, and she was forced to remove her hand from his grip. She shivered at the loss of his warmth. No, this dress wasn't exactly rated for this time of year, but it wasn't like she was going to walk outside in the driving winter wind. She had no plans to leave this hotel.

Besides, it'd been worth it to see the look on Mack's face when she'd crossed the bar to greet him. The way his eyes had lit up—*yes*. That's what she wanted. To feel desirable again, to feel wanted. For too darned long, she'd felt unattractive, unwanted. Roger hadn't looked at her like he wanted her. He'd looked at her like she was just there. No love—no lust. She'd felt like an obligation he had to meet most of the time, if he remembered she existed at all.

She didn't want feel forgotten anymore. She'd lost a part of herself to a failed marriage and she wanted that part back. She wanted to walk into a room and know that her date couldn't tear his eyes away from her. She wanted to know that he was thinking about what was underneath the dress—that he was thinking about her.

It wasn't wrong to need that. She was a grown woman with a sex drive and she was tired of being invisible.

So this was her being highly visible. Going braless helped. Given the way Mack was looking at her, it helped a lot. He hadn't stopped staring at her and he did not look at her as if she were nothing more than an item on his to-do list that couldn't be avoided. He'd made her a promise and he was going to keep it.

She couldn't think of a bigger turn-on.

After they started eating, Mack waited a bit for her to finish her bite. "So you bought a floral shop in the middle of Montana, huh?"

"I did." She laughed. "I found it for sale online and thought, why not? I had my divorce settlement and the cost of living here is a fifth of what it is in Chicago. It's a fresh start, that's for sure. It was a turnkey operation and most of the staff stayed on. For the first year, I was more of an apprentice than the owner. Flo—that's one of the older ladies who works for me—taught me a lot." She shot Mack a funny look. "She tried to set me up with her son. It did *not* work out."

Mack grinned, which took another five years off his face. "Lucky for me."

Oh, yeah. He was loosening up a little bit. He was a wildly handsome man, the salt in his salt-and-pepper hair starting to come in at his temples. He wore a beard, probably because it was the dead of winter. His face had the weathered look of a man who spent most of his times outdoors, but when he smiled?

When he smiled at *her*? When his gaze drifted over her body and his pupils dilated with desire? God, how she wanted his calloused hands to move over so much more than just her hand.

She hadn't lied. She was not looking for another husband. But she wanted to feel more alive than just arranging roses for weddings and funerals could make her feel. She wanted to take the next step to putting her divorce behind her, and that meant something physical—on *her* terms this time.

"So how long have you been in Billings?"

"Almost three years now. I moved out after the divorce was finalized."

Mack thought that over. "When did you join NotMy1stRodeo.com?"

"A few months ago. I had another bad blind date that one of my best clients claimed would be perfect for me." She couldn't help it—she shuddered at the memory of Ryan. "He offered to cook me dinner at his place, which turned out to be eating pizza in his filthy apartment while he watched a World War II documentary. I'll spare you the rest of the details." No one else needed to know about how he'd taken off his socks and picked at his toenails while she was still eating. No one.

"He didn't even cook? That's not right," Mack said as he finished his beer.

"Trust me, the pizza was the best part of that evening. But after that, I decided I couldn't do much worse on my own, you know? And there's something about a cowboy..."

She let her gaze drift over him again. He was a solid six feet tall—hell, everything about him was solid. He filled out his sport jacket and she was dying to know what he looked like under that bolo tie.

"You didn't go out with that one again, did you?"

"No. I haven't had a second date yet." She sighed. "Half of them barely qualified as a first date, you know? I mean, I'm not repulsive. I own my own business. I'm easy to get along with and reasonably intelligent. Who would have thought it'd be so hard to find a decent man?"

"Actually," he cut in, his gaze taking in the full magnitude of her cleavage, "you're gorgeous. But continue."

The way he said it—like it was just a fact that they had to acknowledge, much like they'd acknowledged his wife and her ex—warmed her from the inside out, because honestly? She hadn't felt gorgeous in a really long time. After all, people who knew her—or thought they knew her—were setting her up with the likes of Ryan the Toe-Picker, as if that were as good as a middle-aged divorced woman like herself could possibly hope things to get.

"I..." She took a deep breath, attempting to sound like the self-confident woman she was trying so very hard to be. "Thank you."

He looked confused. "For what?"

"For the compliment. When you realize that your husband cheated on you with younger, prettier women for basically the entire time you were married...well, I felt like I wasn't *enough.* Pretty enough, good enough. Not enough for him."

Mack looked at her as if she'd started speaking in a foreign language. For a second, he looked mad, like he wanted to punch someone—Ryan, Roger, all of them. Then he set his knife and fork down and put both hands on the table. "That man was a fool—all of them were." He leaned forward as he spoke, his voice strong. The air between them almost hummed with tension. "Anyone can see that you're..." His words trailed off again and he seemed to remember where he was. Doubt pulled him away from her.

Oh, no, Karen thought. She wasn't going to let him leave *that* thought hanging. "Yes?"

He opened his mouth, then closed it. She waited. He took a deep breath and pushed back from the table a little. "You have to understand, I met my wife when I was fifteen, and that was it. We married young and I had three sons by the time I was twenty-six. I haven't even looked at another woman much in the last six years, much less complimented them. I don't always remember how to talk to a woman."

"Just talk to me," she said. Her voice came out low. "I'm not sitting over here grading you on style and poise or anything."

"You're beautiful," he said, but he couldn't look her in the eye when he said it. "What do you want with an old man like me, anyway?"

It was a fair question. "First off, you're how old?"

"Forty-six."

"You are far from an old man. Here's what I want from you, Mack. I want you to be real. I want to spend some time with a real man, someone who makes me feel like I'm still a real woman. Like I'm good enough. I can't offer perfection and I'm not asking for it." His eyebrows jumped up as he took that in, but she didn't stop. She was afraid if she did, she'd start to overthink it. So she pressed on. "And you? You already said you're not looking for another wife. What do you want from me?"

His cheeks shot bright red at that question, as if she'd asked him for sex even before the dessert menu had come. But he said, "My youngest is in college now. All three of my boys are grown men, out on their own. I can go a whole week without talking to another person, especially in the winter. It can be a lonely life." He sighed, as if the truth were something best not spoken of. "I guess...I guess I got tired of being lonely." He smirked. "Or Tommy got tired of it for me."

"You came out tonight." A three-hour drive in the darkness of winter. That was quite a commitment for a woman he didn't know. "You didn't have to. You could have said no."

"Could have," he agreed. Then he looked her in the eye. "But I'm glad I didn't."

Karen's heart began to pound. For a moment, she'd thought she'd lost him. The tension between them had receded and she hadn't been sure it'd come back.

But he was sitting over there, one corner of his mouth curved into half of a smile and he was glad to be here. "Me too," she said. Which left only one other question. "So now what?"

Chapter Three

Before Mack could answer Karen's question—and it was a damn good question—the waiter came back and cleared their dishes. He put the bill on the table and, hand to God, Karen reached for it.

"No," Mack said, pulling it away from her.

"I can put it on my room," she protested, her hand still extended like she really expected him to let her pay for his steak.

"Not happening," he replied, checking the total. Yeah, that was more than he usually paid at a restaurant, but then he only ate out once a week after Sunday services, and this place wasn't a Cracker Barrel. He fished a hundred and a fifty out of his wallet and stuck them in with the bill. "Even if I'm not old, I'm still old-fashioned. A gentleman pays for dinner. End of discussion."

Karen's lips twisted to one side, a gesture that was part irritation and part amusement. He wasn't sure if she'd argue the point with him or not, and if she did, he wasn't sure how he was supposed to handle it.

Wait...she had a room *already*?

But instead of listing reasons why they should split the check, she said, "Thank you. Dinner was lovely."

They sat there for a moment, the unanswered question still hanging between them. Now what? In spite of himself, he was having a nice time. Karen was gorgeous, yes—that didn't hurt a damned thing. But this went deeper than that.

Even though he was a widower and she was a divorcee, he felt like he understood her and maybe she even understood him. All the women who attended services with him every Sunday—the school teachers and nurses and bankers who populated the area around Butte, Montana—they looked at him with pity in their eyes, which he hated. Or worse, like he was lost without a woman to care for him and they were just the woman for the job.

He didn't want someone to take care of him. But he missed taking care of Sue—all the little things that he'd gone out of his way to do to let her know he was thinking of her. Notes on the fridge where she'd see them when she woke up in the morning, letting her pick what they'd watch that night—and, yes, flowers.

He smiled at the memory.

"Why don't we walk around a little? I've never been in a hotel quite like this. Doesn't it have a water park or something?"

Karen's face lit up with excitement. "It does. Fountains and everything. Did you bring a suit?"

"No," he said with a chuckle. He retrieved his hat and held her chair for her. She slipped her hand into the crook of his arm. He liked that, liked having a woman by his side. "Lead on."

Her eyebrows jumped up. "This way."

Once they made it out of the restaurant, he asked. "So you're staying here tonight?"

"I am." She led him back toward a pair of doors and stopped to get her keycard out. Once she had the door unlocked, she held out her hand for him and he took it. "After that last terrible date, I wanted to meet on neutral territory," she explained as they walked into the pool area.

The air was warm and humid and heavy with chlorine. Lights under the water made the pool shimmer. It might be below freezing outside, but this place was much closer to a tropical sauna. The cavernous room was completely empty and the water was almost still.

"Cool," he said. "I almost wish I'd packed my trunks."

Karen turned and looked up at him, her mouth curved up in challenge. "You want to go swimming anyway?"

"What?"

"I'll go skinny dipping with you."

Mack felt like his jaw was on the ground because that was both the absolute worst idea he'd ever heard in his life and quite possibly the best one at the same time. He'd love nothing more than to see Karen's nude body covered only with the shimmering water of this pool. "We—we can't do that. This is a public pool."

"There's no one here. The place is deserted," she countered, stepping away from him. She walked over to a table set up near what was probably a snack bar during the tourist season and set her little handbag down. "I'm going in. Are you coming?"

He could not form the words, because if there was one thing he wasn't, it was an exhibitionist. He kept his bedroom door shut and his pants on. Hell, even in the peak of summer heat, he wore a shirt because he didn't want to walk around topless. That was something he saved for his wife, just like she'd saved her body for his.

But before he could protest to that effect, Karen had pulled down a zipper hidden at the back of her dress, revealing the top of what—oh, God—looked like a red lace thong.

Mack grabbed the doorknob of the pool room and made damn sure it was shut, then he leaned heavily against it and watched. What the hell else could he do?

Nothing. Not a damn thing as he watched Karen reach up and untie the bow at the nape of her neck. The dress fell away and then—God help him—she leaned forward and shimmied the red fabric off her hips.

The pool room was so quiet he could hear the fabric shush to the ground, and there she was, wearing only a rose in her hair, a pair of little panties that left absolutely nothing to the imagination and a pair of heels.

She looked back over her shoulder. "Are you sure you won't join me?"

She was right there, damn it all, beautiful and lush and someone he wanted. He hadn't *wanted* in so long that even having a hard-on—and boy, did he have one—was something new and exciting and maybe even a little scary. He was really doing this. This was really happening. "I'll watch. If that's all right with you?"

One of her smooth shoulders lifted and fell. Then she stepped out of her heels and walked toward the steps.

She had to face him to do this.

Mack liked to think he was a strong man. He'd raised a family and cared for a wife until he'd had to bury her. He ran a ranch and managed the cattle and folded his own damn laundry. He *was* strong, for crying out loud.

Or at least, he had been. Right until he got a good look at Karen Thompson wading into a pool in a thong. That red lace thong. It sat high on her generous hips and barely covered the space where her legs met. All of which wasn't quite enough to take his attention away from her breasts. Full and rounded with darker nipples that sat high—even at this distance of almost fifty feet, he could tell that the dress hadn't been lying. She was built.

For the first time in years, Mack weakened. Desire hit him so low and hard in the gut that he sagged against the door. Jesus, he wasn't going to be able to take it as Karen walked forward, her luscious body disappearing beneath the water. He swore to God that he saw her nipples tighten as the water hit her body.

Yeah, that wasn't the only thing that tightened. Mack forced himself to breathe—in through the nose, out through the mouth. Which worked enough that he was able to get his legs back under him and move toward the pool. For a better view. Just to make sure she was okay in there. By herself.

In four feet of water. Yeah, he wasn't even fooling himself with that.

"Are you sure you won't join me?" she asked, her voice soft and inviting. For one wild second, he considered kicking out of his boots and taking her up on her offer.

But crazy as this whole situation was—and it was, hands down, the craziest thing he'd done—he couldn't give himself over to the insanity. Not completely.

Besides, he reasoned, the night was still young. "Positive," he managed to get out without sounding like he was some sex-crazed teenager on the verge of coming in his pants. Then, before he knew what he was saying, he told her, "I want to watch you."

She shot him a coy smile and stretched out her lithe body. The waves surrounded her as she did a modified breaststroke—one that let her keep her head above water. Her legs sliced through the water, and all he could think of was how they'd feel wrapped around his waist.

He dropped down onto one of the lounge chairs that were spread out around the pool and watched as she swam with long, slow strokes. There was no rush, no sense of urgency. She took her time.

Mack adjusted his pants, trying to ease the pressure off his dick. His blood pounded with want and need and lust, driving all doubt from his mind. This might be a sin and he may be buying a ticket directly to hell, but for the first time in...well, years, he felt alive. He was excited and aroused and *ready*. Ready for this woman.

Karen reached the far side of the pool and turned back toward him. She had a hell of a look on her face—a satisfied curve to her lips that promised something so, *so* good.

He leaned his elbows on his knees and watched as she gracefully made her way over to his side of the pool. She lifted herself just far enough out of the pool to rest her arms on the edge, giving him a tantalizing glimpse of her breasts again.

Six years of abstaining seemed to float away in the water. More than six years really. Sue had battled the breast cancer for a couple of years before she'd lost that fight. It'd been so long since he'd looked at a breast and thought of pleasure, of giving and taking and mouths everywhere.

"Last chance to join me," she said in a sultry voice. But she didn't sound like she was irritated he was still dry. She sounded like...like the way he was watching her was just as erotic for her as it was for him.

"I'll wait for you," he told her.

"Then I won't keep you waiting." She pushed back from the side, the water lapping at the rounded tops of her breasts.

He wanted to bury his face in those breasts, suck and lick her nipples and make her gasp with pleasure, and he wanted to do it all without thinking of pain and guilt and heartbreak.

He stood and picked up a towel. He walked over to the top of the stairs and waited for Karen. She stood and the water sheeted off her upper body as she cut through the waves.

Oh, yeah, he was going to make a lot of love tonight. He was going to enjoy himself.

He unfolded the towel and held it wide open for Karen. When she reached the top step, she turned her back to him and held her arms out. Pausing only to admire her backside and that sexy thong, Mack stepped up to her and wrapped the towel around her body. She took the ends from him and held them closed, then pivoted and stepped all the way out of the pool.

And right into his arms. He rubbed his hands over the towel where it covered her back and her bottom. *Slow,* he thought. He had all night long. Jim, his neighbor, was going to feed his horses in the morning, and everything else could wait. The only thing he needed to think about was Karen.

She reached up and placed her palm against his cheek. "I want you to know—it's been almost four years since I've been with a man."

He didn't know why that made him feel good, but it did. Sure, divorce and death weren't quite the same things, but he felt like...like they were both starting from the same place. Starting over. "Those must have been some really bad dates."

She grinned. "They were. But this one's not." She took a deep breath, the front of her towel brushing up against him. "Would you like to come up to my room?"

His dick jumped. Yeah, he'd kind of thought from the moment she'd unzipped her dress that sex would be where they end up. But confirmation of that was never a bad thing.

"I would." Then a thought occurred to him. "But I've only ever been with one woman, and it's been almost seven years since even that. I might be a little rusty."

She stroked his cheek with her thumb. "I'll make a deal with you. You tell me what you like and I'll tell you what works for me. Fair?"

He wrapped his arms around her and held her tight. It felt good to have a woman in his arms again. "Fair." He lowered his head to hers and brushed a kiss over her lips. Just a simple kiss. But there wasn't much that was simple about it. Need—powerful need—flowed between them. His grip on his control—iron-clad control that had kept things like desire and lust and sex on a firm lockdown for year after dry year—started to slip.

The first kiss. His brain compared this to his other first kiss. Back then, he'd been fifteen and nervous and shy—and the braces hadn't helped. He'd kept his eyes open because he could not believe that Sue Jenkins was kissing *him* when she was clearly out of his league.

He kept his eyes open this time too. Well, half-open. He didn't need to stare at a woman who was going to share her body with him. He may be out of practice, but he wasn't stupid. He may not be as young as he once was, but he still had a lot left to give a woman as beautiful and sensual as Karen.

Starting right now. He traced the seam of her lips with his tongue, tasting her and testing. What did she like? That?

Oh, yeah—that. She sighed against his mouth and opened her lips for him. Her arms went around his neck as she pulled him down. He felt the towel start to slip at the exact same moment the door to the pool room was opened. "Okay, kiddo," a man's voice said. "We're...here."

"Oh!" Karen gasped as she simultaneously grabbed for the towel, took a step back and almost fell into the pool.

Mack grabbed her and hauled her up, then he stepped in front of her. She had the towel, which was the important thing here if kids were about. No one else needed to know she was mostly nude underneath it, right?

He started to chuckle at the thought, but her eyes widened in panic. This was exactly why he still had his boots on. He turned to the newcomers—a husband and wife and a young boy, maybe five. "Howdy, folks. The water's great. We were just leaving, so you've got the whole thing to yourself." He aimed that mostly at the kid, because the mom was giving him and Karen a disapproving look and the dad looked like he was going to bust a gut laughing.

"Yeah!" the kid shouted and flung himself into the water with a huge splash.

With the kid's attention elsewhere, Mack pulled Karen forward. He paused long enough to scoop up the red dress and her shoes while she snagged her little purse and they got the hell out of there.

Which meant he was now walking through the halls of a hotel with a woman wearing little more than a towel.

He was not an exhibitionist really—but there was something exciting, something forbidden, about this whole thing. Only he knew she didn't have a swimsuit on underneath that towel. Only he knew what she looked like in the water.

God, he'd never been so hard in his life.

"This way," she said in a breathy, nervous voice, walking swiftly down the hall. They made it to the elevators without seeing anyone else, thank heavens. Karen pressed the button and the door opened up immediately. Mack let her get in first and then he stood in front of her until the door was shut. "What floor?"

"Three," she said and then exhaled heavily. "That was *close*."

The gears of the elevator groaned and they slowly began to ascend, one of those slow elevators that might take two minutes to get three floors.

He could do a *lot* in two minutes.

She opened her mouth to say something else, but he kissed her before she got the chance. This time, he didn't go for simple or sweet. He swept his tongue into her mouth and pinned her body against the wall of the elevator with his and let her feel what she did to him.

He'd never done anything more than kiss in an elevator, but right now—thinking about her little red panties, all wet between her legs from the pool? He slid one hand up under the towel and felt the wet fabric with the tips of his fingers.

"Oh, Mack," she moaned against his skin when he trailed kisses down her chin to her bare neck, her bare shoulders. Droplets of water still clung to her smooth skin, and he kissed them away. She held the towel tightly, but she reached up with her free hand and grabbed the back of his neck. "I like a little biting," she whispered in his ear. "Just a little pressure."

Biting? As long as this didn't get all vampire on him...he skimmed his teeth along the top of her shoulder before biting down—not hard, not enough to break skin. Just a little pressure, like she'd said. At the same time, he felt something small and round and hard beneath her panties and he pushed against it with the tip of his index finger.

Karen's body bucked against his as she gasped.

"Good?" he asked, kissing the spot where his teeth had left a faint red mark.

She clutched at his shirt, breathing hard as he made a little circle over her clit. "Oh, God..."

The elevator lurched to a stop, jolting them against each other. Damn—they were still technically in public. He barely managed to get himself back under control by the time the doors opened. "Okay?" he asked as she stood there, her eyes closed and her chest heaving. At least she still had the towel up, right?

"Room 323," was all she said.

He stuck his head out and did a perimeter check. The hallway was empty, so he took her by the hand and led her toward the room. Walking was a bit of a challenge at this point, because every single movement made him feel like he was going to die the best kind of death. Blood pounded through every single part of his body—his ears were ringing, his dick was throbbing. All he could think about was getting her behind a closed door where no one and nothing would interrupt them this time.

Oh, yeah. He was going to enjoy *this*.

Chapter Four

Karen fumbled the key card out of her purse. She could barely see straight after the way Mack had touched her in the elevator. Hell, even just the way he'd been watching her in the pool...

How long had it been since a man had looked at her with that kind of unbridled lust in his eyes? Like she was the only woman in the world and he could hardly wait to make her his?

Years. Not just the years since the divorce had been finalized, but years before that. Yes, Roger had once looked at her like that, back when they'd first started dating. But it'd lost some of its charm when she'd caught him looking at anything with two legs and breasts that way.

She'd spent the first part of her marriage trying *so* hard to get Roger to look at her like Mack did—as if he not only couldn't live without her, like he wasn't going to make it another ten minutes. She'd waxed and worn skimpy things in public and suggested sex in the kitchen or the car or any place where she thought she might be able to prove that she was enough for Roger.

But it hadn't. All that desperate wildness had never left her feeling desirable—or all that satisfied. Roger had been a selfish narcissist—the thought of giving her what she wanted, what she needed, just never crossed his mind.

Shivering, she fumbled with the key card. "Here," Mack said in a low drawl, "let me get that." He pressed against her back, reached around her waist and took the key card from her.

She saw that his hand was shaking.

And she liked that—that moment of weakness, that physical proof that she had made him literally sit up and take notice of her. Despite all the things she'd tried to use to capture Roger's wandering eye, she had never done anything as crazy as to strip down to her undies and swim for a man.

She almost felt like...like the girl she'd been back before she'd fallen under Roger's spell and lost years of her life to his cheating ways. Wild and carefree and ready for anything.

Ready for Mack.

He got the card in and the door open and then he was gently pushing her through it. The card fell to the ground and, the moment he kicked the door shut behind them, so did her towel.

"God, Karen," he said, cupping her breasts in his hands and pulling her back into him as he leaned against the closed door. His beard prickled against her skin—so, *so* good. "You about killed me down there—so damn beautiful."

She could feel his erection pressing against her lower back, long and hard and hot and for her. Just for her. She didn't have to share him and she didn't have to worry about holding him. Tonight, he was hers and she was his.

He was stroking the undersides of her breasts, heightening her awareness of them, of the way he touched her skin. He watched her as he moved his hands against her, resting his chin on her shoulder as his gaze followed the trail of his fingertips up to her nipples.

She shivered again at the touch, both erotic and sweet. "Cold?" he murmured against her skin.

"Not really. Just..." he rolled her right nipple between his thumb and forefinger. "Don't stop," she moaned. "Don't stop, Mack."

"Mmm." He did it again, this time pulling the sensitive tip with just the right amount of pressure. "Good?"

She had to grab hold of something to keep her knees from buckling, so she latched onto his forearms. “More,” she gasped.

He let go of her left breast and wrapped his arm around her waist. “Yes, ma’am.” Then—oh, God, then—he bit down on that spot where her shoulder met her neck and pinched her nipple. The pressure was just right. Just...right...

“Mack,” she groaned, grinding her hips back against his erection.

“Let me do this for you,” he whispered as he kissed her neck, right under her ear. “I want to know I can still do this.”

He slipped the hand that was around her waist lower, down over the thong she’d specifically bought for just this occasion, down to where her clit was still throbbing from where he’d touched her earlier.

She was whimpering, she realized—whimpering for his touch.

“Do you like that?” he growled in her ear. “Do you like it when I touch you like *this*?”

He brushed his fingertips over her clit as he pulled on her nipple and skimmed his teeth over her neck. She opened her mouth to tell him exactly how much she liked it, but no noise came out. She managed a feeble nod.

“I need more than that to go on, darlin’,” he drawled. “You’ve got to let me know when it’s good.”

And he pressed. He pressed down on the hood of her clit and her hips moved all by themselves as she clung to him. “Oh, yes, yes, *yes*,” she hissed as he began to move in those small circles again, rubbing her clit.

Mack worked her in silence, with a single-minded determination that she was going to come and come right now. “Oh, God,” she whispered as the orgasm began to build, the pressure on the inside of her body matching the pressure he was applying to the outside. “Oh, God, Mack.”

"Yeah, like that. You're so damn beautiful," he growled and then bit down again.

Karen came apart in his arms. Everything about her stiffened and then exploded like a tightly wound spring being freed. All she could do was ride his hand.

Mack caught her as she sagged against him and held her close. "So beautiful," he murmured as he kissed her neck again.

"Oh, Mack," she gasped, trying to get her eyes to focus again. "Oh, that was *wonderful*."

"Not too hard?" he asked, tracing his lips over the warmed part of her neck where he'd been nibbling.

"Just right." She let him carry her weight as her body relaxed. "Wow. Just...wow."

He chuckled behind her. "That's a relief. I was afraid...maybe I'd forgotten how."

A little part of her heart broke for him. Her marriage and divorce—well, Roger had been an asshole, but she'd thrown her lot in with him. She'd been culpable. But Mack had lost his wife and had spent the last six or seven years alone.

This night had started out about her getting over that final hurdle that Roger had thrown up in her life, reclaiming sex as something fun and enjoyable, as something she was worthy of having. That's what she'd been trying to get back with all those failed dates and hadn't. Not until she'd met Mack Tucker.

But now? This wasn't about only her, not anymore. This was about a lonely man who'd almost forgotten how.

She was going to do her damnedest to help him remember. She could give him that.

So she pivoted in his arms. He let her, but skimmed his hands over her body until he was cupping her butt. "I never knew how much I liked these little panties." He grinned down at her as he traced his thumbs along the lace.

"I picked them out just for you," she whispered as she kissed along his jaw. His beard pricked at her skin, warming her up.

She decided that he had on way too much clothing. He still had on his hat, for crying out loud. "What do you like?" she asked as she pulled the bolo tie down and slipped it and the hat off.

"You," he said. "I like you."

She laughed at that and hugged him. "That was a sweet thing to say." Then she grabbed his belt buckle. "But we're past the point of sweetness."

Mack froze as Karen undid his belt buckle. He was still flying high off the climax he'd given her. It'd been freaking *years*, but he hadn't forgotten how to pleasure a woman, how to make her whimper and moan and shake in his arms. It was a damn good boost for his ego that he could do that for this sensual woman—that it was wonderful and she'd been practically speechless, all just from him touching her.

He hadn't lost it. Or maybe he had just forgotten it for a while. But now? Now he had *it* back. Big time.

"What are you doing?" he asked as the button on his pants gave. Because she hadn't started on his shirt or gotten his sports coat off or any of that.

"Your turn," she murmured as she kneeled before him. The buttons on his fly went next. "Tell me what you like."

"Karen," he said, panic beginning to rise up. He was already primed, hard and close. If she went down on him...he wouldn't make it. It'd be over before it started. "You don't have to do that."

She looked up at him, her eyes wide and luminous in the dim light of the room. "We have all night, Mack." She shoved his pants down a little and stroked his dick through his boxer briefs. "This is just the beginning."

He wouldn't have thought it possible, but the idea excited him even more. It'd been decades since he'd been able to really take his time in bed. When the boys had come along, he and Sue had transitioned to quicker, quieter sex with less foreplay and more sleep.

But he and Karen really did have all night long. The idea was mind-boggling.

"Let me do this for you," she whispered as she pulled his briefs down. His dick sprang free and, against his will, Mack moaned.

"Yes, like that," she murmured as she took him in hand and began to stroke—up, down, up. "My God, Mack. Look at you."

"Rather look—" he sucked in air, "—at you," he finally got out as she leaned forward and kissed his tip.

He jerked against her lips, his body more than willing to follow this all the way through.

Karen looked up at him through her thick lashes. "Then look at me," she told him as she took him in her mouth, all warm wetness surrounding him, moving her hands rhythmically over his shaft.

Mack shuddered. It was a lot. Too much. He didn't want to lose it like an eager boy again but—but—

She kept her gaze on his eyes as she swirled her tongue around his tip. He wanted her to stop and he wanted her to keep right on going, right on doing that—

She slipped her other hand lower and cupped his balls, which pulled a low groan out of him. "Jesus," he ground out. He couldn't focus on holding back, couldn't focus on anything but the way she was licking him and sucking him and stroking him. Taking him as he pumped into her mouth.

Then he felt the edge of her teeth rough up against his dick—not a bite, no, but the pressure... "Jesus," he groaned again. He flattened his hands against the door to try and hold himself up.

She moved her hands in counterpoint to her lips, her mouth, and he was not going to make it. "I'm going to come," he managed to say, because even though he wasn't able to think, to control anything but the way his body was screaming to empty into hers, he knew he had to give her fair warning. It was the last gasp of his self-control.

Her mouth relinquished its hold on him and she kissed his thigh, but she kept her hands stroking him, kept pumping until the climax spurted out of him.

"Oh..." he moaned at the release, at the way she slowed down but didn't let go until he was finished.

And he was drained. Yeah, he'd been taking care of himself for a long time, but this...this went far beyond jerking off in the shower. This was *everything.*

"Mack," she said, still on her knees in front of him, still wearing nothing but that little red lace thong, "I don't think you've forgotten anything."

He grabbed her underneath her arms and hauled her up into his chest.

"Good?" she asked. He could feel her lips curved against his neck in a smile.

"Yeah. Yeah, I think you could say that. We've got all night, right?" Because as erotic and sexy as she was, he wasn't as young as he once was. He was going to need a little recovery time.

"We even have part of the morning. At least until checkout."

He grinned. He could think of a few ways to pass the time until he was ready to go again. "Ladies first," he said, motioning to the bathroom.

While she was getting cleaned up, he kicked out of his boots, his socks and his jacket. But then he paused. Should he strip the rest of the way? Or not? It felt weird to just be waiting for her naked, but it also felt weird to wait for her dressed. He wasn't a big fan of nudity—but she'd been mostly nude for a while now, and he didn't like that the clothing situation was so unbalanced, especially not since she'd already seen his dick.

Sucked his dick.

Mack sagged back against the door, his head in his hands. This wasn't like him. He'd gone years and years without doing anything as impulsive as meeting a strange woman and going up to her hotel room for the night. But in a moment of weakness...

In a panic, he almost grabbed his socks and his boots and bailed. He wasn't sure he could face her, not after what he'd done to her and she'd done to him. He wasn't all that sure he could go into that bathroom in a few minutes and face *himself* in the mirror.

He heard the sink shut off. Forcibly, he pulled himself together. This was fine. Okay, at the very least. Sue had wanted him to go on with his life. His sons wanted the same. And if that meant knowing another woman intimately, then...

The bathroom door opened and Karen stood in the doorway, backlit by the lights over the sink. Her gaze flicked over him, no doubt taking in the removal of the boots and jacket. The part of Mack's brain that wasn't paralyzed by guilt was happy to note that she still had on her panties.

But the only thing she said was, "Your turn," as she stepped out of his way. As she passed him, she reached up and trailed a hand over his jaw.

And that...helped. At the very least, it quieted down the guilt and doubt that were trying to take hold of him and focused his attention on her.

Still, as he used the bathroom and washed up, he kept his gaze on anything but the mirror over the sink.

He pulled his pants back up and buttoned them, but he yanked the belt out of the loops. As he did so, his phone shifted in his pants. Even though he'd shut the damn thing off, he could still almost hear the text chime, almost see the messages that Tommy would be sending him.

"Having fun?"

"Don't forget to compliment her!"

"You can do it, Dad!"

Compliment her? He didn't have the first clue what to say. *You give really good blowjobs?* That seemed crude to the extreme. Dammit, he was so out of practice talking in general and to women in particular.

He sighed and looked himself in the eye. "Two adults having some fun, that's all," he muttered. "Nothing wrong with that."

Besides, it *had* been fun. He'd let himself get swept away in the excitement of watching Karen swim, of touching her body and making her cry out. In that moment—and the moment where he'd pumped himself into her mouth, her hands—he'd felt like a different person. Not a dad, not a widower—but a *man.* Alive and ready for a beautiful woman.

His dick twitched at the thought of it all, and Mack almost smiled at himself.

He could still be a man.

After all, they had all night.

Chapter Five

While Mack was in the bathroom, Karen got organized. Turning on the bedside lamp, she dug the box of condoms out of her overnight bag, along with the bottle of lube. She had packed her vibrator on the off chance she did not get lucky with a cowboy tonight and needed to take the edge off.

She left it in the bag.

She was humming, she realized as she pulled down the covers. This was exactly what she'd wanted—to spend the night with a man who looked at her like Mack had looked at her when she'd worked on his body.

In that moment, she'd felt powerful and desirable and special because he was here with her. Not anyone else, just her.

But the longer Mack was in the bathroom, the more she began to get nervous. It didn't help that she was lying on the bed in nothing but a still-wet thong. She got up and adjusted the room's temperature up a few degrees.

Doubts—old ones—crept in on her, so stealthily that she hardly realized it was happening. He was going to stay, wasn't he? He'd taken his boots off. That was a good sign, right? He was going pull her into his arms and look her in the eye and say sweet things to her—about how special she was, how beautiful, all that good stuff. Things that she hadn't heard in almost eight years—not since the honeymoon period of her marriage to Roger.

She wanted those feelings back. She was only thirty-three, after all. She was still far too young to feel like a nun. But she didn't want to feel like all she was good for was her respective body parts. That's how her ex-husband had made her feel—he was only married to her for the pussy and light housekeeping. And he could get pussy anywhere.

She lay back down on the bed on her stomach and forced herself to breathe. She was just out of practice, that was all. It had been years since a man had looked at her like Mack had while she'd been swimming—since another man had brought her to orgasm like that.

Since another man had put her needs, her body, first.

The bathroom door opened and she involuntarily held her breath. Would he stay? Or go? Maybe she should have left the light off. She wasn't some willowy young thing. But then again, she wasn't any more exposed than she'd been when she'd stripped her dress off for him.

He walked out, his shirt untucked but still firmly buttoned. When he saw her watching, he paused and leaned against the wall that divided the bedroom from the bathroom. But he didn't say anything.

Karen shivered as he looked at her. She couldn't tell if that was because of the temperature or her nerves. "Yes?"

A slow grin—far too serious to be called lazy—took hold of one corner of his mouth. "Just admiring."

She exhaled slowly, resisting the urge to suck in her stomach. What good would that do? She was lying on that particular body part, for crying out loud.

Mack shifted and began to walk toward the bed. "Is it all right if I touch you?" he asked.

She stared at him. Hadn't he already? But he stopped when he got next to the bed, waiting on her reply.

"I'd like that," she told him.

Mack sat down on the edge of the bed and lifted up one hand. Karen tensed, which didn't make any sense. She'd asked him to touch her. She wanted him to touch her.

But she couldn't shake off that feeling of doubt.

At least, she couldn't—until Mack touched her.

He started at her hair, pulling the rose out of her up-do and then removing the pins that held the twist. He combed his fingers through her hair, loosening it until it fell around her shoulders in waves.

Then he trailed a finger over her shoulder, down her back and over her butt. He didn't stop there, didn't touch her like he'd touched her earlier. He worked his way down the back of her thigh, her knee—which made her giggle—and all the way down to her foot.

He took his time moving his hand up the other leg. His touch was slow and steady and sensual. Karen closed her eyes and let herself just be under his hand. "That feels nice," she said as he went from trailing a finger to rubbing his whole palm against her bare skin.

"Good," he said. Then he touched her again—but this time, instead of his hand, the tip of the rose brushed over her skin. "How's that?"

The soft petals of the rosebud caressed her skin and filled the air with its gentle perfume. "Lovely," she murmured. The last of her nerves left her and she just let herself enjoy this. This was, hands down, one of the benefits of an older man. He was taking his time. It wasn't all about the fuck—boom, and he was done. There was more to enjoy with him.

Her skin tingled, aware of each movement as the rose kissed the small of her back, the space between her legs, even the soles of her feet. She laughed again and was thrilled when Mack laughed with her.

Then the bed shifted under his weight as he leaned forward and pressed his lips against the top of her shoulder.

"Mack," she whispered as he kissed and licked her shoulder, her back. Then he got lower. He reached her butt and bit down. Not too hard—not enough to bruise—but enough that she trembled in the small place between pleasure and pain. "Oh..."

He traced the bite mark with the rose or his finger, she couldn't tell.

"Harder? Or too hard?"

"Just right. Just..." He touched her other cheek, smoothing his palm over her skin, tracing the edge of the thong. She tensed, waiting for the bite. Waiting for him to mark her.

Her ex had never gotten this part right. He either bit her so hard he bruised her or he didn't bite her at all. And since Karen did not particularly want to be bruised, she'd stopped asking for those little love bites and tried to convince herself that it was healthier if she didn't get bitten. After all, normal people didn't like the little flash of pain that burned bright into pleasure.

"Do you mind? That I like that?" she asked. She didn't miss the way her voice trembled. She didn't want to hear the rejection again, didn't want to feel like her desires were wrong somehow, off. Not right. That she wasn't right.

"Hmm," Mack hummed. He shifted, stood and then straddled her legs. The bed sagged underneath his weight. The contact warmed her legs.

Then he put both his hands on her bottom, massaged her and trailed along the edge of the thong. "Why do you like that?" he asked as he rubbed her. There wasn't any judgment in his voice, just curiosity.

"I don't know," she admitted, relaxing under his touch. He moved over her back, his hands and all their rough callouses kneading her muscles. "I guess...sometimes it's hard to be in the present, you know? You want to be with someone, you want to have great sex, but your mind is too busy thinking about how you forgot to get the dry cleaning and the dishwasher needs to be emptied and on and on and on. And you—well, okay, me—I have trouble staying in the moment. That little bit of sensation—it pulls me back, forces me to be *here*."

She'd never been able to admit that before. She'd had lovers before she got married, some more willing to indulge her than others, but she'd never been brave enough to say *why* being bitten just so worked for her.

"With me?"

She grinned. "With you." Maybe he was the reason. She could be honest with him—with herself—because what was the risk? If it didn't work out, she'd never have to see him again. Their paths would never cross on their own.

But if it did work out...

Mack leaned forward. Instead of biting her on the ass again, he covered the rest of her body with his. With one hand, he grabbed her hair and not-quite yanked it away from her shoulders. Then he bit her, right where her neck met her shoulders.

Everything about her body tightened down in response and she cried out in pleasure against the pillow. There was no worry about why Roger had been an asshole or whether or not blind dates were really worth the hassle of shaving in January or if she'd have enough roses for Valentine's Day or too many.

All there was—all she wanted—was Mack.

"I never much did this before," he whispered in her ear. "You have to tell me if it's okay or not. I don't want to go too far and hurt you."

"Don't stop," she gasped, her words muffled by the pillow.

He wound her hair around his hand and pulled, turning her head so her face was toward the light. "I want..." he said, and then he paused, like he wasn't sure what he wanted or how to ask for it.

"Tell me," she said, shifting her ass under his body. She looked at him as best she could from this angle. The uncertainty on his face made her want to pull him into her arms and hold him, just like she'd held him after the oral sex. "I want to give you what you want, Mack."

He gave her another short tug to her hair. "Yeah," he groaned, and for the first time, he ground his dick against her backside. "That—my name. I want to hear what I do to you. I want you to make some noise."

She smiled up at him. "You bite me like that again and I might just scream."

All the uncertainty bled out of his face. "You are beautiful," he said as he lowered his body back onto hers. The buttons from his shirt scraped over her bare skin, but she didn't care. All she cared about was the hot, heavy bulge pressing against her backside, about the grip he had on her hair, about the way he kissed the area he'd just bitten before jerking her head to the other side and biting down on the opposite side of her neck.

"Oh, *Mack*," she cried, not bothering to muffle her words in the pillow. The place probably was deserted anyway. There wasn't anyone around. She could be as loud as she wanted.

That was as far as the distracted thoughts got before Mack rolled off her and pulled her body with him, until they were spooning. She'd never had her hair pulled like this, but she liked it. It didn't hurt, not really—and she could focus on the sensation.

Mack moved his mouth over to an unbitten spot and began to tease his teeth over her skin. At the same time, he reached his free hand down between her legs and began to stroke the panties.

She bucked in his arms, a high, tight noise stuck in the back of her throat. "You're gonna make me come again," she managed to get out.

His hand briefly left her clit to stroke her stomach, and then he pushed his fingers beneath the lace. "That was the plan, yeah," he growled in her ear before nipping at her lobe. "Put your leg over mine. Open up for me, Karen."

She did as she was told, hooking her leg over his raised knee.

He didn't rush though. He dragged his fingers over her swollen clit and around the edge of her sex several times. "You're already so wet," he mused. "Or was that just the swim?" As he asked, he dipped a finger inside.

Her muscles clenched. "It's you," she got out through clenched teeth. "You do this to me, Mack."

He moved his hand in small circles, his finger barely inside of her. "Do you like it?"

"More," she gasped, trying to thrust against his hand but not quite able to pull it off. He had her leg hooked and he was apparently in no mood to let it go. The pressure was incredible, like the orgasm against the door earlier had only primed her pump and she would explode if she couldn't let go right now, right—

"Do you want to come again?" he asked, slipping out of her to rub her clit. She whimpered. "Do you want me to *make* you come again?"

"Mack," she begged, grabbing at his arm to try and make him get her off. "*Mack*."

"I like hearing you say my name," he said in a low voice. Then, suddenly, he buried two fingers in her, pumping hard. "Like that?"

She whimpered again, her hips trying to match his rhythm.

"Say it, Karen."

"Yes," she whispered, her body straining so hard against the climax that was waiting just out of reach. "Bite me. Bite me, bite me, bite—*oh*!"

Because he bit down on her shoulder at the same moment he thrust his two fingers up into her and she couldn't have held back the scream if she tried. It all broke free in a crystal moment of pleasure and pain and release.

But the moment was too short, and then the beautiful orgasm faded into a warm glow of Mack kissing her neck and lightly rubbing her clit and holding her tight.

"God, you're so beautiful," he murmured.

She felt shimmery with lightness. God, this was so what she wanted—to be able to give voice to her desires, to have them fulfilled instead of dismissed or belittled, to have someone take care of her. She exhaled, sagging back into Mack's chest. "Mack?"

"Hmm?" he replied, still lightly kissing her neck and shoulder.

"Why do you want me to make noise?"

Chapter Six

Mack paused, feeling Karen's slick wetness as he lazily circled her little clit. He didn't really want to let go of her body at this point. He wanted to work her up again and make her scream his name over and over.

Which was probably why she'd asked that question.

It wasn't that he was embarrassed by her question, but he wasn't sure he actually had an answer. "Don't know," he admitted, rolling onto his back. She spun and curled up against his side, which he liked.

He liked it a lot. He'd missed this, holding a woman close, the smell of sex still hanging in the air.

"Did you want it loud before?" she asked. As the question hung in the air, she undid the top button on his shirt.

He sighed, trying to dredge up the memories without getting caught in the loss of it all. "I was married so young, you know. Nineteen. We had a couple of wild years there, me and Sue. Parking by the side of the road and hiding in the cornfields, where no one could find us if they tried." He grinned at the old memories. "Sometimes we didn't even make it to the fields."

"I've always wondered," she said, undoing another button, "if sex in the bed of a pickup truck was worth it. It wasn't something you could try in my Chicago neighborhood—not unless you wanted the cops to show up before you finished," she added. Another button gave.

"Oh, yeah. It's worth it if you have enough blankets," he added. "Blankets, the wide-open night sky, nothing between you. Hell, yeah, it's worth it."

He wasn't sure if he should make some sort of offer. When it warmed up, he could take her out for a drive and they could try sex in the back of his truck. He would, but he didn't know if they'd be together or not in another five months. This might just be a one-time thing, and if so, he was okay with that.

Really.

She got his shirt unbuttoned and pushed it open. Which did not get him any closer to being naked, what with his long underwear. "Sorry," he said, disentangling himself long enough to sit up and strip the whole mess off. "Used to dressing in layers for the winter."

"Understood." She waited until he was finally shirtless. Then she reached up and traced the muscles on his back.

He wasn't as young as he once was, but ranching had a way of keeping him in decent shape. Or at least decent-enough shape. He hoped.

Her touch was light and soft against his skin, and he had to close his eyes to take it all in. It'd been years since anyone had touched him. Oh, sure, he shook hands and got clapped on the back at church and, yeah, he hugged his boys.

But this? The way a woman's hands felt caressing his body? It was almost too much for him. He was hard and ready and he wanted to roll onto her and bury himself in her body over and over until his release left him sated and spent. To hell with all this foreplay, all this talk.

Except...except he needed the foreplay and he especially needed the talk. He needed to feel this human connection with Karen.

He jammed his feet under the covers and pulled them up over both of them. Then he lay back down in her arms, marveling at the wonder of it all. Her arm went around his waist and she held him. It was somehow even more intimate than the things they'd done.

"We had Mark—he's the oldest—when I was twenty one. Nicky was a year and a half later, and then Tommy almost two years after that. Three kids by the time I was twenty-six." He shook his head. "Tommy's almost twenty-one now. I look at him now and I can't believe I'd been married for two years and had a baby on the way at that age."

"Was your wife the same age?"

"She was a year younger than I was. That's why we didn't get married until I was nineteen." He sighed again. "And once you have three little ones who need to eat and sleep and play, you change. *We* changed. We didn't spend all night doing...this," he said, waving his hand over the bed. "No more parking in the middle of nowhere, no more wild sex in the back of the pickup. It became...quick. Quiet. We had to be fast and not make any noise because we didn't want the boys walking in on us, you know?"

"I understand that."

"And Sue got sick and...well." He cleared his throat. "The boys grew up and left home, and since then it's been...quiet. It's been real quiet."

A bit of that quiet settled over them. He reached up and covered her hand with his. He just held her.

He was tired of the quiet. Been tired of it for a long time. He'd taken to leaving the TV on all the time, even while he was sleeping. The news, the weather, whatever show happened to catch his fancy. If he wasn't working, he was listening to other people talking in some vain attempt to push back against the crushing silence.

Karen squeezed him tight and then she was moving, sliding out from his arms and straddling him, which gave him a hell of a view of her breasts. She shifted her hips back and forth against the zipper of his pants. "I think," she said, her voice breathy as she stroked his chest, "that it's time to make a little noise."

Just the sight of her up there—the promise of her body riding his—pushed the silence and disappointment and loneliness of the last few years out of his mind. Because how could he think of anything but Karen? Of the way her breasts shifted when she moved her hips, of the way her nipples tightened when he traced his finger in small circles around the darker red parts?

"Yes, like that," she moaned when he went from circling to tugging on those nipples, gently pulling them toward him. Her head fell back. "Oh, that's good, Mack."

His name on her lips...yeah. He half-sat, half-pulled her down to him so that he could use his teeth on her. She ran her fingers through his hair and held him against her breasts as he sucked and nipped and licked at her, her nipples getting harder and harder in his mouth as he got harder and harder beneath her.

"God, you feel *so* good." She was panting as he slipped a free hand down her back and palmed her ass again. She still had on those little red panties because, as much as they'd done to each other, they still hadn't gotten naked yet.

"Take these off," he demanded and then, just because he could, he squeezed her ass in his hands.

She jolted against him, her eyes wide with what he hoped was desire. "Then I get to strip your jeans off. Deal?"

His blood began to hum. "Deal."

She sat back on her heels and then rose to her feet to stand over him. Moving so slowly it hurt him, she slipped the little panties down her legs, lifting one foot and then the other before she dropped the little bit of fabric over the side of the bed. She stood over him again and he stared up at her as he rubbed his hands over her calves.

"You are *beautiful*," he told her. And she was. Her figure was lush and rounded, the kind of body a man could get lost in.

Because he felt a little lost in her right now. He wanted to touch her again, to scrape his teeth over her skin, to make her shiver and shake and cry out his name over and over.

Her grin faded a bit as she looked down at him. When she shifted her weight, it gave him one *hell* of a view. "It's been a long time since I felt beautiful."

"But you are," he told her. He sat up and pressed a kiss against the top of her thigh. "Everything about you is perfect," he murmured, leaning up enough that he could reach the spot between her legs.

He scooted her legs a little farther apart so he could have the best access. Then he licked her. She tasted sweet with a slight hint of chlorine from the pool.

"Mack," she said, grabbing his head again. "At least—*oh*—at least let me take your pants off."

"In a minute," he told her. "You already did this for me. I'm just returning the favor." He flicked his tongue back and forth over her little clit. It was red and swollen and oh so slick from when he'd already touched her.

"God, that feels so good," she groaned. Her legs started to shake. "Mack." When he didn't stop, she said with more force, "*Mack*. If I don't have you inside of me right now..."

He pinched her clit between his tongue and his teeth. Not much pressure—certainly not a bite in the true sense of the word. Just the touch of teeth on flesh. Just for her.

"*Oh!*" she screamed and her knees gave. She buckled onto him so hard that he barely had time to lean back and catch her.

When he folded her into his arms, she bit down on his shoulder, and in that moment, he understood. Just another layer of sensation, another touch on the skin. "I want you on top," he managed to get out. "I want to watch you ride me."

"Pants," she whispered. "Condom."

"Yeah." He lifted her off and undid his pants. As quickly as he could, he shucked the damned things off and grabbed the box of condoms from the bedside table.

His hands shook as he tore open the packet. There was still an air of the unreal about this whole thing. Was he really in a hotel room with a woman he'd just met, the taste of her sex still on his tongue?

Karen took the condom out of his hand and rolled it on, which pretty much answered the question. Because while his head couldn't quite grasp the realness of the situation, his body sure as hell recognized reality when presented in the form of a woman who made him want things, made him want to do things that he'd forgotten he used to want.

Once the condom was on, she mounted up and kissed him. He could feel the tantalizing warmth of her sex against his dick, but he wrapped his arms around her waist and kissed her back. Because this wasn't just about sex. Maybe it never had been.

She lifted herself up and his dick sprang to attention. Slowly, she lowered herself back down onto him, her body stretching to take him in.

"God, you feel good," he got out in a hoarse whisper, his face buried against her neck. It was all he could say.

Because the feeling of being surrounded by that warmth, that wetness—it wasn't like he'd forgotten. How could he have? He'd never been an angel. He hadn't been a virgin when he'd gotten hitched. He'd liked sex early and often.

But the sensation of a woman's body closing around his, her muscles twitching with pleasure around him—it was as if he'd put that memory away so he wouldn't have to think about what he didn't have anymore.

And now he had it back.

She leaned back and cupped his face in her hands. Her eyes were wide with desire, with need. For him. "I'm going to ride you *so* hard."

Sounded good to him. She pulled his arms away from her waist and lifted them over his head. He was forced to lie back, but her breasts were right there, moving back and forth with every single one of her movements.

He caught the tip of her nipple in his lips and began to suck her.

"Yeah, like that," she moaned and then...then she began to move. None of those little shifts of her hips back and forth, no subtle shimmies.

She rode him, her ass rising and falling on his dick with enough force that, even if he'd wanted to say something—even if his mouth hadn't been busy with her stiff nipple, pulling and nipping it until she was saying, "Yeah, Mack. Oh God, yeah," over and over again, he couldn't have spoken. All there was, all there could be, was his body and hers and the way they moved together, faster and harder and then, when he didn't think he could take it, harder still.

She let go of his wrists to grab his head and move him to her other nipple. "Like that, yeah," she said as he sucked her tender skin into his mouth. "Oh God, you feel so good inside me."

He filled his hands with her ass, pulling her farther apart so he could drive harder up into her. He dug his fingers into her skin, which made her moan his name even louder. "Mack—oh, *Mack*!"

He pumped harder, faster—the whole time, all the noises she made pushed him closer and closer to the edge. "Oh, God. Mack, I'm going to—you're going to make me come," she gasped.

"Come for me," he said, squeezing her ass harder. She sucked in air and ground down harder on him. "Come for me, Karen."

He managed to catch one of her nipples in his mouth again and held it between his lips as he looked up at her. She met his gaze, her eyes glazed over with lust.

Then he pressed his lips together.

A jolt of what felt a hell of a lot like electricity shot through her. Her mouth dropped open and a noise that was part scream, part moan and all sex rolled out of her.

Mack fell back against the pillows and, grabbing her hips, he thrust up as hard as he could while her orgasm held her tightly all around him.

"God—God," he groaned, and even he didn't know if it was a prayer for release or a prayer that it would never end.

Then his climax ripped through his body, pushing him through several final thrusts as he emptied everything he had into her.

She fell forward onto him, her skin warm and damp with perspiration. He wrapped his arms around her and held her, not wanting to break the connection between them.

He didn't want it to end.

But it had to, he knew that. He pulled out before he lost the condom, but he still didn't let her go. They lay like that for several minutes, panting and catching their breaths.

Through the post-sex haze, he became aware that Karen was stroking his hair, slowly and gently. He smiled and shifted so he could kiss her. "Amazing."

Which wasn't a strong-enough word to describe how he felt, but it was the best he could do. But already the high was fading. He was up past his usual bedtime and he wasn't used to having this much sex. He was going to be stiff in the morning, that much he could already tell.

But it was worth it. God, it was worth it.

She leaned up enough so that she could look at him. "Will you stay the night with me?"

He grinned, because he didn't think he had much of a choice at this point. If he tried to drive off into the winter night, he'd probably pass out from sheer sexual exhaustion and crash the truck or something.

Plus, if he woke up with her—and he wasn't too sore—they'd get another shot at sex again. And he'd like another shot.

"What time is checkout?"

The smile she wore was huge and made him feel good. He'd put that smile there. He wasn't too old or too out of practice. He could still take care of a woman.

He was still alive. It was a hell of a feeling.

"Eleven." Finally, she pulled herself off him and stood beside the bed. "Wow," she murmured, getting her balance. "Just...wow, Mack."

"Glad to hear it." Wow. Yeah, that about summed it up.

She went into the bathroom to get cleaned up. Mack took care of the condom and tried to arrange the pillows. He might have been nervous about sleeping with a woman after so long, but the post-sex exhaustion was pretty severe.

Tonight, he'd sleep and he wouldn't even mind the silence because Karen was next to him. And in the morning, he'd wake up, make love to her again and then...

And then he'd go home. They both would. He'd go back to his ranch, to his quiet house and his cows and horses and the infrequent emails from his sons. And Karen would go back to her florist shop.

And that would be that.

Maybe it wouldn't be. They were only three hours apart. Maybe...

The bathroom door opened and he shook all the *maybes* out of his head. Sleep first, then morning sex.

Everything else could wait.

Chapter Seven

After all those years of sleeping alone in bed—because the sleeping-alone thing had started well before her marriage had officially ended—seemed to disappear as Karen curled up in Mack's arms. She wanted to keep the light on, to keep touching him. He was solidly built, a bunch of muscles that didn't come from a slavish gym routine, but from an honest day's work. She wanted to run her fingers through his dark chest hairs.

But she didn't. If he'd been up since five something that morning and she'd kept him up until past ten having the kind of wild, crazy sex that she'd been dreaming of having for years and years—well, she wasn't surprised when he started breathing evenly a few minutes after she shut the light out.

So she just lay there for a while, savoring the feel of his strong body moving into deeper sleep.

She was going to be sore, that much she knew. Mack was built like, well, a Mack truck. And he knew how to bite her just right. She could still feel the way his calloused fingers had dug into her backside. God, what a ride.

It'd been the kind of sex that a woman would have trouble walking away from. She hadn't been lying—she wasn't looking for a marriage, especially now that she knew more about Mack's wife. She didn't want to try and replace a woman he still obviously loved and always would.

But to have Mack in her bed, in her arms?

She wasn't sure she wanted to kiss him goodbye and be done with it either. Mack had exceeded every single one of her fantasies about a strong, silent cowboy. He'd put her first and made her feel beautiful and special—and that didn't even take the orgasms into consideration.

The feeling of Mack inside of her, Mack grabbing her, Mack biting her—it'd made all those little pops of orgasms she had with her vibrator look like child's play. There was no way she could replicate all of those sensations on her own.

She thought back to her last date, with the Toe-Picker, and the ones before that with the colorless, hopeless boys trapped in men's bodies. She couldn't recreate the orgasm Mack gave her on her own. Hell, she didn't know if there was another man in the greater Montana area that could do that for her.

She'd gone looking for her fantasy cowboy and—as unbelievable as it still was—she just might have found him.

Now what was she going to do?

Morning came early. Or, at least, it felt early to Karen. The bed shifted and she became aware of the dim light filtering into the room around the edges of the curtain.

Then she was alone in the bed. She heard the bathroom door click, and for a moment, she couldn't quite remember—oh. *Mack.*

Just thinking of what he'd done to her body last night made her muscles clench—which made her realize how danged sore she was. Which was a good sign. She hadn't dreamed the night of wild sex.

She'd really and truly managed to find herself an honest-to-goodness cowboy, and he was everything she'd ever dreamed of—only better.

Smiling to herself, she managed to roll over, pull the covers up to her chin and check the clock.

6:08. In the morning.

Lord. She normally slept until about seven thirty. The shop didn't open until ten, which left her plenty of time to sleep in, work out and shower before she surrounded herself with the beauty of every flower she could have delivered to this part of Montana.

What time had Mack said he got up? Five? Yeah, five. He'd slept in until 5:15 the day before, she remembered him saying. And...he got up at four in the summer?

Lord.

The bathroom door opened again, and she managed to get her eyelids open to about half-mast—which was enough to see the naked form of Mack Tucker emerge into the dim light.

If she'd been able to, she would have whistled. The man was masculinity personified. Those muscles. That chest hair, that beard. He wasn't cut like a man who lived in a gym, but there was no missing the fact that this was a man who used his body every single day.

Languid heat began to build between her legs, erasing the temporary soreness. *Hers*. He was hers for at least the next few hours. "'Morning," she murmured sleepily.

"'Morning," he said as he climbed back into the warmth of the bed. Her arm went around his waist and she curled her body around his. He pulled her in tight and kissed her on the top of her head.

She sighed into him. "I suppose you're going to tell me that you haven't slept in this late in...years, right?"

He chuckled. "Nope." He moved his hands over her back, rubbing in slow circles. "I'd even go so far as to say decades."

She let her fingers trail through the hair on his chest. "Do you think you can stay in bed for a few more minutes?"

He tilted her face up. "I was counting on it." Then he rolled her onto her back, his broad chest covering hers, and kissed her.

She let her hands explore his back because she had not gotten enough of touching him last night. His muscles twitched under her hands, heightening her awareness. His body reacted to hers—he was aware of her on a fundamental level. That was something she'd been missing for years and years—the feeling that she was important to a man because she was *Karen*, not because she was an available female.

She shifted her legs and looped them around the back of Mack's—and was rewarded with a deep moan of pleasure when his already-hard dick brushed against her clit. He leaned up on his forearms and thrust against her, his dick sliding over her clit, teasing her. "You feel so good," he groaned as he leaned back down and kissed her again.

Then he captured her lower lip in his teeth and bit down, just a little. Just right.

She moaned into his mouth as the tension seemed to pull at her body and push it back all at the same time. "You like it like that, don't you?" he whispered as he kissed her cheek, her neck—and he bit down again.

"Yes. Oh, Mack," she gasped as he shifted and thrust against her and put his teeth to her skin. She shuddered as he slid over her again and again. The pressure was building, pushing back against her clit. How could she need him this badly already? She'd gone years without sex, and years before that only having sex once a week.

But now? He'd given her three explosive orgasms last night and she was well on her way to another one this morning. She needed more. She needed more of *him*. "You drive me crazy," she whispered, shifting her hips against him.

"How crazy?" he asked, leaning back to look at where the two of them met but weren't joined—not yet. She looked with him, looked at how his body looked hard and was covered in her wetness because she was already so ready for him. "God, look at you, Karen—look at how much you want me. Look at how much I want you."

She tried to open her mouth, tried to tell him she was watching, that she was seeing everything about him and everything he did to her—but nothing came out but a high whimper that got stuck in the back of her throat. She clung to his shoulders, trying to pull him in, trying to get that pressure on her clit to release so she could think again.

Because when he said things to her, things like, "Jesus, you're so damn sexy, babe," she couldn't think, couldn't speak—couldn't do anything but cling to him and watch his beautiful body torment hers with raw lust.

He flexed again, the tip of his dick sliding up and back over the folds of her flesh, and she wanted more. More than this teasing touch. More than a little pressure on her clit. She wanted all of him, right now, hard and fast and wild.

"You want that?" he asked, his voice hoarse as he flexed and drew back.

She nodded.

"Tell me," he demanded. "Tell me what you want."

"Mack," she got out. "*God.*"

He pulled back, farther this time, and slammed his hips down, grinding his dick against her. "*Say it.*"

"Fuck—me. Oh—fuck me. Fuck me *hard,*" she begged.

He growled, a sound of satisfaction and lust. "Such dirty words out of your pretty little mouth. Is that what I do to you?"

"Yes, oh—yes," she gasped as he slammed his dick against her clit again. "Oh God, *please* fuck me."

"You want it hard?" His voice was raw, like she was pushing him past his point of reason just as he'd done to her. "You want me to fuck you *hard*?"

"Please," she almost wept. To hear him say it—to know he was going to do it, going to do it to *her* because he was a man who kept his promises. "Please, I need to come. *Please.*"

Then she felt him press against her, felt her body widen to take him in. She gasped. He was right there, hot and hard and ready to give her what she so desperately needed. He was going to fuck her so hard that she wouldn't be able to sit for a week without feeling how he'd pushed her to that place where pleasure and pain were one and the same.

And then, right on the brink of giving her everything she'd ever needed, he pulled back. "Yeah," he said, almost to himself as he snagged another condom from the table. "Sorry. Got carried away there."

"It's okay. I did too." She lay there, watching him roll the condom on, mentally smacking herself. She wasn't some naïve girl anymore. She knew damned good and well that at this stage condoms were non-negotiable. And yet, there'd been a moment where she'd been so blinded by need that she'd wanted him to hold her down and take her.

Oh, hell, she still wanted that.

When he had the condom on, she grabbed him by the hair and jerked him down to her.

"Where were we?" he asked, and he actually managed to pull off an innocent look.

She laughed in spite of herself and then he kissed her, rough and demanding. "Oh, yeah," he said as he leaned down far enough that he could capture one of her nipples in his mouth. "I was just about to fuck you. *Hard.*"

"Yes, yes, that," she whispered. "Rough and hard and dirty. Oh!" she cried out as his hot mouth tugged on her nipple, pulling it out. The spike of pain made her shudder in delight. "Oh, please, oh..."

She dug her nails into his back, trying to spur him on, but he grunted. "Oh, no you don't," he said, leaning back to grab her hands. "None of that."

Then he pinned her hands over her head with one of his and—finally—he positioned himself against her and began to thrust.

Last night had been a little slower, them getting to know each other's bodies, what the other wanted and liked. But not this morning.

Mack held her down and drove into her with an almost savage fury, and she liked it. Liked how she was completely at his mercy and he was still doing exactly what she wanted, exactly how she wanted it.

"Like that?" he grunted, slamming into her again.

"Yeah," was all she was able to say. "Yeah."

And then, just when she thought she couldn't take much more, he started to nip at her with his teeth, all up and down her neck, her shoulders—as far as he could reach without pulling out of her. "Scream for me, babe," he whispered in her ear, right before he bit her lobe.

So she did, because he gave her no choice. He pushed her until the orgasm took control of her body, tightening down in a moment of utter, perfect clarity that drove her voice out of her. "*Mack*!" she cried, arching her back into him. Then everything about her went limp and soft.

He growled against her skin, thrusting harder and harder until he froze, his body deep inside hers. Then he collapsed onto her, panting hard.

Karen got her hands free and wrapped them around him. "God," she whispered. "God."

"Good?" He actually sounded worried about it as he leaned back enough to trace a fingertip down the side of her neck. "Not too rough?"

"God, no. Just right." She pulled him back down into her arms. "I didn't...I mean, I've had orgasms before, but, Jesus. I think that's the first time sex has been better than my fantasies."

He rolled off of her but didn't let go. He pulled her with him, keeping the skin-to-skin contact between his chest and her breasts. His strong arms encircled her and he stroked her hair, and she felt warm and cared for and *safe*. It was a wonderful feeling. "That's...well, that's good."

"It's *great*. And you?" She giggled. The euphoria from her climax was actually making her lightheaded. "I made you say those things... I can't believe you *actually* said them."

"Yeah. Me neither." He exhaled heavily. "But it was—*whew*." He leaned his head up and grinned at her, and in that moment, he looked *so* much younger—like the weight of the last few years had finally lifted off his shoulders. She could see the reckless man who'd have sex in cornfields and pickup trucks, wild and young and, yeah, maybe a little careless sometimes.

"Did you ever used to talk like that before? With your wife?"

"I don't—" He paused—and the pause just went on. He stopped stroking her hair. "I don't know," he finally admitted, sounding like she'd punched him instead of asking a question about his sexual past.

She didn't like how he suddenly sounded shell-shocked. So she kissed him, kissed the boy he'd once been and the man he'd become.

And she kissed him so he wouldn't have to fumble around for words because she got the feeling he was too shocked by having said *fuck* in front of her that he simply did not know what to say next.

"Breakfast after this?" she asked.

"Yeah," he agreed. "And after that..."

The words hung in the air, casting a pall over the afterglow. Because after that...

She didn't want this fantasy to end.

But it might have to anyway.

Chapter Eight

He hadn't packed anything. Not even a toothbrush. He'd gone to the trouble of making sure that Jim from the next ranch over would be able to feed the horses, but he hadn't packed an overnight bag.

Yeah, he wasn't exactly on the ball here.

While Karen got cleaned up in the bathroom, he got dressed in yesterday's clothing. His legs ached—hell, his butt ached from all the thrusting—and he was spent. As late as he'd slept, he could easily roll back under those covers and sleep for another few hours.

But she'd suggested breakfast, and the day wasn't getting any younger—just like he wasn't either. So he got dressed and, as he did that, he thought about what would come after breakfast.

Something had happened this morning, something that had pushed him to a place he might have known once, a long time ago—back before the kids and the cancer, back when he and Sue were two kids crazy in love and unable to keep their hands off each other.

He couldn't remember if he'd ever told Sue he was going to fuck her hard, or if she'd ever told him to do that to her. They'd done some pretty crazy things—including not always using a condom, which had lead to a few anxious months here and there. But...had they talked like *that*? He didn't know. He didn't like not knowing—not being able to remember that about him and Sue. He didn't like it all.

He sat on the edge of the bed and pulled on his boots with more force than he technically needed. That's not what this night with Karen had been about—forgetting Sue. He didn't *want* to forget her. She was his wife and he still loved her.

Last night—this morning—it'd been about...

Well, lust. Not that there was anything wrong with that.

But if there wasn't anything wrong with it, why did he feel so *not* right? Why did he feel like he'd betrayed Sue?

He was going around and around with himself when Karen came back out of the bathroom. Instead of the stunning red dress, she wore a pair of jeans and the kind of turtleneck sweater where the neck part hung low, so he could still see a few small marks that he'd left on her. Her hair was still down, still hanging in long, loose waves around her shoulders.

Something inside shifted as he stood and stared at her. Like...like last night, she'd been out of his league, the kind of woman he could safely lust after because there was just no way that someone as refined and classy and impulsive as Karen Thompson would ever fit into his quiet world of early mornings, earlier evenings and a whole lot of cows.

The woman standing before him now with a wide and happy smile on her face was still Karen. Even after less than twelve hours with her, he felt like he'd know her anywhere. But this version looked like a woman who might want to spend a little time out in the middle of nowhere that was his part of Montana. Like she might be comfortable with an old man like him.

She looked like she would belong.

That made everything worse.

Her smile faltered a little. "You okay?"

"What? Oh, yeah." He forcibly shook the mess of thoughts out of his head. "My head, it's still a little fuzzy from sleeping in so late." Yeah, fuzzy. That was one way to describe it. He tried to give her a grin. "And other things."

She looked at him a little bit longer. He didn't miss the hint of worry that pulled at the corners of her eyes. "Do you still want to grab some breakfast? I know you probably need to get home."

Her voice was level when she said it, but he heard it anyway. The sound of a woman who was used to disappointment getting ready to deal with more of the same.

And despite the fact that he wasn't actually sure if he was okay or not—that there was something about this whole experience that left him wondering what the hell he was doing—he couldn't disappoint her. Not her.

So he closed the distance between them and pulled her into his arms and held her. It wasn't sexual, not really. It was...

Intimate. And that, more than anything—that scared him. Because he'd only ever been intimate with one other woman.

What he was feeling wasn't panic, because Mack Tucker did not panic, for God's sake. He hadn't panicked when Sue had been diagnosed, and he hadn't panicked when she'd gotten sicker and sicker. Well, not much anyway.

So whatever this was, it wasn't panic. Absolutely not.

Which did not explain why, instead of saying the smooth thing, the thing that Tommy would probably tell him to say, something like I've got time, he said something else entirely. "I need to get back."

She was stiff in his arms for a second, as if his words had stabbed her right in the back.

"It's a long drive," he went on stupidly, because more talking could only make this worse. "And I'm sure you need to get to work soon too."

She sighed and, for a brief moment, she hugged him back. "I understand. I...I had a wonderful time, Mack. This was good for me. I hope..." she took an even deeper breath, "I hope it was good for you too."

He leaned back and looked down into her eyes. There was so much there—hope and worry and caution. He cupped her cheek in his palm. "I'm still—" He sighed. He wasn't sure he could explain anything at this point. The first rule of holes and all that—when you're in a hole, stop digging.

So he kept it simple. Or tried to anyway. "I'm still trying to figure this whole thing out."

"I know." She turned and kissed his palm. "When you get a little bit more figured out, you can call me. If you want." She closed her eyes and swallowed. "If you want to see me again."

That hit him low, like a punch to the gut, because he was disappointing her. Hell, he was disappointing himself, and that went against everything he believed. Because he'd taken a beautiful, vibrant woman to bed and now, in the cold light of a cold day, he was going to cut and run. That wasn't the kind of man he was.

Or was he? Because he also wasn't the kind of man who took a woman to bed, not anymore.

Or he hadn't been. Not until Karen Thompson had walked into his life.

He didn't know. He just didn't know.

But he couldn't let go of her yet either, because once he let go, that was it. That was him walking off into the sunrise. So he kissed her and she kissed him back. Not the fevered kissing that had made him lose his mind this morning, but something sweeter. Like she knew how hard he was trying and she appreciated the effort.

Then the kiss ended.

She stepped away from him. She didn't meet his gaze.

And damn it all to hell, he couldn't just walk out the door. He couldn't be a callous bastard, but he didn't want to throw off a half-hearted, "I'll call you," because he couldn't make a promise to her he couldn't see his way to keeping.

But he owed her something, something more than a goodbye kiss. "Let me get your bag."

Her lips pulled down into a frown, but then she nodded. She shoved her things into the bag and grabbed her coat, he snagged his hat and they walked out into the hall in silence.

The elevator—the same elevator where he'd pinned her against the back wall and touched her through her panties—was a special kind of hell now. And because he couldn't look at her and not think of all the ways he'd touched her, he shifted the bag to his other hand, took hold of her hand and held it tight, as if that was the riskiest move he'd made all night.

She held his hand back, which he decided meant that she didn't hate him for not exactly turning out like the cowboy of her fantasies. Not much anyway.

They walked out of the hotel like that, like a couple heading out for a big day together. She led him to her car, a little sedan that didn't look rated to Montana winters, and he put her bag in the trunk.

This was it—the last possible moment he could redeem himself. He could still take her to breakfast. He still could say something. *Anything.*

"Karen," he began before he could talk himself out of it.

She paused and turned to look back at him. "Yes?"

And he wanted to tell her everything, how he couldn't remember if he'd ever talked dirty to Sue and he was too old for her anyway and this was all too much for him because he loved his dead wife. Because it was just too much for him. *It was.*

But he couldn't.

He cleared his throat. "I had a real nice time too."

That got him something that was supposed to be a smile and just didn't make it. Not even close. "Good. I'm glad to hear it."

Then she got in her car and he turned to his truck and began the long drive home.

Alone.

Chapter Nine

"Karen?"

Karen paused on her way back to her little office in the rear of Bergman's Floral Creations. But she didn't turn around. Flo was a genius with baby's breath but a bit overbearing, in a motherly sort of way. Which was exactly the kind of thing Karen was not in the mood for. Not after watching Mack drive away from the hotel without a look back. "Yes?"

"Everything okay?"

Karen steeled herself and tried to wipe the disappointment off her face. No, actually, everything was not all right. She'd just spent the night in the arms of a man who made nearly every single one of her fantasies come true—except for that one about sex in the back of a pickup truck—and she didn't think she'd ever see him again.

"Fine." She turned and gave Flo what she hoped was a sympathetic smile. "Have we gotten confirmation on the rose order? Valentine's Day is coming up fast, and I don't want to be left empty-handed." There. That was a perfectly reasonable thing to say, especially because Flo hadn't quite let her forget that during her first year as the owner of this store that was exactly what had happened.

Flo stared at Karen. Flo's hair was in the permanent helmet of old-lady curls and the same work apron she'd probably been wearing for the last thirty years was tied around her waist. "Bad date?"

Bad? No. It'd been a wonderful date. The only bad part had been when it ended.

She would have thought that rejection wouldn't sting this much. After all, years of living with the realization that Roger didn't love her, had never loved her, had trained her well. Not to mention that string of bad first dates with losers and creeps. She should be a pro at rejection. It shouldn't hurt at all. But it still did.

"I don't think we'll be seeing each other again." Which neatly sidestepped the goodness or badness of the date itself and stuck to the facts. "He's a widower and I don't think he's ready to move on."

Flo shrugged. "Widowers are tough. Some move on too fast, some never get over it."

Then the phone in her office rang and Karen gratefully hurried to answer it. It was the flower wholesaler, calling to confirm her rose order.

Karen was grateful for the distraction of work. She threw herself into the pre-Valentine's Day preparations with a vengeance. Which was how she normally handled the holiday. Work kept her from reliving the lousy Valentine's Days she'd muddled through with Roger—with the *expensive* piece of jewelry in a Tiffany box that had invariably proven to be the $99 cheap mall-store special that he'd transferred into the bright-blue box on his own, the dinner where he'd boldly and loudly professed his love in front of the rest of the diners but never when they were alone. Oh, and the way his phone would *always* ring at some point in the evening and he'd hurry out of earshot to talk to a *client* who was always his latest girlfriend, calling to tell him how much she loved him.

But this was different. She wasn't trying to drown out the memories of being neglected, misled and ignored. She was trying to not think about the way Mack Tucker had watched her swim, the fire in his eyes when he'd made her cry his name. Because to think of that would be to want it—him—again.

The days turned into a week, then two weeks. Every time the phone rang, she stupidly hoped to hear his rough voice on the other end, asking to see her again. Telling her he couldn't stop thinking about her. That he missed her.

Mack didn't call.

She knew he wouldn't.

Mack turned on his phone, saw the text messages from all three of his boys as well as all the missed calls, and shut that sucker right back down.

He knew what they wanted. They wanted to know how his big date had gone and whether or not Mack was getting on with his life.

He didn't want to talk about the date. He didn't want to talk about Karen. He didn't want anyone to know how he'd tucked his damn tail between his damn legs and run like a coward.

He didn't want to tell his sons that he'd almost forgotten about their mother.

So he kept his phone off. He didn't turn on his computer, just in case one of the boys tried to video-chat with him or whatever the kids were calling it these days. He let the machine pick up his landline.

He didn't tell anyone about the date. He didn't even go to church for a few weeks because he didn't know how he was supposed to sit in the house of the Lord and listen to the preacher talk about sin and forgiveness.

He didn't even turn on the television, aside from catching the weather because impending blizzards were something that no rancher in his right mind would ignore. But instead of leaving the TV on all the time just to fill the silence, Mack turned it right back off.

The silence was punishing, but he deserved it.

Karen probably hated him, but he deserved that too.

One snowy day, when he'd made sure his cattle had water and feed and that was all he could do, he couldn't take it anymore. He dug out the shoeboxes full of photos, the album his mom had put together when he and Sue had gotten married. He flipped through decades of snapshots.

He started spreading the photos out over the kitchen table, organizing them by year and by memory, forcing himself to remember everything that he might have forgotten.

There were the photos of his senior prom. They'd slow-danced to every single song, unwilling to part for anything, even a catchy tune. They'd already been having sex for about four months then, and he'd decided that night that he was going to marry her just as soon as he could, because he knew it was never going to get better than this.

And the photos of her senior prom, then their wedding photos from just two weeks later. Her prom dress had been her wedding dress because her momma had refused to spend more money on another dress so soon, so she'd gotten married in that. It hadn't mattered to them. They'd been adults and they couldn't wait a minute longer. The rest of their lives had been waiting for them.

The rest of Sue's life anyway.

He stacked the pictures of Sue's growing belly when she had Mark, then the ones of her with a big belly and a toddler in her arms. Nicky. And then Tommy, a squalling little ball of red in her arms in the hospital, with Mack leaning over them both, his arm around Sue. Years of Halloween costumes and Christmas mornings and new boots for the boys.

He found the professional photo they'd had done for their tenth anniversary, because Sue had lost as much of the baby weight as she could and was finally ready to have her picture taken again. He'd felt ridiculous being posed by the photographer, but even he had to admit the results were worth it.

Slowly, order was restored to the piles of photos, but Mack couldn't bring himself to put everything back into the boxes. He *had* to look at all the photos now—the table was covered in them. He *had* to remember. He couldn't allow himself to forget.

There was one last box he pulled out from under the bed. It wasn't overflowing like all the other boxes had been.

Mack sat down at the table and opened it.

There weren't as many photos in this one. Instead, there were bracelets from hospital visits and a copy of the first clean doctor's report, followed by the results from a year later that the cancer had come back. The scarf Sue had used to cover her baldness was in here.

And down at the bottom was a photo. He didn't remember seeing this one before. Sue was in her hospital bed, wires and tubes and death lurking at every corner of the frame. Mack was in bed with her, his strong body curled around her weak one.

She'd turned her face to his and their foreheads were touching. Her hand, the one with the IV lines running into it, rested on top of his. Their eyes were closed.

Tears ran down Mack's face as he studied the picture. He didn't know when the photo had been taken, but it couldn't have been more than a few weeks before she died.

And Sue...was smiling. She was *smiling* in the picture. Her eyes were closed and half-sunken into her head and she was about to die and leave him for forever, and still, she smiled. He couldn't take his eyes off of it. Of her.

Something made him turn the photo over. There, on the back, was Sue's handwriting. It was jagged and slanted, none of her normal strong curves to be seen, but he recognized it anyway.

"See how happy you make me? Be happy, Mack. Be happy."

"I don't know how to be happy without you, babe," he whispered to the photo.

It didn't answer him. Of course it didn't, because there was no answer to be had.

Mack put his head down on the table and cried.

Chapter Ten

"Dad?"

Mack started from his brooding at the shout. "What?"

"Dad!" Tommy burst into the house, tracking in snow. "Where the hell have you been? We've been worried sick about you."

Mack gaped at his youngest. "What are you doing here? You're supposed to be in school."

"Yeah, well, you didn't text me back." Tommy stomped his feet, getting more snow everywhere. "You haven't returned my calls, or Nick's or Mark's. You're not online, you're not answering your phone. What the hell were we supposed to think?" He shed his coat and draped it over the couch. "We decided that one of us had to make sure you weren't frozen to death somewhere out on the ranch, and I was closest. What the hell have you been doing?" He turned and saw all the photos piled on the table. "I mean, seriously, Dad, what have you been doing?"

"Nothing. Just...remembering."

"Jesus, Dad. We thought you might have been kidnapped by your date or something, and you were here *organizing photos* the whole time?"

"Hey, you watch your tone."

Back in the day, that rebuke would have gotten him a, "Sorry, Dad," or something.

But not now. Mack was starting to realize Tommy was *pissed*. "For God's sake, you could have at least sent us a text to let us know you weren't dead or anything. Do you have any idea how worried we were?"

Mack stared up at his son, his youngest. He always thought of Tommy as the baby. But he wasn't looking at the littlest of the three right now. He was looking at a full-grown man. "I'm...I'm sorry, son."

Tommy glared at him for a moment and then it passed. He sank onto the couch across from Mack's recliner. "So what happened?"

"I...I can't talk to you about it." The thought of explaining anything that had happened with Karen to his own kid...no.

"Come on, Dad. You've been a hermit for weeks now, organizing old photos and—" He stood and walked over to the table and picked up the top photo. The very last one. "Oh. You found this one."

"You know it? I didn't remember it." Which was the problem, wasn't it? That he was forgetting the love of his life?

"I took it, Dad. You two were asleep and you looked... Well, I didn't know if you guys would get another chance like that. So I took a picture and showed it to Mom." His voice softened. "She told me—"

"What?" He stood and went to his boy. "She told you what?"

"She told me to put it in with the other stuff and you'd find it when you were ready."

Was this what that was? Was he ready? Ready for *what*?

"You didn't tell me about it." It came out as an accusation, but Mack couldn't help it.

"She told me not to," Tommy replied easily. "And if you think I'm the kind of man who'd go back on a promise I made to my dying mother, well—"

"No, no," Mack quickly replied. "I just..."

They stood in silence for a few moments, staring at the last picture of Sue Jenkins Tucker.

"So tell me what happened that sent you into hiding to dig all this up," Tommy said quietly. "Was it that bad?"

"No." *"Be happy, Mack. Be happy."* "She was actually wonderful. Beautiful and smart and nice." Then, because he felt he owed Tommy a compliment, he added, "You picked well. But don't ever sign me up for another dating website again, okay?"

"Okay," Tommy said with a chuckle. "If she was all that, what happened?"

How could he stand here and tell his son about sex with a woman who wasn't his mother?

Tommy sighed. "I don't really want to know the details, Dad. *Ew.* But I also don't want you to lock yourself away like this. It's not healthy. Suck it up and tell me what set you off."

Mack spun and walked back into the living room. "I—I spent the night, all right?"

"Good," Tommy said. "Good for you."

"It's not though. Don't you see? It's not good. It's not good at all."

"Why the hell not?" Tommy demanded. "Look, it's been six years, okay? It's not a bad thing if you move on. It's not a bad thing to go out with a pretty woman—she was pretty, wasn't she?"

"Yeah, but that's not what made her special," he snapped.

"Then what the hell was it? You've spent the last six years acting like you died with Mom. Six years of barely living at all, and for what? That's not what Mom wanted. I heard her—do you remember what she told you the day before she died?"

"She told me to go on with my life," he said bitterly. "That, I remember. But I—I'm forgetting other things. Me and Karen—we—things happened. Things happened and they were good things and she asked if I'd ever done anything like that with my wife and I couldn't remember, okay? I couldn't remember."

Tommy stared at him for a long, quiet moment. "And that's why you ran away?"

"Yes!" He was shouting, but he couldn't stop. "I *know* it's been six years. You don't have to tell me how long it's been because I know it every single damned day that I wake up and she's not beside me. Six of the longest, darkest years of my life because, even though she died and left me, I still love your mother and I don't *ever* want to forget her. And when I was with Karen, I...forgot."

He dropped back into his chair and covered his face with his hands. For so long, he'd kept it together because he had to. The boys had needed him to be strong after they'd lost their mother. The cattle had to be fed and worked. He had to go on. He couldn't stop.

But the boys were men now, grown men. They didn't need him anymore, not like they had.

And Mack was all alone. With nothing but his memories.

"So what you're saying is you were *not* thinking about your dead wife while you were having sex with another woman."

"Jesus, Tommy."

"No, I'm serious, Dad. That's it, isn't it? You were able to let go of Mom for just a little while and be in the moment with someone else and you...what? Think that makes you a bad person?"

Mack managed to level his meanest glare at his son. "I am *married.*"

"You *were*," Tommy corrected. "Damn, man. Have you at least called her? Karen, I mean."

"No." Admitting that was harder than he thought it'd be.

"Why not?" He was irritated again. "You're kind of coming off as a jerk here. I know you're not all up-to-date on your dating protocol, but sleeping with a woman and then not calling her or sending flowers or something—that's a jerk move."

"I couldn't." There was an expectedness to the silence that followed. "I didn't know what to say."

Tommy sighed. "You thank her for the nice time. You compliment her. You ask her out again. No one is asking you to get down on one knee and pop the question, for God's sake. That was one of the reasons I picked her. She expressly did not want to get married again. But you don't have to spend every waking moment remembering every single thing you and Mom ever did, you know. Letting go of Mom for a while doesn't make you a bad person. It makes you human."

Mack didn't have an answer for that. Tommy sat back down on the couch. "None of us—not Mark, not Nick and not me—would think less of you for that. You're not erasing Mom's memory. You're just not living in the past anymore. And if you can't see that..." He abruptly stood and thrust the new photo into Mack's hands. "If you won't listen to me, listen to *her*. And turn your damn phone back on."

And he left. Tommy walked right back out as suddenly as he'd walked in, nothing but small puddles of melted snow on the floor to tell Mack the boy had been there at all.

Mack stared at the photo, at Sue's smile. And then he turned it over in his hands and read the very last thing his wife ever wanted to say to him over and over until it burned into his memory.

"See how happy you make me? Be happy, Mack. Be happy."

Be happy.

He couldn't let her down.

Chapter Eleven

The chime over the door jingled as Karen was double-checking the day's deliveries against her inventory list. She glanced at the clock—four-fifty. Almost closing time. "Welcome to Bergman's, we'll be right with you," she called out, trying to sound perky about the late arrival. The shop had been incredibly busy. Flo was pulling ten-hour days and Julie, who normally worked part-time on the weekends, was pulling down 40-hour weeks right now.

Which was great. Valentine's Day sales accounted for almost a third of her yearly sales. Yay for love.

Not for the first time, Karen's thoughts turned around and ran smack-dab into Mack Tucker. She hoped he was doing okay—if anything, the fact that their date had been so close to Valentine's Day had probably only made things worse. This could be a lonely time of year.

But she had let it go. Or tried to anyway. She hadn't called. She'd sent one email, but he hadn't replied. She hadn't even contacted his son, the one who'd set him up on that dating site.

She had deleted her profile though. She wasn't ready. That much was clear.

She just had to get through the next week. Then she could process it all with a little more distance.

She finished the inventory check and set the clipboard down. "How can I help you?" she asked, heading out into the front of the shop.

And she ran smack-dab into Mack Tucker.

"Mack!" She gasped as she tripped backwards.

Two strong hands went around her waist and steadied her. "Karen," he said. He looked...a little older, maybe a little sadder. But then his mouth curved into a smile. "It's good to see you again."

"It is? I mean, yes. It is." She cleared her throat, trying to get her brain to work. It wasn't easy with his hands around her waist like that. "I...didn't expect to see you. In the store. Today." *Or ever,* her brain helpfully—but silently—added.

"Yeah." He let go of her and took a step back, his gaze drifting over her floral apron and her sensible sneakers. She wished she looked better—that she'd been able to plan ahead for this. Oh, to have on a cuter shirt and the chance to make sure she didn't have any errant leaves in her hair. "Well, about that. I need to order some flowers."

"You do?" She gave him a confused look. "Don't you have a florist in Butte?"

"Oh, yeah, there's a couple. But they didn't have what I needed." Again, there was that grin, sly and nervous all at the same time.

"What is it you need?" She didn't mean it to come out quite like that—like a double-entendre—but she honestly didn't know how else to say it at this point.

Why was he here? Had he come to apologize or ask her out again or was he just in town and had an hour and was looking for a quick screw?

That last thought made her a little mad, which was enough to at least get her mouth closed. She stood up straighter. This man—this kind, loving man—had cut and run after a really good night of sex. She was no one's fuck buddy. And that was final.

"I need something that tells a woman that I'm sorry," he began, his gaze never leaving hers. "I need something that tells a woman I found her to be the most beautiful, exciting woman I've talked to in years, and that I really do like her. I like her a lot. I need something that tells that woman that I do believe in hope even when I might feel hopeless."

She gasped, which made him smile. She'd told him that when she'd told him about buying this florist shop. Flowers gave her hope.

He hadn't forgotten.

"And, if possible," he went on, taking a step closer to her, "I need it to say something about how, even when the days are quiet and the nights are dark, that I know there's still beauty and grace in the world, even if I'm too danged dense to realize it at the time."

"Oh," she whispered, her heart beating wildly. "I don't—carnations, maybe? Or lilies?"

He chuckled as he took another step toward her. "I'm sorry. I've been a fool about it, about you." He reached out with one hand, still cold from the outside, and caressed her cheek. "I don't have a good excuse, except to own up to the facts. And the fact is, I panicked. When I was with you, I wasn't thinking about my wife, and that scared me."

"I never wanted to replace her," she told him, her voice shaking.

"I know. I mean, I know that *now*. But at the time...I guess I got it into my head that making new memories with you would somehow erase the old memories with Sue. I didn't talk to my boys. I didn't talk to you. I holed up in my house and forced myself to only think of her." He gave her a weak smile. "That's where I've been for the last several weeks. Until my boys got so worried about me that Tommy left college and came home just to make sure I hadn't died."

"Oh, Mack. I didn't want to change your past. I don't even want to change mine, as crappy as it was in parts. Who we were then, that's what makes us who we are now."

"It's something I'm figuring out," he admitted. "I behaved like a jerk. A first-class jerk. I had an amazing time with you that night." A hint of blush hit his cheeks. "And that morning."

She felt her own cheeks flush. "I was worried it was something I'd done."

"You did. You made me feel alive again. And I wasn't ready for it then." He leaned down, his mouth just inches away from hers. "But I think I'm ready for it now. I think I'm ready to be happy again." He swallowed. "I didn't know how to say that on the phone. So I drove up to say it in person. I screwed up. I'm sorry. I hope you can forgive me."

She threw her arms around his neck. "Of course I do."

He kissed her then, long and hard, and it just felt right. It felt right to have him back in her arms, to know that even though he'd screwed up, he'd step up and take responsibility for it, instead of casting blame everywhere but at himself.

He leaned back and looked her in the eye. "I want to try again. Dating. I'll drive up to see you and you can drive down to see me, and we'll get to know each other. No rush, no pressure. Just two adults who enjoy being together. If you want. I can't offer you perfection, Karen. I can just offer you me as I am."

She tried to look stern. "On one condition."

"Yes?" His eyes widened in what might have been panic.

"The next time you get scared like that, tell me. Or tell someone. Call your sons. Promise me that you won't ever disappear like that again. I've been worried about you."

He pulled her into a tight hug. "I promise. I won't disappear. It wasn't fair to you and it wasn't fair to my family." Then he leaned back, a glint in his eye. "And I always keep my promises."

She kissed him again, tasting his mouth, his tongue, taking in everything she'd missed about him for the last month. It wasn't a declaration of love—but it was something better.

A declaration of honesty.

The kiss deepened and her body began to tighten in response to his—right until the sound of someone clearing her throat behind them made them both jump. Karen spun to see Flo standing in the doorway, her arms full of lilies. "Don't mind me," she said with a grin.

"Beg your pardon, ma'am," Mack said, which made Karen laugh. It was, hands down, the most old-fashioned thing she'd ever heard him say.

Flo gave him a motherly look. "You the widower?"

All the color drained out of Mack's face. "I am."

"About time," Flo huffed. "Took you long enough."

"Ma'am?" Mack said again, giving Karen a terrified look.

"Mack Tucker, this is Flo Allen. Flo, this is Mack."

"Pleased to meet you. Now go on, you two," Flo said. "It's almost closing time anyway. I've got this."

Karen opened her mouth to protest, but Mack took her hand in his and squeezed it—not too much pressure but enough. *Just right,* she thought. *He was just right.*

"Thanks, Flo," she said, pulling off her apron and dashing back to the office to grab her keys.

"Where to?" Mack asked the moment the door had closed behind them.

"Would you come home with me?" Then she held her breath, waiting for his answer. "Would that make you happy?

He smiled down at her. "You have no idea how happy that would make me. And I promise you this, Karen, I'll do everything in my power to make you happy too."

Then he leaned down, kissed her and nipped at her lower lip with his teeth. Just a little pressure that set her body on fire.

"It's still too cold for the pickup truck," he whispered against her mouth. "But if there was something else you wanted to try..."

She yanked him toward the car. "Come home, cowboy."

So he did.

And he kept his word.

She was *very* happy.

About the Author

Award-winning author Sarah M. Anderson may live east of the Mississippi River, but her heart lies out west on the Great Plains. With a lifelong love of horses and two history teachers for parents, she had plenty of encouragement to learn everything she could about the tribes of the Great Plains.

When she started writing, it wasn't long before her characters found themselves out in South Dakota among the Lakota Sioux. She loves to put people from two different worlds into new situations and see how their backgrounds and cultures take them someplace they never thought they'd go.

When she's not helping out at her son's school or walking her rescue dogs, Sarah spends her days having conversations with imaginary cowboys and American Indians, all of which is surprisingly well-tolerated by her wonderful husband. Readers can find out more about Sarah's love of cowboys and Indians at: www.sarahmanderson.com or Facebook (Sarah-M-Anderson-Author).

You can also find Sarah at Twitter: @SarahMAnderson1, Goodreads: www.goodreads.com/SarahMAnderson or contact Sarah by snail mail at Sarah M. Anderson, 200 N 8th ST 193, Quincy, IL 62301-9996.

Look for these titles by *Sarah M. Anderson*

Now Available:

Men of the White Sandy
Mystic Cowboy
Masked Cowboy

Anything for a Cowboy

Jenna Bayley-Burke

Dedication

For Donna, Sarah and Heidi, who believed I could.

Chapter One

"You're not divorced."

Jacy Weston cringed as her best friend peered over her shoulder. She should have been finished long before now, but registering online dating profiles was a tedious task.

"Well, I'm not married. And I thought it would be harsh to kill off someone just so I could register for notmy1strodeo.com. I only have three options—divorced, widowed or complicated." She pushed her red hair behind her ears and tried to refocus.

Carly took chair from the dining room and joined her at the antique secretary where the computer lived. "So choose complicated."

"I think that means you're sneaking around. I don't want someone who'd go out with a married woman." Jacy kept her eyes on the screen. With her profile complete, she could finish this mess and head back to work vaccinating the herd before her brothers wondered what she was up to.

"Catch me up. What the hell are you doing?" Carly pulled her dark locks over her shoulder and started braiding them.

"Signing up with the site Slade's using. It's designed for people who lead a country lifestyle. If I have to just have lunch with one more boring metrosexual who starts saying howdy and yeehaw as soon as I tell him I live on a ranch, I'll start sedating them. So I'm trying to find a guy who understands that the actors in spaghetti westerns aren't cowboys."

She secured her thick braid with a band she'd been wearing around her wrist. "Slade said the site was worthless."

"My brothers all have the attention spans of a fly on a horse's ass. Besides, this site is less of a time suck for women because the guy does all the work. Or at least starts the conversation. He tips his hat, and it is up to you on how to respond. Wink, smile or look away."

"It tells the guys to look away? I can't imagine your big brother taking that very well."

"Who cares? This way I can be the one to weed out the creepers. I want to get my first time over with, but not enough to bend over for some loser."

Carly held up a hand. "Whoa there, sister friend. Two things. People have sex differently than animals, and since when are you interested in giving up your V-card?"

Jacy turned to her best friend. "I know how people have sex. But I don't want some big production. Just over and done with and no longer a topic of conversation that guys think is either a challenge or a code word for commitment. Virginity is something for the young. I mean, in this day and age, being a thirty-year-old virgin is ridiculous."

"Or a sign of character and good upbringing."

"More like overprotective brothers and a veterinary program that left me no time to sleep let alone date, and now an insane work schedule with the practice covering three counties and my responsibilities here at the ranch." Jacy shook her head. "I should've listened to you and done it that spring break we went to Lake Havasu."

"Yes, your first and only spring break. You studied the entire time." Carly sighed. "Is this really just about your birthday?"

She shrugged. "It's a milestone birthday. Think of it as the gift I'm giving myself."

"That's some seriously creative reasoning. Let me find you a few options. Your first time shouldn't be with a stranger."

"Oh, no, I'm not going to embarrass myself with someone I have to see again. Besides, you know my brothers have scared off every guy in our age group in this county and all the neighboring ones. I didn't get asked for a date once in high school. Remember the way they ran off guys when we were in college? No one local, no one hoping to bag the Weston daughter to get themselves a job on the ranch. That's why I filled out the profile as if I'm from Southern Oregon instead of here in Opal Creek."

"You've put a lot of thought into this devirginizing plan of yours. I mean, you've divorced yourself and moved. Are you still a veterinarian? Did you change your name?"

She'd shortened her last name from Weston to West but didn't care to own up to it. "I'm going to be me, just a few counties south. I want a moment to be something other than the good girl from Weston Ridge, you know?"

"Not really. I grew up in a trailer, remember? I can't see being part of the Weston Ridge legacy as a problem. Or why you'd want to toss away your first time now. You've waited this long."

"I should have experimented the way everyone else did. Now it makes me a freak."

"That's not what makes you a freak." Carly smiled, her dark eyes twinkling. "Driving three hours south to bust a hustle does."

"I don't want it to be some big event. The first time is always awkward and horrible, why not handle it now and move on with my life?"

"My first time was lovely."

Jacy cleared her throat. Things had been awkward enough when Carly and Ace had been together, and two years post break-up things still hadn't returned to normal. "We're not discussing my brother. Any of the four of them, not in this conversation. And you're not to tell them either."

"Yeah, I'm sure Ace would love to not speak to me about your sex life. But I think this is a horrible idea. You've never even gone below the belt with a guy. You think you're really going to be able to lie back and think of England with a stranger?"

Jacy logged out of the program and then stood to face her friend. "I don't have a booty call waiting the way you do. Guys do not take a number for a chance at a make-out session with me. I have to do something."

"If I'm your bad-girl mentor, then you're never going to be able to pull this off. Hell, I couldn't do it, and I exercise my flirt muscles at every opportunity. I mean, you're going to meet this dude and get naked with him an hour later. And then what? Drive home?" Carly gave a shudder. "Unless you're more like your brothers than I realized, casual-sex Fridays are not your thing."

"I'm not planning on making this a thing. Just a one off."

"Then let's go out this weekend. We'll hit Duke's and let guys buy us drinks until you're ready to be an orgasm donor."

"I hate bars. And drunk dudes I've known since the sandbox do not appeal. I hate going to the meet market, which is why I shop for my arm candy online."

"Right. It has nothing to do with being socially stunted because you prefer animals to people."

"Case in point."

"Ouch. I want it on record I think this is a bit over the top."

"Noted. Now I'm going to get back to pissing off cattle."

"Mama," Ray called from the back door. He didn't have time to be summoned to the house today. Or any day, really. He hung up his hat and then pulled off his boots before making his way to the kitchen.

Of course, she was right there, cutting his sandwich on the diagonal the way she'd always done. As if he came to the house for lunch on the regular. He ought to be at the bunk house with the crew, making sure they were ready to head out and repair the south fence.

Ray poured the lemonade on the table into the glasses she'd set out, then pulled out her chair. His mother carried the plates over and took the seat he offered. He joined her and tucked into his sandwich. The sooner he got back out on the ranch the better.

"Busy day?" She watched him eat until he felt under inspection.

"The south pasture fence needs mending, the farrier is due by three and I promised Lad I'd get Chewbacca out of his way."

"Did he pay the stud fee yet? Because if not, he can feed that bull until he settles up."

"We worked something out." He settled easier into his chair. If all she wanted to do was talk business, he'd be out the door before the hands finished with lunch.

"Ray, we cannot support half the county. The farrier doesn't take payment in kind, and neither does our crew."

"Mama, we're having a good year. Lad had to take a loan to fix his barn. It's the right thing to do. They're good neighbors."

She let out a long sigh. "Well, somebody raised you right."

"Tragic, ain't it?" He finished off his lemonade and poured himself more.

"It's too bad you don't have children of your own to raise."

There it was. He picked up his dishes and marched into the kitchen. He'd suspected she was up to this again.

"You haven't been on your September date. You promised."

"You blackmailed me into that promise. You have two other sons to needle for grandchildren. Bother them."

"They're not ready. You will make someone an amazing husband."

"Yeah, Kendra sure thought so." Four years had passed and the failure still gnawed at him.

"Oh, let it go. The whining can't last longer than the marriage. Besides, Kendra's painfully stupid."

"Says my mother. Who faked tears to get me to sign up for a dating website."

"They were real." She put on a pout worthy of the crocodile tears she's shed at her last birthday.

"I don't have time for this. Notmy1strodeo.com is nothing but a collection of women with baggage I don't want to carry."

"You promised one date a month for a year."

"And after this year you promised to never mention dating to me again. If it's going to happen, it'll happen."

"You spend all your time with cowboys, cattle and horses. There's no way to meet women in your life. I had to take action."

He raised a brow, not wanting to tell his mother most of the dates the site brokered were nothing more than a call to action. Which he'd learned quickly not to answer unless he wanted to deal with a woman blowing up his phone for weeks afterwards.

"Just tip your hat at your top three and be done with it. There's still time to get a date for Saturday. And who knows, you might like her and have a second date next weekend for your October. Imagine that, Ray. A second date."

His brothers really needed to man up and get girlfriends so their mom would get off his back. He'd tried marriage, failed spectacularly, and had no desire to repeat the mistake. But since his younger brothers were off playing rodeo cowboy and country songwriter, he knew the odds of either growing up any time soon were long.

"I already logged you in and searched through the new members."

"Mama, so help me, if you pretended to be me—"

"I don't catfish. I'm just trying to save you some time."

"How do you know what catfishing is?" He settled into the wooden chair in front of the kitchen desk where his mother made her office.

"I'm more current than you, cowboy. You don't even have a television in your cabin."

The screen showed his mother's choices, three brunettes who looked too similar to his ex. He'd had a type but had learned five years ago it was the wrong one. He refreshed the options. A blonde equestrian standing beside her show horse. Too much work. Another brunette using the confederate flag as a dress. Not going there. A fresh-faced redhead with an impish grin.

He clicked on the profile of the vet from one county over. Divorced, no kids. Hadn't been married a year. Sounded like someone he knew all too well. He tipped his hat and logged off.

"Did you choose three?" His mother turned his way as he made his escape.

"It's handled."

"You made a date already?"

"Mama, you'll get your September date if I have to go hang out at Trophy Room. I'm not spending another year like this one."

"Me either," she muttered, returning to the dishes.

Chapter Two

Jacy locked her bedroom door, which she hadn't done since she moved home after vet school. With both her younger brothers back at the ranch, she didn't dare check notmy1strodeo.com downstairs. She lay atop her made bed and smoothed her hand across the first and only quilt she'd ever made. The collection of horse fabric had been clever to a pre-teen, but it seemed too busy now. But since it had taken her six months, she'd use it until it fell apart.

She opened the dating app on her phone and groaned. This dating thing was worse than a desk job. She propped herself against the pillows to peruse the hat tippers. She immediately set a filter to weed out everyone over fifty. Should have been more careful about that.

Cowboy number one had a great photo. He seemed to have been snapped unaware, staring out at a grassy pasture, a wide grin lifting his stubbled cheeks. Divorced, under forty, married less than a year, no kids. Ray Mitchell's light brown hair had a little curl and his body looked great beneath the gray T-shirt. In fact, his whole profile made her think twice about hers. She shouldn't have used the headshot her mother had snapped for the veterinary clinic website. Maybe she could get Carly to take one that showed more personality.

She shook her head. No, this wasn't about showcasing herself. This was just about finding someone to hook up with. She winked at his profile and then scrolled to the next. And the next, and on until she'd told more men to look away than she'd thought possible on a profile that had only been active for six hours.

A woodpecker knock sounded from her phone as the app lit up with a message alert. It took her a minute to figure out how to access it.

"Duck or Beaver?"

When she saw the simple question, she had to smile. Most guys opened the conversation by either telling her she was beautiful or asking if her hair was naturally red.

"Black and orange forever!"

She'd much rather talk about her alma mater than discuss her hair. Unless he was a duck, because the school rivalry in Oregon was enough to keep him from being a contender. One university was known for football and lawyers while hers actually taught useful things.

"Animal Management '05"

"Pre-vet med '09 and DVM '13"

She pulled her bottom lip between her teeth and bit down. Thank goodness she'd thought to shorten her name. He'd been on the OSU campus with Ace and Slade, but before she'd made it there. Bullet dodged.

"Did you Steer-a-year?"

"No extracurriculars. Worked weekends as a vet-tech, so didn't have time for any clubs."

"Clubs at OSU mean something different than at most schools."

"Thank goodness."

Her eyes widened and she wanted to reach into cyberspace and grab the text back. She didn't need him knowing she hated places like that. Maybe he was looking for a fun type. Girls who wanted to sleep with a guy right off probably did that kind of thing.

"Agreed. Waste of time."

"I'm more of the up-early than the late-night type."

"Me too. Can I call you? I hate texting."

Her hopeful heart gave a squeeze and then kicked up a notch. She needed to ask him out, put her plan into motion. She texted her number and prayed he didn't have a squeaky voice.

The dinner bell sounded on her phone and her heart jumped. She cleared her throat before answering in what she hoped was a nonchalant tone. "Hello?"

"Jacy? It's Ray." He had one of those warm whiskey voices that she found so sexy.

"Hi." Think of something to say. Something worldly, interesting.

"Hi."

"I don't know what to say." She couldn't help the laugh. He joined in and her pulse skipped at the sound of his mellow baritone.

"I don't know who came up with internet dating, but they should have also developed a way out of awkward conversations."

"Right? It's all a gamble until you see the person up close and can see if they even resemble their profile. And even then, some computer nerd who never had a date wrote a program that thinks you and this person will get along. And then you go home thinking you've been punked by a TV show." She wrinkled her nose. Rambling, so attractive.

"You've just described my last year. Do you look like your picture?"

"Mostly. My mom did it for the office website. What about you?"

"My mother took it when I wasn't looking. She liked it."

She cleared her throat. This could be a deal breaker. "Do you live at home with your mother?"

He gave a chuckle. "I'm not one of those. We're on the same property, but I have my own place."

Which meant he had a bed. She sighed in relief. "I can't judge. My mother is down the hall and I've got two brothers downstairs." Crap, she sounded pathetic. "But it's only because I'm mobile for work. Sometimes I don't make it back home for a few days, so taking care of my own place would be a challenge."

"You don't have to defend yourself."

"I know. I'm just nervous. I'm bad on the phone."

"So I'm not a fan of texting, and you're not into phones. I guess that means we'll have to meet in person."

She pumped her fist in the air. "I'd like that."

"Where will you be this weekend?"

She pouted, not sure what he meant.

"You said you had to travel for work."

"Oh, right. I'm at the wildlife park outside of Roseburg until Saturday morning."

"Okay. Do you want me to drive up there or would you like to come here on your way south?"

"I'll come there. Where do you want to meet?" A heaviness settled in her chest. She'd told him she lived on the opposite end of the state. If she went to him, her drive home would be an extra two hours. But if he came to her, there was a chance someone at the park might mention something. Lying sucked hard.

"Um, depends on when you're free. Becky's for coffee, Trophy Room for drinks?"

"Coffee is good." That way she could still get home at a decent hour. She was expected to be home on Sunday, and if they went out for drinks, she wouldn't be. Though she might be more relaxed if she knocked a few back before trying to knock boots. He spoke before she could change her answer.

"Becky's at eight?"

"That sounds great." She had so much to Google. Ray, directions, Becky's. This was why she'd never tried to get laid before. Too damn much work.

"Thanks, Jacy." He took a deep breath. "I'm going to be disappointed if your hair isn't actually red."

She tugged on her standard-issue ponytail. "You won't be disappointed. I promise."

Becky glared down at Ray as she poured his coffee. The disapproving expression had to be courtesy of his mother. She'd worn a matching one for the last two days, insisting that coffee wasn't really a date. She'd been so ornery about it, he'd tried to arrange to meet Jacy last night, but she'd been on mustang watch at the wildlife park an hour north.

"Thank you, Miss Becky." He leveled his gaze at the cafe owner, wishing the town wasn't small enough for everyone to know his business.

"She's late." Her ruddy face pulled lower. "Probably thinks you were kidding about coffee."

"She's on her way." He ran his fingers over his phone, where he'd found a picture of a newborn zebra and her text, *"Running late"*, when he awoke.

"You sure? Because I put aside cinnamon rolls and I don't want to waste them."

He flipped over the empty coffee mug beside his and gave his best smile. "Warm them up."

"Cream and sugar?" She laid the sarcasm on thicker than the meringue on her famous pies.

"We'll find out soon enough."

After an exaggerated eye roll, she made her rounds sprinkling sweetness on all the other customers in the crowded restaurant. Next time, he'd tell his mother *after* the obligatory date. He didn't need the opinions of women who hadn't dated this century on what constituted a date. Life had changed since dinner and a movie. No one took that kind of time anymore. Dating sites did the weeding out, and coffee or drinks decided if you might actually be worth a few hours. He didn't like it anymore than they did, but the game played on.

Trailers and RVs lumbered down the highway in front of the restaurant. The parking lot had filled up as he'd waited. He sipped the scalding coffee and stared out the window, wishing he cared less. They'd had two abbreviated conversations since he'd asked her to coffee. Both times, she'd been in the middle of some sort of animal emergency. Maybe a colicky cow or lame sheep had trumped him again.

A giant black truck pulled off the highway, topped by an equally oversized cabover camper. Curiosity had him wondering just where that behemoth would park, until he spied a red-haired driver heading right towards his motorcycle and blocking it in. Not that he could make a run for it, but still.

He'd bet the roof light bar could illuminate an entire barn. Her truck made his look like a pasture wagon. He stood as she disappeared from sight and grinned when she pushed open the door. A vision even more enticing than her profile photo had hinted at.

Long red hair gleamed over her shoulders and she looked younger than twenty-nine with her fresh face smiling and makeup free. A blue and green plaid shirt covered most of her, a white tank top and dark jeans took care of the rest. She was shorter than he'd figured, with unexpected curves that had him wishing he'd pushed for a dinner date. She walked towards him, her smile brightening with every step of her mud-speckled boots.

"Ray?" She held out her hand. He took it in his, impressed by her firm grip. "Sorry I'm late. I meant to be on time. And then there was no parking space so I've blocked someone in."

"It's my bike, so you're in the clear."

Her pink cheeks darkened. "I'm so sorry. I wasn't trying to trap you, I promise."

"Don't worry about it." He motioned to their booth and glanced back at a gaping Becky. His mother would hear about the pretty redhead before Jacy had her first sip of coffee.

Jacy bumped into the table as she slid in, apologizing again. "I'm messing this up, aren't I?"

"It's fine, really. Animals can't tell time. I get it."

"Thanks. I didn't expect anything to happen while I was on watch. Having extra vets come in is really a precaution. I've been there a dozen times before with nothing to do but watch monitors. And then we realized the zebra was foaling so we headed out. It's so amazing to watch them foal naturally, without intervention. We waited to make sure the foal could stand and nurse. She let us close enough to iodine the umbilicus before she decided the show was over. It's one of those things that makes me think we ought to let horses foal in the field, but then I think of postnatal infections and what would happen if the mare needed help and we didn't know and birthing onto straw rather than dirt and—" She sighed and pulled her bottom lip between her teeth. "I'm rambling. Sorry. I do that sometimes. Okay, all the time."

"It's fine. Better to talk about animals than the weather." He reached out and rested his fingers against her flannel-covered arm. He liked that she was talking, filling in the usual silence that came before the job-interview portion of a first date.

Her shoulders relaxed. "I'm excited. And nervous. And severely under-caffeinated."

Ray motioned toward the coffee, noticing how her hazel eyes shone. "There is coffee."

"Good." She wrapped her hands around her mug and lifted it. She took in a deep breath and smiled. "This stuff is so strong I'll wake up in two minutes. I'll drink, you talk."

"I don't have anything as interesting as a zebra happening in my life. My morning was chores and this afternoon I have to reposition a bull."

"What kind?" She sipped at the coffee Becky served cowboy strong without wincing.

"Angus with enough Brahma to make him punchy. Bones spent two years on the circuit, so he likes to show off."

"They're fun to watch, but treating them is a nightmare."

"Bones puts on a good show, but he's highly motivated by food. Back in his day, he was impossible, but that's the point of a bull. I wouldn't want to draw a mild one."

She set her empty mug down with a clunk. "You rodeo?"

"Not since college, and that was team roping. Bones is the first bull I trained. Why? Are you against the show?" As a bucking-bull breeder, he'd always been involved in the circuit. But there was more money in providing the livestock than trying to out-cowboy some dude in pearl snaps.

"No, I just didn't realize you were in the game. I work some of the shows, that's all."

"And like any smart woman, you've learned not to trust a man married to the rodeo. I get it." From her fake smile, he guessed that's what had ended her short marriage. He couldn't blame her a bit. "I'm not much for going to the show myself, unless it's to see how our stock is performing."

She gave a shrug as Becky appeared with giant warm cinnamon rolls dripping with icing and a refill of coffee.

"Anything else for you two? Cream, sugar?"

Jacy nodded, her shining hair swirling around her shoulders. "I would do anything for a plate of bacon."

Becky pointed her coffee pot at him. "If you'll go out on a second date with this one, I'll bring you a mountain. What do you say, Ray? Think she'll see you again, or should I up the ante and bring out pig candy?"

He leveled his gaze at her until Jacy's lilting laughter broke through. "By all means, bring on the big guns."

"I like her already." Becky gave him a wink before retreating to the kitchen.

Jacy scooped up some icing with her fork and brought it to her mouth. She had soft full lips, perfect for kissing, or other things. Her eyes closed and she gave a little moan that sparked something in places that shouldn't be active this early in the morning. At least not in public.

"Oh, that's good." Her hazel eyes glistened as she looked over at him. "Do you always get special treatment here, or is the waitress showing off for me?"

"It's all for you. Usually, I get told I have to eat in the kitchen because they're full. Becky's had this place since I can remember, and she's friends with my mother."

"Who you don't live with, but she knows you're on a date. Or coffee. Because some people don't consider coffee a date. Especially with girls who show up late and then block your only escape." Her gaze dropped to the cinnamon roll and she worked at uncoiling it. "I should have said something quippy about how the next date is up to you, right? I'm not really up to speed on the dating treadmill. It never seems to go anywhere, so I tend to fall off as soon as I get started."

"I prefer to think of it as jumping off. Why use a treadmill when you can walk and actually get somewhere." He cut into his roll and steam escaped.

"Exactly. Make the date, sit down, have the job interview and then repeat. Who needs it?"

"Apparently, us." He grinned as her smiled brightened and a laugh bubbled up. She had a full-body laugh, the kind that required everyone in the vicinity come along for the ride.

She straightened her face in what had to be mock seriousness. "Can we skip the interview part? Because you're totally hired."

He lifted his fork and she knocked it with hers in a mock toast. They talked about nothing and everything while Becky eavesdropped under the guise of keeping their plates and coffee mugs full. He got to hear about her escape from a buffalo stampede while he offered up his bull-wrangling misadventures.

Awkwardness dissolved and he couldn't take his eyes away from the way her hands flailed when she talked, or how she closed her eyes in enjoyment after the first bite of whatever decadent treat Becky bribed her with.

"I think I'm going into a carb coma." Jacy leaned back against the booth, her alluring hazel eyes dancing in delight.

"So if I let you nap, does that mean lunch would count as a second date?"

"I think that depends on if I'm napping alone." Her voice shook as she spoke. Her pink cheeks darkened, the blush creeping down her neck and towards her shoulders.

He tilted his head, unsure just how to read the comment. "I think it's best if you rest up now. I was thinking we'd go on a ride later."

Chapter Three

"Yes, please." Her eyes widened and she tried not to smile too big. She'd done it. Propositioned this dream of a man and he'd taken her up on it. Her virginity would be a thing of the past by nightfall, and with the way he put her at ease, she just might enjoy it.

"I'd love to get out and enjoy the sun while it lasts. Forecast calls for rain on Monday." He reached into his back pocket and pulled out his wallet. "I'll text you directions to my ranch, unless there is someplace you'd rather ride."

"Your place sounds great." She wanted to keep him talking, keep him giving her that little shiver from his deep baritone. "I'll pay for breakfast. I'm the one who kept ordering more stuff."

He wrapped his hand around her arm and her pulse broke into a run. "You really think Becky would let me out of here if you paid? She hasn't grabbed me by the ear in twenty years, but I wouldn't put it past her."

With a smile, he rose and strode to the back of the restaurant where Becky had retreated. Watching him walk away caused an image of him taking off that black T-shirt and unbuttoning his worn jeans to slide through her mind. The knowledge she'd soon uncover the promise of what lay beneath wrapped around her like a fog of lust.

If her brothers hadn't been running off every man who'd come her way since her boobs appeared, she might know how to flirt. Might even be able to make the transition from breakfast to horizontal heaven immediately. After all, there was a bed in her mobile office. But she'd rather be in his, where they wouldn't be distracted by passing through the equipment she stored in the camper.

She wanted Ray and his smoldering sexiness. She wanted to gaze into his sky-blue eyes and let him do what she didn't know how to. And if that meant waiting until this afternoon, hell, she'd waited this long. What did a few hours matter?

The next time Ray moved Bones, he'd be using a tranquilizer. The behemoth rocked against the sides of the horse trailer as if he were in the chute, ready to unseat the cowboy who dared climb on his back. Ray prepped to release the beast, noting how much damage he'd have to repair on the inside. The damned bull had turned himself around.

Two of the hands arrived to help. No matter how old the cowboy, they all had a thing for watching a wild bull. And Bones gave a good show. But he was domesticated now. Just like Ray had been able to bribe him into the trailer with food, he'd do the same on the way out. Even wild things knew when they had a good thing going.

True to form, Bones barreled out, aiming for imaginary targets as he bucked and twisted his way into the field. But as furious as his rage was, after a few snorts and hoof stomps, he sampled the grass and then ignored the cowboys watching the revolt.

With a shake of his head, Ray returned to his truck to grab the sign and a hammer. On one side of the gate he attached a sign he'd made in high school shop class.

Do not enter this field unless you can cross it in six seconds. The bull can make it in seven.

Deke and Crosby both gave a chuckle. They'd worked the ranch since before Ray had taken over after his father's stroke. The older cowboy spoke first.

"I can't believe that sign has held up."

Ray shrugged. “It may have had a little help in the paint department.”

“Maybe you should have gone with grey instead of black,” Crosby said, resetting his tan hat. “Old Bones is getting a little long in the tooth.”

As if on cue, the bull looked up and gave a snort.

“I don’t know.” Ray stepped up on the fence. “Bones, you getting too tired of getting your rocks off to earn your keep?”

In response, the bull turned and laid out a load of manure.

“See that, Crosby?” Deke said with a laugh. “The old bachelor ain’t never gonna settle down. Too bad you boys can’t screw your way into old age. Y’all need to find women on the regular.”

“Ray bagged himself a redhead this morning,” Cros offered by way of deflection.

“And that is why you’ll be riding fences with Bones for the rest of your life. You like to gossip with old women and objectify the young ones.” Ray locked up the trailer, an uneasy feeling coiling in his gut. He shouldn’t care that the rumor mill had fast forwarded his date into the dirty zone, but he couldn’t help it. Jacy West wasn’t the usual kind of woman that you could date and forget. She had something about her that made a man curious for more. The way she filled out her jeans was just a bonus.

He’d liked her far more than he’s expected to. She’d looked all glossy beauty queen in her photo, but her reality was comfortable jeans and dirty boots. It had instantly made him comfortable. Plus, he’d never met a single woman who could speak intelligently about irrigation one minute and real estate the next. He had to see her again, or else he’d risk building her into something she was not. Riding with her today would likely tug her off his pedestal of the perfect woman. He’d known forever that perfection didn’t exist, but like a shooting star, the dazzling glimpse of one had you yearning for more.

"You hitting Trophy Room tonight?" Deke asked as he joined Crosby in the UTV.

"No, I had the morning off so I have stuff to catch up on." Like asking Jacy for a second date.

Jacy left her truck running while she hopped out to open the gate. The crisp fall wind swirled around her, kicking up dirt on the gravel drive. It smelled like rain, but she hoped it would hold off until after their ride. The weather could go all to hell for all she cared, so long as she accomplished her mission.

Her gut quaked, and she pressed her hand there. Carly had been right on that she wasn't exactly cut out for this sort of thing. But she liked Ray, and that should make it easier. It had to, because she didn't have it in her to try this particular experiment again. As she lifted the latch, she glanced down at a wooden box made to look like a tombstone. The weather-beaten thing even had rocks in front of it for effect. She read the inscription.

Here lies the body of poor old Nate. The last SOB who forgot to shut the gate.

Jacy grinned as she opened it. She loved the tone of this place already, from the mailbox built to look like the main house, the tombstone and the arcing metal stretching across the drive stating it was Rocky Ridge Ranch.

She hopped in and scooted the truck through, then returned to close the gate. Not that she thought she'd end up like Nate. But it was protocol. If you open a gate, you close it. Back in her truck, she wiped her hands against her jeans before gripping the steering wheel. She'd been fine driving out here, but then she drove to places like this all the time. Now that she was here, her nerves were announcing the difference. Sure, she was here to see a man about a horse, but this time it was the man she wanted.

The winding drive moved past a garden her mother would love on one side, and the rise of a hill on the other. The road ended between the house and a horse barn, with several other outbuildings joining to make the place feel like a small town. She parked the truck and found her phone, hoping she could call Ray and not have to play some door-to-door knocking game.

Only Carly had found the time to load Jacy's inbox with two dozen texts. Jacy shook her head and dialed Carly's number, mentally preparing for more warnings and advice.

"Did you do it?" Carly didn't bother with hello.

"I'm at the ranch, but I haven't got out of the truck yet."

"You don't have to do this. You could leave right now."

"Cool it. I want to go on a ride with Ray. And I'm hoping that leads to more. I only stopped to call you because you seem obsessed."

"I'm worried about you. You're hours away with a guy you met online and your original plan failed to execute. Plan B is an even worse idea. He's a person now, not just a dating profile. And you like him, I can tell. Sex can't be zipless when emotions are involved."

"I'm taking this one step at a time. There are more steps than I realized, but I found the guy, I met him, liked him, and now we're going riding off into the sunset. Just because I want to have sex doesn't mean I can't let him think he's charming me horizontal."

"There's nothing sexy about laying down a horse blanket in a hay field. Trust me."

"Noted. But trust me here. I'll do what I want, when I want. But so help me, if you text me again tonight, I won't be sharing any details."

"Call me if you need me. No matter how late it is when the deed is done and you're driving back."

Ray emerged from the stable and excitement jolted through her body. A ball cap with the logo of their alma mater shaded his eyes, focusing her attention on the way his lips curved in a wicked grin. She ended the call quickly and then tucked her phone into the center console. She didn't want any interruptions. She wanted some time with her cowboy until he had her feeling calmed down and turned on, the way she'd felt this morning. Then she'd do anything to make Ray her first.

Ray knew his smile was probably a bit too wide, but it matched Jacy's. He pulled off his gloves and stuck them in the back pocket of his jeans as he crossed the gravel yard to meet her beside her mammoth truck. Just like earlier, he felt that instant tug of desire, the urgent longing of man for woman. Every stray thought since he'd left her had been about her naked. And standing here with her flaming-red hair, worn jeans and a white tank top, she slid into every fantasy he'd ever had.

"You found me," he said, instead of asking to skip the ride and take things indoors.

"The directions were spot on." She put her hands in her back pockets, drawing his attention to her breasts. He forced his gaze up to the watercolor swirl of her hazel eyes. "How long do you think we'll be out for? Should I take a coat?"

"I'm not taking one." He rubbed his hand against the back of his neck, suddenly all hot and prickly. He'd prefer she not cover up, but that was for selfish reasons. Good thing one of them was practical.

"Then I won't either. I tend to run hot."

Her words hit him right in the libido. But like this morning, he didn't know how to read it. He didn't want to jump too far ahead and risk getting kicked out of the game entirely. He nodded and walked back towards the stable. She fell in step beside him.

"Who am I riding today?"

Him, if he had anything to say about it. He clenched his fists and dragged his dirty mind out of the gutter. Since he'd sworn off dating-site hookups six months back, he hadn't bothered with sex, a fact his body had decided to alert him to today. He hadn't been this focused on bedding a woman since his first time.

Ray cleared his throat as they entered the paddock. "I saddled Little Joe for you. He knows this place better than I do. Plus, he's as smooth as we've got since Candy's getting ready to foal."

She stopped beside him and reached for the gelding paint. "And who is this handsome fella?"

"No flirting with my girl, Hoss." He patted the horse's neck and undid the cross ties keeping the youngster in place. Joe whinnied in his stall.

"Let's make him jealous," she mock-whispered before mounting his horse in a smooth movement.

"Seriously?" He spoke more to Joe than anything, since Jacy had ridden Hoss smoothly into the corral. He climbed onto the horse his mother usually rode. "You better keep up, old man."

Out in the corral, Deke had Candy on a lead and a boot on her front leg. "What happened there?" he asked his foreman.

"I was just telling the doc here, Candy's about to throw a shoe, but I don't want to bother her with the farrier until after she foals." Deke gave him a wink.

"She has another month." He looked down at his father's horse, a melancholy mare who'd had her way with a wild mustang while grazing. That, or immaculate conception. He sure as hell wasn't about to breed a twelve-year-old who'd had stillbirths her last two seasons.

Jacy turned toward him. "I'd be surprised if she makes it the week. Do you see how she's gone wide, and her teets are full?"

He didn't, but cattle were his bread and butter, not horses. "Good call, Deke. Mind getting the gate?"

Deke looped Candy to the fence and pulled the gate wide. "You should see how Bones is doing. I think he's looking for a way into the alfalfa field."

He cast the older man a look as they passed through. He didn't need any advice on the best places to take a lady on his own spread.

"So, Bonanza?" Hoss moved in close to Little Joe, as they often did when his mother took her Sunday ride with Ray.

"The names? Yeah, my granddad started that tradition. This is actually the sixth Little Joe."

"You just recycle the names?"

"Usually. The Bonanza bunch are more pets than anything. Hoss is the only one that's working the ranch. We keep a half dozen ranch horses up top." The animals turned towards the road that led up to the ridge without the slightest guidance from him.

"Ray, when you said you'd like to go on a ride, I didn't count on it being on a carousel." She wrinkled her button nose and grinned over at him.

"They're used to the route. I take my mom out on Sundays to show her what we're working on. It's something of a tradition from when my dad was running things."

"So when you took over the ranch, you took over that too."

"He kept it up for the first few years, but after the second stroke, he had a hard time balancing and took a spill." He lifted his ball cap and turned it around backwards before replacing it. He hated to think about that awful day. "He broke his hip, and since he already struggled to walk, the recovery has been long."

"Well, if you're trying to impress me, it's totally working."

His shoulders relaxed at the change of subject. "Yeah, it's a nice spread. My great grandfather started with the first hundred acres right off the highway. The house is his original homestead, just added to. My grandfather picked up the back forty in a card game, no joke. Dad snagged the land beneath the ridge pasture by pasture until he doubled the size of the place. I bought the parcel across Salt Creek, complete with a herd of wild mustangs that started crossing the river as soon as the title was signed over. The natural breaks in the land make it easier to maintain the bulls, especially in the winter when boredom makes them punchy."

"Ray?" She waited until she caught his gaze. "I was talking about you, not your ranch. It seems our generation is giving up this kind of life, not gravitating towards it. Agriculture is about more than fields and livestock. The connection to the land and the balance of family, that's something you can't fake or force. You either feel it, or you don't. And you do."

He blinked and rubbed away the tightness in his chest. "Good lord, woman. That is the hottest thing anyone has ever said to me."

She parted her soft, pink lips, her eyes wide with bewilderment before she threw her head back with a laugh so full it seemed to come up from the ground. The sun dripped butterscotch over the red waves of her hair. He couldn't help but join in.

"Ray, honey, if that's your definition of hot, I can blow your mind with awkward sentiments. I can't flirt for shit, but saying things that border on the uncomfortable is my specialty."

His laugh was all his own this time. "I see you completely differently. You're all relaxed comfort from where I stand."

"No one has ever accused me of being relaxed before. It's the oddest of compliments." She tilted her head with a confused narrowing of those pretty eyes.

"You must have some tragic war stories." They crested the top of the ridge and the horses headed towards the new barn, the sweet smell of manure swirling around them.

"War stories?" She sat up higher, taking in the set-up.

"You know, flakes you've dated, exes you've shed."

"Ah, I refer to those as tales of woe. You have no idea what it's like to show up at a restaurant to find the man you're meeting is wearing more makeup than you. And jewelry. And tighter jeans."

He nodded in camaraderie. "It's the ones who seem to have put up pictures of their daughter and not themselves that freak me out."

"And the ones who have been drinking the crazy sauce, or who try to get grabby."

"I apologize on behalf of all men."

She shrugged. "I usually wind up having to apologize, or administer first aid. With four brothers, I don't exactly hit like a girl."

He pulled Joe to a stop beside the working pens and Jacy circled Hoss around until she was facing him.

"Too much? I tend to over share." She sat up taller in the saddle, her hazel gaze wide and clear. "If it helps, I've never done any permanent damage. And by the looks of your nose, you've broken it before, so you know a bloody nose looks worse than it is."

He rubbed the bridge of his nose. "This is the standard issue Mitchell nose."

She covered her mouth. "Shit. Sorry. Shit, I shouldn't be swearing."

"Why the fuck not?"

"It's not ladylike." She gave an exaggerated sigh. "I'm a complete disappointment in the girly department."

"Can't say I agree with that." He gave her a look that brought a blush clear to her shoulders.

"Can I rewind the last five minutes and not be so weird?"

"No rewinds in life, babe."

"How about fast forward to the point where you forget I insulted your nose, confessed violence against assholes and admitted my intolerance for metrosexuals?" She turned Hoss toward the pens. "Tell me about your barn, or Bones the bull."

He moved Joe to ride beside her again. "This is my new barn, went up this spring. Twice as big as the old one because our heifers had a fertile season, and the old one had bats." He gave a mock shudder.

"Bats are a sign of a healthy farm."

"Yeah, until one flies into you. Then they've got to go."

"You know they'll come back, right? There are measures you can take, but bats serve a purpose."

"This is not my first rodeo, remember?"

She arched a brow. "Clever."

"Two bat houses on the south side of the barn, and fake snakes on the rafters inside."

"Fake snakes?"

"Yeah. You want to see?"

"Do I want to go in your barn and see your snake?" She gave a quick laugh and then pulled a serious face. "I mentioned how I break noses, right?"

"You're going to bust my balls this whole day, aren't you?"

"I'm much better at ball busting than flirting. Way more experience."

"From where I'm sitting, you're no slouch on either count."

"Well, you're sitting on your mother's horse, so I'll take that with a grain of salt." She nudged Hoss past the barn, to the crest of the hill. She turned and looked back at him. "You have a whole other operation down there."

He caught up to her. "We work the cattle in different areas for different things. Those pens are for the loading and when we separate the yearlings from the heifers and calves. That barn is smaller, the road is wider, and that's a scale house instead of a tractor shed." He pointed to the east. "And that is Bones."

"You put a bucking bull in a wooden pen?"

"Hey, bull expert. I know my animal."

She held up her hands and wiggled her shoulders. "Sorry, rodeo boy."

"Okay, sassy pants. On the other side of the scale house is my next moneymaker, Church. He'll be ready for the circuit by summer."

"You named a bull Church?"

"Even better. Church Bingo."

"Oh, you win. You win all the things."

"Naming bulls is a skill. Broken Bones, Drill Sergeant, Colonel Crush, Second Thoughts, Crime Scene and Bones McCrackin. Bones is his sire. He did great on the circuit this year."

"Church Bingo is your best." She looked past him, her forehead wrinkling in concern. "There isn't a cloud in the sky, but there's that rain electricity in the air. Do you feel it?"

"I think that's me. Come here." He nudged Joe closer with his knee and held out his hand.

"Are you going to try and show me your snake?" She slid her hand into his, anticipation arcing between them.

"I'm not looking to get my nose broken." He leaned closer and her gold-tipped lashes fluttered closed. She tilted her chin up, a Mona Lisa smile on her pink lips. He brushed his mouth against hers for a fleeting whisper of a kiss. He didn't want to push too far, too fast, and risk scaring her off. "Thank you for meeting me for coffee."

"Oh." She blinked quickly, as if something were in her eye. "Thanks for asking me."

He tugged her hand to pull her near, letting the kiss linger until she parted her lips. "And thank you for coming here for a ride."

"Cowboy, if that is your idea of a kiss, we're going to have trouble." She shook off his grasp, turned Hoss toward the valley and let him run.

Chapter Four

A wide shadow spread across the field, darkening the bright green alfalfa. A cold wind blew against her back. The sweet smell of the pasture faded as the pores of the earth opened up to welcome the rain. Jacy reined Hoss in, listening to the clapping of hooves as Ray caught up to them. She didn't want to get caught in a downpour, but waiting out the storm at Ray's would get her mission back on track.

She hoped. He looked at her like he might want to take it there, but his kisses at the top of the ridge had been practically chaste. And she was so damned tired of being that girl.

Ray pulled Joe to a stop in front of her just as a lone raindrop hit her cheek. Both horses sniffed the air, alert to the change in weather. Lightning flashed and the animals pawed the ground. A moment later, a clap of thunder had Little Joe dancing sideways.

"You're going to have to take a rain check on seeing the creek."

She nodded, fat droplets splashing onto her shoulders. "Is your place nearby?"

He shook his head. "My cabin is between the creek and the homestead. Joe's not going to settle until he's back in his stall. If you don't want to get wet—"

"Don't worry about me. Let's just get the horses back where they're comfortable."

"Hoss is fine in any weather. But Joe's decided he's a delicate flower."

"It takes all kinds of kinds." Lightning lit up the sky and the rain began in earnest. Ray turned and let Joe run, the boom of thunder quickening his pace.

Hoss kept pace with them, the two animals urging the other on. It was the kind of ride she used to love as a kid but never had the time for now. Nothing felt better than the spontaneous rush, the clamor of hooves, the cool rain showering around them.

Too soon, they were back at the corral. Jacy jumped down and opened the gate. Ray gave her a look, but she shook it off. He was the one on the spooked animal. Hoss followed close behind them while she closed the gate and then ran to the cover of the horse barn.

She pushed her wet hair out of her face and sucked in air, taking in the familiar smell of fresh hay and aged wood. It smelled like home and soothed her nerves. She spied Ray as he slammed the gate to one of the paddocks before marching her way.

"You're really something, you know that?"

"So I've been told. We should brush out the horses and—"

"They'll keep." He stopped in front of her, his gaze locking with hers before it drifted south.

She looked down. Her white tank top was translucent and clinging to her just as her see-through bra was. Her pink, puckered nipples were as visible as if she were naked. Her cheeks heated, but she fought the instinct to cover up or crack a joke. She could tell by the way he clenched his unshaven jaw that she had his full attention.

His nostrils flared as he raised his gaze to meet hers once more. She wanted to say something, to ask for what she wanted. But before she could find the words, he wrapped one arm around her ribs, lifted her off her feet and moved them across the floor and into the tack room. He kicked the door closed and didn't stop until he'd lifted her onto a workbench. He set her down hard. She reached her hands back against the wood to steady herself.

Excitement prickled along her damp skin. No one had ever looked at her like this. The predatory gleam in his blue eyes had her warring between terrified and electrified. She had to make this happen. If she didn't take the risk, she knew she wouldn't be daring enough tomorrow, or ever again.

She reached out and fisted his T-shirt, pulling him to her. She channeled everything into her kiss, and when he took the back of her head in one large hand and deepened it, she recognized his desire matched her own. She parted her legs and he pushed closer until the hard ridge of his cock pressed against the seam of her jeans. She wrapped her legs around him, anchoring him to her.

Thunder roared, and he broke the kiss but kept his forehead against hers, his rough breaths against her face. He gripped her hips, pressing his cock harder against her, then took her tank top and pulled it over her head. Her wet hair clung to her shoulders as he undid the front clasp of her bra. He licked his lips as he looked her over.

"I didn't expect this when I asked you here." He traced his finger along the pink of her areola. "I didn't expect you at all."

She slipped her hands beneath his black T-shirt, feeling the physique she'd only seen outlined before. She pushed the material up. He looked as good as he felt, all hard planes and lean muscle. When she got to his chest, he hauled the shirt over his head and dropped it behind him. A smile spread across his face and he pulled her into his arms and held her close.

She reached up and wrapped her arms behind his neck, loving the way his sparse chest hair teased her puckered nipples. She brushed her lips against his, the way he had up on the ridge. She pressed her lips to his until he tried for more. She leaned back and he tried to follow.

"It's not nice to be teased, is it, cowboy?"

He slid his hands between them, filling his palms with her breasts. He rubbed the pad of his thumb back and forth over her nipple. "I can't decide if you're the angel or the devil. I see you one way and think I have to go slow, get to know you, do things right." His other thumb teased her neglected breast. "But then I turn my head and all I can think is how good it will feel to be inside you."

She gave a little whimper and rolled her hips, her clit swelling at his words. "Who says it can only be one way?"

"I've never known anyone like you." He rolled the tight buds between his fingers.

"I am a one of a kind." She pulled the ball cap off his head and threaded her fingers in the soft waves of his hair. She pulled him to her and kissed him with an urgent message. They wanted the same things. Only she wanted it all, right now.

He leaned her back against the bench as he kissed his way across her mouth, down her neck and to places she'd only dreamed about being kissed before. He pulled one peak into his mouth, his teeth and tongue working it with an erotic rhythm. She moved against him, letting the pleasure build until thunder rolled and her breath caught. Her heart stuttered and her whole body tightened and relaxed, squeezed and released. Pleasure and the sweet heat of orgasm swirled between her legs and then radiated out to the rest of her body.

Ray chuckled and pressed himself harder against her. "You're amazing."

"You're not too bad yourself." She brought him to her for another kiss, the weight his body on hers building a delicious tension.

He slid his fingers into the waistband of her jeans and tugged. Her pulse tripped and trepidation shook her insides. She'd gotten him all worked up, but this was the part where she'd need him to be slow and easy and careful. He tugged again and the waistband slipped from her waist to her hips.

She choked down the fear and awkwardness. "Do you have protection?"

"Nope." He tugged again and her jeans slipped to her thighs.

"Then we can't." She placed her hand against his chest and his heart raced beneath her palm. She had a condom, but she'd left it in the truck. Maybe on some subliminal level, she wasn't as ready for this as she thought.

"I gave you that orgasm." He placed his hand between her thighs and she instinctively tried to close them. Only his body was in the way. "It's only fair that I get to taste it."

She gasped as he slid his fingers along her wet lips. She wrapped her hand around the thick muscles of his biceps and met his gaze.

A soft voice broke the spell. "Son, are you in here?"

Ray's eyes closed and he pursed his lips. They broke apart and Jacy slid off the workbench, pulling her pants back on as she looked for her bra.

"We got caught in the rain, Ma. We're just pulling on the dry shirts we keep in the tack room." He shook his head and pulled open a cabinet. He grabbed a black T-shirt and pushed it over her head before she could reach for it. She found her wet bra and put it on, the material like ice against her heated skin. The shirt fit her like a muumuu, but it was better than see-through.

"Is Jacy staying for dinner?" his mother called out.

Ray scrubbed his face with his hand, so Jacy opted to answer.

"Thank you, Mrs. Mitchell, but I have to get back home."

"It's like we're twelve," Ray whispered.

"Are you sure? It's no trouble at all." His mother sounded so nice, Jacy felt guilty for turning her down. But a session of meet the parents could derail her plan completely.

"Ma!" He opened the door and stepped out. Jacy cringed because he hadn't bothered with a new shirt yet.

"I'm just trying to help." She crossed her arms over her chest. Her blue embroidered tunic set off her eyes and complimented her curly gray bob.

"But you're not." He cleared his throat. "Jacy, this is my mother, Lynn. Ma, this is Jacy, who I am sure would rather have met you when she isn't wet from getting caught in the rain."

"It's good to meet you, Jacy. Maybe next weekend, you can stay for dinner." She gave Ray a because-I'm-your-mother-that's-why smile before heading back towards the house.

"You do not have to have dinner with my parents." Ray pushed a hand through his hair, which settled in a million different directions.

"Why? Is she a horrible cook?"

"No, because I want to try and do this right. I was hoping we could go out for a nice dinner, maybe a movie or drinks after."

She wiggled her shoulders. "Are you asking me out on a date?"

"Of course. You rocked this one."

"Okay." She grabbed courage with both hands. "Maybe next time you'll be a little better prepared."

"I'm not sure anything can really prepare me for you." He stepped to her and pressed his hands to either side of her face. He brought his mouth to hers for a kiss that was sweet and soft and warm, nothing like the fiery hunger of moments ago.

"Is that supposed to tide me over?"

He shook his head. "It's to make you want more."

"Are you okay? Did you bang it out like wild monkeys or did you come to your senses?" Carly's voice filled the cab of Jacy's truck as she drove down the highway.

"This was the preamble. I'm going to see him again." She set the cruise control and smiled. He wanted more of her, and she was desperate to give it to him.

"Wait, what? I thought this was a one-time thing. Remember, you didn't want emotional drama."

"It's not drama. I liked him. I like how I was with him. Being with him wasn't a performance. Aside from insulting his nose, I didn't embarrass myself. I was barely awkward."

"What's wrong with his nose?"

"Nothing. He's perfect." In so many ways.

"Oh, sister. This does not bode well for you."

A prickle of unease crept up her spine. "What are you talking about? I found an amazing man who actually likes me. That's a win in any playbook."

Carly cleared her throat. "Did you tell him you're not actually divorced? Or that you live three hours away? Or that your vagina needs a housewarming party?"

"It didn't come up. And it won't matter."

"Because you're only into him for his pleasure potential, and once you get what you want, you'll never see him again, right?"

"That was the original plan, but he's...I don't know how to explain it. He's perfect." Her body warmed just thinking of him.

"This is what I warned you about. You can't separate sex and emotion. You probably can't tell if you're feeling things for him because you want to sleep with him or the other way around. I really don't want to see you wrecked by this."

"Well, aren't you just a bag of sunshine." She didn't want to argue with Carly, especially when she couldn't disagree. This could be a disaster, but she had a good feeling it could be something special. "He's going to take me out again next Saturday. I'm going to need your help making me irresistible. Maybe I'll even wear makeup."

"You're going out with him the night before your birthday? Are you going to bring him to the party your mom has spent months planning? You can't cancel on her."

"It's too soon to toss him into the fire with my brothers. The party isn't until after church, so I'll have plenty of time to get back."

"I can't believe you've put your virginity on project status."

"I can't believe I waited this long to do it."

Busy with the line of cows at Donaldson's Dairy, Jacy ignored the dinner bell ringing twice, but the wolf-whistle signaling a new text message proved too much. She removed her gloves before reaching for her phone. Putting the thing on vibrate was the least she could do for the ladies giving her the stink eye while she checked their udders.

"You left your tank top. Let's meet for coffee and I'll bring it to you."

Jacy smiled at her phone. It had to be a good sign that Ray was thinking of her first thing the next morning. She held out her phone and nudged the old girl beside her. The Holstein looked up just as she snapped the selfie.

"Coffee with you would smell a lot better than a dairy farm. But these girls have my full attention today."

"Nice coveralls."

"I like to keep my farm fashion current."

She cringed and looked down at the dark brown canvas. She had to remember that Ray wasn't her friend, he was a man she needed to want to see her naked.

"Tomorrow?"

"I have a date with a pig."

"Hey now, I'm a nice guy."

"Actual pig. He has his own blog."

She scrolled through the pictures on her phone and sent him one of Chester. As pigs went, he was a looker.

"Your pig is better at social media than I am."

"He's an educator, so he has to know how to talk to kids. Emoticons help."

He sent her a smile. *"That's the best I can do."*

She replied with a wink. *"See you Saturday."*

Chapter Five

Of all the things she did as a veterinarian, Jacy liked office days the least. A marathon of paperwork and tedium, only broken up by backyard chickens and pet goats. Luckily, she only had one day of it a week, since the partners in the clinic liked staying close to town so they could head home for chores and dinner with their family.

Which suited her just fine. She'd rather be helping animals than stuck in meetings, and her chores at home had dwindled to nothing but vet tasks. She turned the country music up loud and pulled out of the parking lot, heading out of town. It only took twenty minutes to get to Weston Ridge, the perfect distance to shift her mind from work to play.

After dinner, she was headed to Carly's to prep for her date this weekend. She'd realized it was technically her first old-fashioned date. Every other guy had been just coffee or a beer, things that had come up on the spur of the moment, not something to plan for or look forward to. Or fear. Because she hadn't worn a dress since she could remember. And Carly thought she should. But she didn't know how to walk in a dress, and then there was makeup which always made such a big mess.

The music stopped and the caller ID on her phone announced, "Call from Ray."

A jolt of excitement sizzled within. He'd managed to text or call every day since she'd left him. Not that he was much of a talker, but it warmed her to know he was thinking of her as obsessively as she was of him. She pressed the button on her steering wheel to let the call through.

"Ray, you know if you keep calling me every day, I'm going to get used to it."

"You go ahead and do that." His smile came through in his voice. "What are you doing tonight? I have a shopping list a mile long, so I have to go into town."

Her excitement fizzled. Little things like this kept coming up, reminding her that he thought she lived much closer to him. "Dinner with the family. I'm completely committed."

"Maybe we should move our dinner up to Friday."

"That's tomorrow, and I have to do dirty work."

"Dirty work?"

"Examining steers before they get processed. It's a holistic farm-to-plate operation, so they'll need me as long as there is daylight."

"Ah, well. Can't blame me for trying. I ought to get on your schedule for next weekend right now."

"Um, about that."

"Babe, if you're playing hard to get, you're hammering it home. You don't have to pretend to have to wash your hair."

"Aw, it's not that. But I'm shadowing at a bison ranch in Sisters next weekend. It's not part of my rotation for the practice, so I'll have to make it up to you the following weekend. Unless you've tipped your hat at someone more available."

She meant it as a joke, but it came out harder than she'd planned.

"I haven't been on the site. Have you?"

"Cowboy, I'm having a hard time juggling you."

"Well, maybe you shouldn't."

She gasped and cornered a bit too sharp on the curve.

"Damn, I mean you shouldn't bother with the site. This is why people should talk in person."

She cleared her throat, not sure what to say. She had no intention of ever using the site again, but she wasn't sure she should own up to that just yet.

"We're still on for Saturday, right?"

"Yes. I don't want you to think it's you. Large animal vets travel a lot for work since farms are so spread out, and I want to learn as much as I can while people are open to teach me. The partners in the clinic don't get offered the same opportunities because it's assumed they're too busy with the practice. I haven't had enough experience working with bison, and this outfit is doing elk as well, and the whole thing is just fascinating."

"I'll either get used to it or you'll just have to move closer."

"It's good to have options." That annoying niggle of guilt returned with a vengeance. She'd have to get on with another clinic to be closer to him. "What do you want me to wear?"

He gave a low chuckle. "You don't want me to answer that."

"At dinner. What should I wear to dinner?" The zing of excitement returned. After their date, they'd be together. It seemed understood between them, which set her at ease. She wouldn't have to try and force anything, it would just happen.

"Whatever you'll be comfortable in. I'm thinking of ironing a shirt."

"Fancy."

"After calling you all week, it's the least I can do."

"Are you going to call me tomorrow?"

"After dark?"

"Scandalous, I know. How about we go really crazy and I'll call you so you can take the drive with me again."

"Again?"

She put the truck in park. "I was driving home. I have to get the gate."

"Okay. Three more days."

"Seventy-two hours."

"Not that we're counting."

Ray leaned against the wheel well of the restored 1950 Chevy pickup and watched people leave the rehab clinic. They served all kinds here, some ran out of the place in workout gear while others were in wheelchairs. Three times a week, his mom drove his dad into Medford to the state-of-the-art facility, and while the old man's progress had slowed, every little win mattered.

While he waited, he pulled his phone from his pocket and texted Jacy a quick, *"What are you up to?"* As much as he had hated texting before, he'd done plenty of it this week. Because of the nature of their work, they both kept odd hours, and the messages helped keep the conversation going. He'd only been talking to her for a week, but her stories and opinions made things more interesting and enjoyable.

"Herd check at an Asian water buffalo dairy. Don't trust them enough for a selfie."

"Buffalo dairy?"

"You know, mozzarella, super premium ice cream."

"I'm bored and playing chauffer for my old man." If anyone had told him last week he'd be taking a selfie with his dad's pickup, he'd have laughed like crazy. He sent it and checked the parking lot to make sure no one had spied him.

"Gorgeous, but if you want ice cream, you'll have to take your shirt off."

His bark of laughter caught more attention than his selfie. *"Tomorrow."*

"I'll bring it to you tomorrow, if I get a hot shot today."

So not happening. No matter how much he liked how her mind worked.

"Blackberry, hazelnut, cherry, and sweet cream. All you have to do is send a little man chest my way."

"Sweet cream. Not buffalo."

"I just screamed a little."

"What are you doing with my truck?" Rick Mitchell's gruff voice caught him by surprise. "What the hell did you do there?"

Ray followed the direction his father's cane pointed. "Running boards. Factory stock, not custom. You're welcome."

"Caught by my old man. Thirty hours." He shot the quick text to Jacy before tucking his phone away.

His father struggled towards the truck, but Ray knew better than to help. "Took a couple months to get here, but it should make it easier for short people to climb in."

Even the old cowboy's drooped eye glared at him.

"I was talking about Ma and Ryan. What's got you so punchy?"

"Where's your mother?" He placed both hands on his cane, as if he'd rather walk home even if he had to drag his sagging left side through the dirt.

"A retirement lunch for one of her music-teacher friends. I overheard the call and talked her into it."

"So you could get at my truck like some vandal?" He shuffled towards the door and leaned on his cane to inspect the running boards.

"Dad, maybe we should have you checked out for dementia, because I'm not the son who steals cars. That's Rowdy. I'm Ray, the good one."

The glare returned with a vengeance. "I wish my mother had never started that."

Ray let his grin widen. Grandma played favorites and he'd loved it. "Hey, she loved you best. Every generation has one of us."

"Oh yeah? Then where are my grandsons? Still getting poured down the drain?"

"Ugh, Dad." He winced, because a passing stranger heard that one and the woman's mouth had dropped open. "We're supposed to hide our crazy when we're in town."

"At least she knows you're available." He shuffled close enough to lean on the truck while he used his good arm to pull open the door. He sighed and looked back at Ray. "You should go get my physical therapist. I want credit for this."

Ray moved to stand behind him, a little unsure the running boards would be enough. Rick had only recently mastered the steps at home and it took him a half hour to make it up to the front porch.

"You know, this will be easier on the driver side. Give me the keys."

"Nice try. But I'll tell you what. You get in, and I'll let you drive once we're through the gate."

Rick set the base of his cane on the floor boards and used the leverage to make it up on the running board. With a little twisting and another push off the cane, he plopped down on the seat.

Ray closed the door and circled around to the driver side. He climbed in as his father fastened his seat belt.

"You're staring." Rick reached out and thumped the dash. "You're not driving Miss Daisy. We have things to do today."

"I didn't know you were working on the seatbelt thing." He knew his father hated all the little ways he had to be looked after. That was why he worked so hard at physical therapy even though doctors had told him to adjust to the new normal. Rick went after his independence with the same tenacity he'd used to make a name for 3R as a bucking-bull breeder.

"It's a lap belt. Don't get all soft. Do I need to drive or are you going to be able to suck it up, buttercup?"

Ray started the truck and shifted it into gear. “To think I was going to take that mouth of yours to Becky’s for lunch. I even called and asked her to prep you some sliders.”

“Well, if you called, we have to go.” He sat up straighter in the seat. For years, burgers had been off the table since he could only eat with one hand. Becky put the tiny burgers on special over the summer and Rick had welcomed bacon cheeseburgers back into his life with gusto.

“If we must.”

“She’s going to ask about that girl, you know.”

Ray guessed as much. “Doesn’t mean I have to answer.”

“But you’re taking her out tomorrow, right? Your mom said you’re planning on staying the night in town.”

Ray shifted in his seat. He did not want to discuss his plans with anyone. Hell, he hadn’t even told Jacy he’d chosen a hotel restaurant in case they wanted to get to know each other better after dinner. He guessed from the way she flirted that she might, but he didn’t want to presume.

“It’s your first second date all year.”

“I’m sorry. Did you change bodies with Mom today?”

“It makes your mother happy. And Deke said she’s a pretty girl, so there’s no harm in seeing where things go. That’s all I’m saying.”

“First off, she’s not a girl, she’s a woman. She’s a veterinarian, not some teenager. And I have to see her in town or else we’ll be followed around by all you nosy Nellie’s.”

“The food-animal vet here has to service three counties.”

He cast his dad a look that screamed cease and desist.

“I’m just saying...a good vet is hard to find. Would be damned convenient to have one closer. Plus, the upstairs of the house hasn’t been used since Kendra got her walking papers.”

Ah, yes, the ex-wife who’d thought his cabin too small and rustic. What’s life without wi-fi and cable?

"There's even my old office in the shop if she wanted to start her own practice."

"Dad, it's our second date. I'm not rushing into another marriage that seems like such a good idea but in reality is a nightmare. Besides, she has a practice two hours from here, and we both know I'm not good at long-distance relationships."

"That wasn't you. Kendra is a slut. She used you for money and fooled the lot of us. But you can't blame all women because you got hooked by a rotten one."

He'd thought supporting Kendra's decision to get her degree was the right thing to do. He'd even moved her into the studio apartment off campus and tried to be understanding when she said she had too much studying to do to come home most weekends. Hell, if she hadn't gotten pregnant and if he hadn't done the math, things might have turned out differently. Though, since the baby was Chinese, he would have clued in at some point.

She'd left him with a lot of regret and a strict abhorrence of liars. Hypocrisy and half-truths started out small, but the more lies the mark believed, the deeper the duplicity could go. Internet dating brought them out of the woodwork, from fake pictures to an age being a decade off. And he'd fired good hands at the ranch for lies he would have settled with a conversation before. Lies were the gateway drug to betrayal, and he was never going down that road again.

Chapter Six

"Do you smell like barn, or is it your boots?" Carly wrinkled her nose as she held open the door to her trailer.

Jacy sat down on the step and took off her boots. "I took a shower after dinner."

"Thanks for that. And no working in my clothes. I want you to look good for tomorrow night, and the effect will be ruined if you're covered in shit."

"I feel more attractive already." She got up and followed her best friend inside. "Sorry I didn't have time to go shopping."

"We do need to work on your wardrobe, but this limits your choices to sexy and sexier. At a store, you would have found something more *Little House on the Prairie*, when you need *Sex and the City*." They walked into Carly's bedroom, where she pulled open her closet.

"I'm not looking for a makeover. I just want to borrow your black wool slacks and a sweater or something. And a pair of shoes that aren't sneakers or work boots." Her phone vibrated in her pocket. She smiled as soon as she checked the simple message.

"Twenty-two."

"Is that him?" Carly had a dress in each hand, a strapless red and a bright blue with the sides missing.

"Yes, but no to both of those. I don't know how to sit in a dress, or get in and out of a truck. And if I ever wear a dress again, it will be a whole dress. Those seem to be missing vital parts."

"That's the whole point." She tossed them on the bed and grabbed two more. A strapless black and one more lace than dress.

"I'm two seconds away from cinching up my mom's pants and wearing one of her tunics."

"You're the one trying to get laid. Speaking of..." She took a wrapped box from her dresser and placed it on the bed. "Some things you can't borrow."

"My birthday's not until Sunday."

"You don't want to open this at the party, I promise."

Jacy undid the pink bow and then opened the box. She peeled back the tissue paper and gasped. The strapless white lace bra and panties were like nothing she'd ever owned. Not at all practical, because while the underwear covered, they didn't cover anything up.

"Send him a picture of that. I dare you."

Jacy's cheeks heated and she had a twisty feeling in the pit of her stomach. "I can't do that."

"Then give me your phone and I'll do it. Unless you want to make the first move, you want him on edge. After last week's failure to complete the transaction, this is your last chance to leave your virginity in your twenties."

Except the timeline didn't matter as much anymore. If it took months to be with Ray, she'd wait. But that would mean extending her cover story, and she struggled with it already.

"Don't give me sad eyes. With the way you two are on the phone constantly, I'm sure he's as moony as you. Which means your original plan of a zipless encounter with a stranger is shot to hell. He's not a stranger anymore, and you're going to want to be with him after, not walk away."

"I know. I need to tell him about my profile on the site. I don't want him to find out any other way."

"Well, yeah. But not tomorrow."

"I think I'm going to open with it, so we can discuss it over dinner. He's wonderful, and I want things to work out. I think he's the one."

"Well, that escalated quickly. You're going to need to dial down this sudden call to matrimony. Take this one step at a time. It might turn out that he's not all you're building him up to be. Let him seduce you with the fancy restaurant and all. Talk logistics with him the next day, when he's all satisfied and happy." Carly went back in the closet for a dress fit for Marilyn Monroe and another that rivaled one for Jessica Rabbit.

"It's like you don't know me at all." Jacy put the lid back on the box and pushed it aside. "Anything that you wear to church would be fine."

"At church, most of the people are in jeans, so I only look nice in comparison. And while you're looking to get biblical with Ray, you're not taking him to church."

"I need to be comfortable so I can relax and have the nerve to go through with it."

"Don't worry about that. You want him bad," she said from the closet.

"I do worry. I've never done this before." Carly was right. She needed him to want her so bad he didn't notice her awkwardness. She shored up her courage and took a picture of her lingerie.

"Good girl." Carly beamed from across the room. "Now send it before you over think it."

She winced as she did, because that message couldn't be brushed aside as teasing or flirting. "Okay, now can I wear what I want?"

"Of course not. Trust me about the dress. Have I ever steered you wrong?"

"You steered me into a ditch once." She grinned, remembering how her fifteen-year-old self thought her best friend could teach her to drive. The lesson had lasted all of five minutes.

Carly rolled her eyes and held out the latest two options. "Which do you think would make him drool more? Naughty cowgirl or the sweet seductress?"

She got up to get a better look at her options. An A-line white eyelet dress with a wide leather belt, or a ruffled floral with spaghetti straps. She'd feel exposed in both, though she tried to reason that she'd be covered up less in a tank top and shorts.

"Come on. You can borrow my bluebird boots with this one." She wiggled the floral number.

"I'm not sure I can pull off ruffles." But she did love the leatherwork underlay on Carly's dress boots. Not that she'd ever be able to feel comfortable in something like that.

The white dress joined the pile on the bed. "This is soft, not frilly. The pattern is tiny purple hyacinth, you love those."

She took the silky material in her fingers and tried to picture herself in it. She just couldn't see herself in spaghetti straps with ruffles at her knees.

"Humor me and try it on. Consider it my thank you for making sure you don't show up for a sex fest wearing your standard issue black briefs and white bra."

"Ray seemed to like my bra, thank you very much."

"No, he liked your boobs. Trust me. You'll see a difference." She took the dress off the hanger.

Wearing a dress would surely prove her point faster than arguing. Jacy stripped down, trying to ignore that Carly had been spot on about her underwear. She slipped the dress on, mortified that it came to mid-thigh.

"Oh, honey," Carly whispered. "That's the one."

She shook her hcad, and pulled at the ruffled hem. "I won't be able to bend over, and I'll have to cross my legs when I sit."

"That's kind of the point. Men can be rendered stupid by a woman crossing and uncrossing her legs."

"That's above my pay grade. I just need him to think I clean up nice." Her phone vibrated to life atop the box.

Carly clapped her hands and grabbed the phone. "I told you that would get him hard."

The heat of her blush seeped from her cheeks to her ears and down her neck. "Can we not talk about his, um, business?"

"Hon, his business is your business now." Carly turned the phone to show her what he'd replied.

His bare, muscled chest was as enticing as his smile. She grabbed it and covered the screen. "That was not meant for you."

"Go on, you have to reply. Tell him you licked the screen or that he gave you lady wood. Or you could up the ante and send him a picture of your boobs."

Jacy sat on the bed, hiding the screen from her best friend. The idea that Carly had seen the photo made her a little queasy.

"About time." She typed quickly.

"I'm still learning to selfie. Took me a couple dozen tries to get that one."

"Worth the effort."

"Your turn."

"I only do live shows."

"You're killing me."

"I better go. I need you alive."

"Twenty-one."

Jacy sighed and hid the phone inside her box of tricks. With Ray, the flirtation came easy. Nothing felt stilted or forced. She hoped she could pull off this sex thing, because she'd hate to lose the easy way they had with each other.

"Look at that, sitting down in a dress and the world can't see your cookie." Carly smirked and held out a gift bag.

"It's longer than I thought, but I don't like being so bare up top." She took the bag and peeked inside. Makeup.

"Don't make that face on your date. It's fugly." Carly reached around and pulled the band holding Jacy's ponytail. "Problem solved."

Her hair fell just below her collarbones, making her feel a bit less bare. "I can't believe I'm going to wear a dress."

"That's the easy part." Carly handed her a mirror. "Pay attention. I'll do one side of your face, then you'll do the other."

Jacy sucked in a breath. She's rather catch an angry bull than deal with mascara.

Ray set his forearms on the stable door and leaned in for a better look. As if on cue, Candy lay down on the straw and her water broke.

Deke shook his head as he knelt down and wrapped the mare's tail. "Sorry, man. I wanted to be wrong about this."

"Dad says she always foals after dinner." He scrubbed his face with one hand and reached for his cell phone with the other. With the vet three hours away, he didn't have much choice but to stay. Not with the way Candy's last two deliveries had gone. "I wish the vet hadn't been a month off on the due date. Candy's never been early before."

"I'm hoping for a better outcome this time. She was so depressed last year."

"Yeah, the old girl was so forlorn she let the first mustang she found knock her up." He shook his head. "She planned this. We need to face it, our Candy is a love 'em and leave 'em type."

"She does like the wild ones." Deke stood and walked to the stable door. "Did you get the time when her water broke? The last time she didn't progress for an hour before we went in. Maybe helping her sooner is a better idea."

Ray nodded. "I'm going to make a few calls and see if I can find someone to help her."

"You're going to call your lady, right?"

"Yeah, I'll have to get a rain check. She was raised on a ranch, so she'll understand." And he'd be tormented by two more weeks of her teasing. If he could make it that long.

"You should ask her to come."

Ray leveled his gaze at the older man. "I'm not dating her to take advantage of free vet services. It's too big a favor to ask this early."

"It doesn't hurt to ask." Deke shrugged and turned towards the horse. The discomfort showed in her breathing, but her body lay calm.

Ray marched outside, the sky still bright. He'd planned this night like a scene from one of those romantic movies women liked, and instead he was going to give Jacy something more like a disappointing comedy where no one laughed. His shoulders slumped and he leaned against the wall of the shop. A part of him wanted to head into town and let Deke handle Candy. But it was a small part, one he'd stomped down since taking over the ranch at twenty-five. Shards of immaturity had been swept under the rug then, but on occasion, they still poked at him.

He looked at the last message on his phone and winced. The number two, sent moments ago. He dialed her number, wanting to hear her voice to make sure she understood that what was keeping him away did indeed have something to do with wild horses.

"Hi there, handsome." Her voice lilted into his ear, so happy and light.

"Have you left yet?" He cleared his throat, not wanting to say what he needed to.

"I'm on my way now. Why?"

His throat tightened, making swallowing hard. "Babe, something's come up." When she didn't respond, he knew he needed to explain more. "Remember Candy, the mare you said would foal in a week?"

"Oh, no, did she lose another one?" Her genuine concern eased his tension. She'd understand, wouldn't turn it into some dramatic episode.

"Not yet, but her water just broke. So we'll know soon."

"What does your vet say?"

"He's hours away doing herd checks in Bly, so the connection is spotty. He says to let her try and intervene if we have to."

"What about your back-up vet?"

"At the Beaver football game. It's fine, Deke and I have done this before."

"Was her last birth vet assisted?"

"No, before the stillbirths, she had four healthy foals without anyone even knowing. She knows what to do better than we do."

"I'll be there in a half hour."

"That's not why I called. I wanted to tell you that I'm sorry about tonight. Could we try it again next weekend?" He pulled his tan hat off his head and then resettled it.

"I have the bison ranch."

"I'll come to you this time. Or maybe we could do a couple days at the coast." He tried to think of something better to offer, to entice her. "I'll come up one night after work and take you to dinner if you want."

"Whoa there, cowboy. As much as I want to let you talk to see how much of your time you'll offer up, I'm not being cagey.

I'll see what I can rearrange. But I'm in for a trip to the coast. Especially if it's stormy and we can watch the waves crash while we stay warm behind a window."

"I like the way you think. But I can never tell if you're trying to tempt me or if my mind is just in the gutter."

Her sweet laugh slid through his mind, easing the disappointment. "Candy will have foaled and be comfortable by morning. Can we meet up for lunch?" he asked.

"I can't. I have an appointment in the afternoon. When I look at my schedule, I'll find some time, I promise."

"Ray?" His mother's yell from the house caught his attention.

"Jacy, thanks for understanding. I better get back to it."

He turned off the phone and crossed the gravel to the house. "Something wrong, Ma?"

"We were just wondering how Candy is." She shoved her hands into the pockets of her cardigan.

"We? Or is Dad sending you out as proxy?" He braced his hands on his hips and stared up the steps.

"I asked a question, son. Answer it." For as much as his mother looked soft and pliable, underneath the cozy veneer, she was tough as nails.

"Her water broke. I'm going to call around to a few breeders and see if I can get a lead on a vet. Remind Dad he was the last one to help her with a successful delivery."

She sighed and wrapped her arms around her middle. "Give him a break. He doesn't like to be seen like this."

"He had a stroke, not some disfiguring accident. Besides, it's just me and Deke. We could use his experience with her."

"Ray, we taught you to never judge a man until you've walked in his shoes."

He looked at his boots and then back up at his mother. "Mom, I live in his shoes."

Chapter Seven

Jacy climbed out of the truck and circled around back to the camper, careful not to kick up dust in the gravel and dirty Carly's boots. She opened one of the storage boxes that also served as a step up into the camper and grabbed one of her pairs of rubber boots. And then she cringed. All of her coveralls were drying in the laundry room at home. She looked down at the dress and shook her head. She tended to over prepare, but since she'd planned on spending the night with Ray and then racing back home, she hadn't counted on him needing her in a professional capacity.

She slammed the box closed and opened the one marked equine. She lifted out the medical bag and added in supplies she might need. Just the basics for now. After she examined Candy, she'd restock and beg Ray for some clothes to ruin.

Gravel crunched behind her and she turned to watch a clean-shaven Ray walk her way. His plaid button-down was tucked into his snug jeans, the sleeves rolled up to his elbows. Heat bloomed on her cheeks as she realized how much tonight meant to him too.

He stopped inches from her and the world narrowed to his icy-blue eyes. He stared so intently at her mouth she wondered if he might kiss her. Instead, he took her hands in his and looked her up and down.

"I didn't call to get you to come help, but I'm glad you're here." He shook his head, released her and took a step back. "You're beautiful, Jacy. Did you wear this for me?"

"My reasons were purely selfish. I wanted you to look at me like that."

He took another step back, his hands in fists by his sides. "I have never wanted to kiss someone so badly in all my life."

"You should do something about that." She took a step towards him, until he held up his hands.

"I want to, but I need you to be a vet right now. Candy's not progressing. We tried to check her and it pissed her off, so she's standing up and I can't get her to lie back down."

"I'll give you a pass on dinner, but you should always kiss me hello." She sat on the storage box and exchanged Carly's dress boots for her rubber ones. "Before I leave, I want my kiss, plus a bit more as interest."

"It's the least I can do."

"It really is." She took her bag and they started towards the stable. "I want to check her, but after that could you grab me some clothes I could ruin?"

"Take my shirt." He'd undone two buttons before she could stop him.

"If you have your shirt off, I might not be able to concentrate."

"Really?" He grinned, his eyes crinkling at the corners.

She hit his arm with the back of her hand. "You have the same problem."

"I think I have a more serious case. We should start working on a cure."

"Or helping your dad's horse foal. It's quite the dilemma."

"I think most people would take the easier option."

She shrugged. "It might be easier, but it wouldn't be right."

"Ain't that the truth." He led her to a large stall, the floor covered with a thick layer of straw. Inside, the beautiful roan swayed in obvious pain while Deke whispered to her.

"Is your dad here? He'd have the easiest time getting her back down now that she's agitated."

His shoulders stiffened. "I already asked."

"Then I'll ask him, and borrow something to wear from your mom."

Deke snapped his gaze on her. "You don't want to do that."

"Why not? I'll replace anything I ruin."

Deke and Ray exchanged a look. Ray shook his head slightly and backed away. "I'll try again."

Ray hadn't even made it up the porch steps before his mother opened the door. She stepped outside and moved to close it behind her. Her blue eyes went wide as he pushed past her and marched to the living room. Rick looked too cozy in his recliner.

"You need to come help with Candy." He widened his stance and stared down his old man.

"There's nothing I can help with." He lifted his left arm a few inches to punctuate his point.

"If you don't come with me, Jacy's going to come in and ask you herself. Is that how you want to meet her?"

"I can't do it!" His father's face grew red as he shouted. His mother stepped between them.

"That's enough, Ray. Now that Jacy's here, I'm sure she'll handle everything. Vets don't like owners getting in the way."

He stepped to the side, ignoring her usual attempt to diffuse things. "Mom, she needs some clothes to change into. She came dressed for our date."

"I'll bring her something." She turned to face him and crossed her arms over her chest.

"Just grab something. I'll take it to her."

She tossed a look back at Rick and then huffed a breath and headed towards their bedroom.

Ray leveled his gaze again. "Let's go."

"Remember who you're talking to." With his good arm, he pushed himself up taller in the recliner.

"Remember who you are. You can't keep your life on hold, waiting until you get to one hundred percent. I'm not asking you to do anything but try to calm a horse. Your horse."

He shook his head. "By the time I make it over there, it will be over already."

"I'll carry you. Actually, that's a great idea. You can come willingly or I'll toss you over my shoulder."

"Ray!" His mother rushed into the room. "That's enough. We're all worried about Candy, but let's not take it out on each other."

He took a deep breath, and wished the strokes hadn't taken more than his father's use of the left side of his body. The man he'd looked up to was hidden away somewhere in there, and he'd spent years trying to coax him back. Nothing worked.

Rick used the control on his recliner to lift it and help him stand. "We'll do this three-legged, the way we did at Ryan's graduation. Just like then, if I cough, you come help me."

"Got it." He braced his arm around his father's back and then slid his boot beneath his dad's slipper. He took the sweats his mom had brought out in his free hand. "Let's do this."

She held open the door as they found their rhythm. By the time they made it to the stables, Rick was breathing hard. Ray's gut tightened as he wondered if he was doing the right thing, pushing like this.

"Good to see you, boss." Deke cut a glance into the stall. "It's not looking so good."

"We can hear you," Jacy's voice filtered out from inside. "Ray, did you get your dad?"

They hustled to the door, finding Candy still swaying. Jacy stood behind her, exam gloves pulled up past her elbows. To say her dress was ruined would be an understatement. Rick coughed and they made their way into the stall. The horse walked towards them and Ray held his breath until the old girl rubbed her nose on Rick's OSU sweatshirt.

"Kneel down and see if she'll go with you." Jacy instructed. "The foal is breech, and by the look of the legs, a couple weeks early."

Rick started to kneel, taking Ray with him. Candy stepped back and then crumpled into the straw beside them. Rick sat and scooted closer, whispering to the horse. Jacy got to work, delivering the foal before he could figure out a way to help. She stayed with the colt, rubbing its face with a towel until it began to squirm.

Right there, in the mess of life happening around them, he knew he loved her. For her gentle calm in a crisis and the way she made him laugh, for the way he'd felt this last week and how she'd kissed him without holding back. He wanted to tell her and didn't care who heard, but confusion twisted her features.

"When did she have her last ultrasound?" Jacy stood and peeled off her gloves. She pulled a stethoscope from her medical bag and knelt beside the mare.

"She didn't have one." The look she gave Ray could have turned him to stone. "We're not horse breeders. She got pregnant the natural way, and no one was any the wiser until she went wide. With our horses, we let nature take its course."

"Did she at least have her shots?" She moved the scope to different places on the horse's belly, which had begun to seize with new contractions.

"Of course. We just don't heavily monitor."

"I'm not accusing you." She got up and returned with fresh gloves. "Ray, can you keep the first one awake? It's been a long labor, but he can't sleep until we get him standing and he eats."

His dad swore under his breath.

“What do you mean the first one?” Ray dried off the little black colt, admiring the white blaze and stockings.

“Candy has a secret baby. Which explains why they’re early and why she carried so wide. Let’s just pray she ate enough, and that her milk comes in fast.”

Ray looked back at his dad, who shook his head as he whispered to his horse. Even Deke wore a grim expression. They all knew that twin pregnancies were rare for horses and seldom resulted in live foals. Time, space and nutrition were working against them already.

“Good news,” Jacy said with a smile. “This one is in the right position.”

The colt wriggled in his arms, trying to find his feet. “Babe, he’s okay, right? He seems fine, just a little small. He’s even trying to stand up.”

She didn’t answer, just focused on the next foal, pulling him free after a few contractions. This black colt was feistier from the start, kicking free of his sac and vocalizing. Candy responded with a whinny and lifted her head to look at her babies.

“I’m so impressed with this mare right now, I can hardly stand it.” Jacy removed her gloves and sorted through her bag. “Mr. Mitchell, how is she? Do you think she’ll stand to nurse, or should I milk her?”

“Call me Rick.” He cleared his throat. Ray went to his side and helped him to stand. The mare looked up at him, checked on the colts and stood. She leaned against the wall, but she was up. “As a brood mare, she’s the best I’ve ever had. Even her maiden season, she didn’t need any help.”

“If Blaze over here hadn’t been breech, it might have gone that way this time.”

It took him a moment to realize she wasn’t playing with the smaller colt but examining him. When he found his feet, he headed straight for Candy, who licked and nuzzled him.

An hour later, the mare lay with her colts on clean straw, all fed and tended to. For the next forty-eight hours, they'd have to be watched round the clock and monitored with a list of instructions Jacy had dictated. Deke volunteered to take the first shift, and Ray's folks even wanted a turn.

Jacy wiped her eyes as she carried her bag out of the stall and set it on a table in the tack room. She shivered, and he realized she'd spent the last three hours in clothes that were soaked through. There hadn't been time for her to change into the clothes he'd brought. He caught her just as she wiped her eyes again.

"Babe, is there something you're not telling me?" Her hazel eyes widened, sending him on alert. "The colts are all right, aren't they?"

"I hope so. It's an absolute miracle, a once-in-a-lifetime kind of thing. I want this to be a story we tell for years, but I know so much of what could go wrong."

He pulled her into his arms and held her close, trying to warm her cold fears. "Lots of things could go sideways, but most of the time things happen the way you plan them to. Like how we're together tonight."

"Are you kidding me? I'm disgusting. I need a hot shower and clean clothes."

"This is so far from what I planned." He held her tighter, until she wrapped her arms around him. "Will you stay the night?"

"Yes, I want to be close in case they need anything. I'll be sure to check them in the morning before I leave, and I'm going to try to come back Monday and clear my schedule for Tuesday. I can run some blood work and I'll call if it seems they're not getting enough colostrum."

He pulled back and waited for her to look up at him with her mascara-rimmed eyes. His pulse jumped, but he pushed through the fear of being turned down cold. "I want you to stay with me."

"Oh." Her mouth formed a perfect circle around the word.

"I'm not pushing for anything. But you're here, and I was really looking forward to being with you." She looked at him like he was trying to sell her a bridge. "How about if you check out the cabin, take a shower while I grab us some dinner from the house, and you can decide where to sleep after."

"I can't believe you want to be around me when I'm covered in horse."

"I mentioned the shower, right?"

Chapter Eight

The cowboy had fluffy towels. Jacy wrapped one around her body and squeezed her hair dry with the other. His bathroom had a porcelain soaking tub and a walk-in shower tiled in river rock. When Ray had led her to his cabin, she'd expected rustic inside as well as out. Instead, she'd stumbled upon a cozy oasis that had calmed her nerves.

She peeked out the bathroom door to see if Ray had returned with dinner and her change of clothes, but everything was still. She stepped out into the single room, more master suite than anything. His log-framed bed sat high in the middle of the space, while bookshelves lined the back wall. The kitchen area reminded her of a wet bar with the half-sized fridge and tiny sink. A leather club chair perched in the corner by an armoire that must serve as his closet.

The wide planks of the floor were cold beneath her feet. She didn't want to rifle through his things, but she didn't want to greet him in a towel even more. She borrowed a pair of knit wool socks and a flannel shirt. Expecting him to open the door any moment, she slipped them on quickly.

After she'd hung her towels to dry, she wasn't sure what to do with herself. The only places to sit were the bed and the chair by his bookcases. She opted for the chair but got distracted by his shelves. Shelves of Zane Grey and Louis L'Amour, Hemmingway and Faulkner, plus a collection of works on agriculture, food and cows.

The front door pushed open and Ray stood there with a smile. He must have showered at the house, because his hair was a mess of damp curls and he'd changed into a T-shirt and plaid pajama pants. He held a metal lunchbox in one hand and a roll of clothes in the other.

"You look good in my shirt." He kicked the door closed and set the lunchbox on the chopping block he used as a counter. "So good I'm thinking my mom's University of Oregon sweatshirt can wait until morning."

She pulled a face. "Your mom is a Duck? I'm so sorry."

"We try not to judge her slip in judgment. She hadn't met Dad yet and learned the error of her ways. Plus, she was on scholarship, so they were paying her to be there."

"Well, if they were paying, I'm glad she took their money." When she stood this close to him, the overwhelming awareness that she wore nothing beneath his shirt had her libido raging. And she had no idea what to do about it. "What was her scholarship in?"

"Music, same as my youngest brother, Ryan. He went there too. We don't talk about it."

"Unless we beat them in football. Or basketball. Or anything."

"The Oregon Civil War rivalry can get pretty heated." He toed off sneakers he must have put on at the house.

She pulled her hands into the sleeves of his shirt. "Did I take too long in the shower?"

"No, I showered at the house because I needed pajamas. I only keep what I use here, the rest of my clothes are at my folks."

"You usually sleep naked, don't you?" Her pulse thrummed as she glanced over at the bed, thinking about how he climbed beneath that quilt every night. The same quilt she'd be sleeping under.

He nodded. "I want you to be comfortable."

"I'm starving. What did you bring for dinner?" As segues went, it sucked. But she didn't know what to say or do. She had this wonderful man right next to her, about to share a bed, and the way things were going, they were having a slumber party.

"My mom makes savory hand pies. They're faster to grab than making a sandwich."

While he pulled out a plate and unpacked their dinner, she tried to think of what Carly would do. Not that she'd ever find herself entrenched in the friend zone with the man of her dreams. Carly knew her effect on men and used it accordingly. What had she said? Get him on edge and he'll make the first move. If only she knew how.

Ray held up a mason jar of lemonade. "Do you want your own glass or can we share?"

"Sharing is good." She wanted to hit herself on the forehead. She brought lame to an all new level.

He took the plate and jar to the bed and sat down, stretching his long legs out in front of him. She had no idea what to do next. Flirting she liked, but putting all that sass into motion proved impossible.

"Stop looking at me like I'm the wolf in grandma's bed, intent on stealing your cookies. There's no other place for both of us to sit." He patted the quilt beside him. "I don't bite, it's not my kink."

"You're just saying that so I'll ask what your kink is. And I don't think I want to know." She climbed up on the bed, too aware that she didn't have on any underwear.

"I want to know yours." He handed her the bread as big as her entire hand.

"I don't have any." She peeled off the edge of the hand pie and peeked inside. A puff of steam escaped with the smell of apples and cheddar and ham.

"It must be me then." He tucked into his dinner like talking sexual kinks happened all the time.

She ate in silence, careful not to touch him when he passed her the tart lemonade. She wanted him to make love to her and she wanted to come clean about everything. Her profile, her virginity, how hard she was falling for him, all of it. But she didn't know where to begin on either count. He got up to take the plate to the sink and she wanted to pull him back, keep him beside her until she could figure out a way to make this happen.

He turned off the overhead light as he returned, leaving only the warm glow of his bedside lamp to illuminate the room. He came to her side of the bed and took her hand.

"Would you be more comfortable if I slept at the house, or in the chair?"

She squeezed his hand and shook her head. "I want you close. This just isn't what I expected."

He pulled away and went to his side of the bed. "The cabin is pretty rustic, but it's just me here, and that's how I like it."

"This place is an oasis. It's not that." She turned towards him and tucked her legs under her, covering her knees with his flannel. "I thought tonight would be an escape from reality, where I could be a shinier, sexier version of me, and you'd be so excited to be with me nothing would be awkward."

He pushed her still-damp hair behind her ear. "You definitely looked the part."

"And now it's just me, no makeup, my hair a lank mess, and half my mind is still in the stable. I feel selfish for wanting to sneak away with you when I should be the one watching those colts."

"Oh, babe, Deke won't let anything happen to the twins." He pulled her close to his chest. "I owe you a special night in town. And a new dress."

"We owe Carly a dress. I don't own any."

He slipped a finger beneath her chin and tilted her head up to look at him. "You really did wear that dress for me."

"I figured it would up my odds of seeing you without a shirt on." She tried for a teasing smile, but his face went serious. Her stomach clenched, knowing she'd pushed too far.

He released her, gripped the back of his shirt and pulled it over his head in one swift movement. He set his hand on her flannel-covered knee and gave her a look that would have dampened her panties had she been wearing any.

"Babe, you want my shirt off, just ask. It's a standing invitation whenever we're alone."

"Let's make it a rule that your shirt comes off whenever the cabin door closes." His broad, muscled shoulders drew her gaze first, then the light hair that highlighted the hard contours he'd earned through work, not a gym. She reached for him and pressed her hand to his chest, his nipple hard beneath her palm.

"No shirts in the cabin. Fantastic idea." He undid two of her shirt buttons before her nerves kicked in again.

She wrapped her hand around his, stalling his progress. "The lingerie got ruined too. It's just me under here."

"I know. My mom is working her laundry magic on it."

"Your mom has my panties?" She set her head on his shoulder with a groan.

"Relax. She won't be shocked. We're too old for her to think we're celibate virgins." He laughed, but the sound didn't warm her like usual.

Instead, she sat up tall and looked into his forever-blue eyes, wishing she'd already told him. All of it, every half-truth and white lie. She didn't want anything between them, but now wasn't for explanations. She still had a few more hours of twenty-nine left. She'd spent too long keeping the door to her sexual side locked tight. The celibate virgin of her youth needed to step aside for the passionate woman she wanted to be.

"Okay, I shouldn't have said that. You're young and beautiful, and I'm an idiot."

"No, you're right. I'm turning thirty." She undid the next button herself. His breathing got shallow, though in the warm glow of the lamp she was in shadow. "And I'm sure she thinks we're—"

"Please don't talk about my mother right now."

She snickered. "Do you have something better to do?"

"You." He finished undoing the buttons and then pushed the material off her shoulders. His work-roughened hands against her skin, man against woman, aroused the tide of desire she felt whenever he was near. He set his forehead against hers and her anxieties drowned in the warmth of him. This was Ray. This was right. This was what she'd been waiting for.

She kissed him then, his face in her hands, only the slightest roughness of stubble beneath her palms. She leaned into him and his chest hair teased her nipples. She tasted him, the earthy maleness she remembered from last week, along with a new excitement as he stroked her tongue with his.

He kissed his way to her ear, his breath making her shiver. "Let me make love to you, Jacy."

"Yes." Her voice sounded rich and throaty, as different from her usual tone as she was about to be. He released her and stood. She prayed she hadn't actually whimpered out loud.

He pulled back the quilt and blankets to the foot of the bed, arranging the pillows behind her. He pulled a condom packet from his pocket, shed his pants and then joined her on the bed, easing her back against the pillows. She didn't have much of a chance to admire his toned stomach, firm thighs or the thickness between.

He kissed her without hesitation, as if this was what he was born to do. The solid heat of his body against hers flooded her senses. She couldn't get enough of the warm scent of his skin, the drugging taste of his kiss or the rough slide of his hands as he touched her. She wanted it all, to soak up layer upon layer of their lovemaking. She reveled in the sensation of that gorgeous body she'd admired pressing her into the bed. The weight of him a comfort and a heady reminder of the power he had over her.

With his hand on the back of her neck, he lifted her head and fanned her red hair against his white pillows before releasing her. "This is how I imagined you."

"You thought of me like this?" She slid her hands along the sculpted muscle of his arms and shoulders, exploring what she'd only dreamed of touching.

"You thought of us too." He lowered his head, trailing warm, wet kisses down her neck.

"I think I've wanted you forever, I just hadn't found you."

He groaned and covered her breasts with his hands, squeezing and pushing them together. "I love your breasts. When we got caught in the rain, I could see your nipples, and I had to taste them, had to feel them beneath my tongue."

He dipped his head and gave each nipple a long, slow lick. She lifted her arms overhead as he played with her, pleasure coming at her in waves. She loved it all, the soft feathery strokes of his lips, the swirl of his tongue and the pull of his mouth as he suckled her.

"And then you showed up in that dress with the straps I could slip down. I could feast on you anytime I'd like."

She arched her back and hummed her pleasure. He slipped his hard thigh between hers, bringing just enough pressure against her center to ease the building ache. She closed her eyes and dove into the sensations. He traced his hands over her body, followed by whispered kisses and teasing nibbles. She'd never felt so feminine, sexy, beautiful. She'd shelved those parts of herself to focus on everything else, and it was as if his touch gave those gifts back to her.

He moved his attentions down her stomach, across her hips, to her thighs. She parted her legs as if it were the most natural thing in the world to open herself to him. The bed moved as he shifted his body. He tilted her hips to one side and rested his head against her inner thigh, letting her upper leg rest on his shoulder.

And then he kissed her. Nothing prepared her for the storm of sensation. She reached for him, pushing her hand into the soft waves of his hair. She gasped for breath and grabbed the edge of the mattress with her free hand, needing an anchor to steady herself. She moved with his mouth, the rhythm of his talented tongue. She couldn't help the moans that escaped as her legs began to quiver. He stroked her deep inside and her breath stalled. Waves of pleasure washed over her, so hard and fast she felt swept away by the undertow.

Ray moved over her as she caught her breath, protecting them before he shifted her body onto her back. She opened her eyes as he lowered himself onto her, his thick erection cradled against her slick heat. She rocked against him, so sensitive to the pressure there. She looked up at him, intoxicated by the way his desire for her showed on his face.

She locked in on his pale-blue gaze and slid her leg out, moving her foot over his calf, thigh and around his hip, opening herself to him. After the pleasure he'd showed her, she wanted him to find the same kind of release.

He pushed inside and she gasped, pulling in a sharp breath. The stretching sensation wasn't painful, just foreign. She focused on his gaze as he eased in, rocking into her with exquisite control until she'd taken all of him.

"You're so tight." He rolled his hips, pressing into her but not thrusting as he began a slow rhythm. "It's been a while, huh?"

She closed her eyes, not wanting to pretend with him in this. She wrapped her other leg around him and ran her hands across his back, to the hard muscles of his tight butt. She urged him to quicken his pace. He pushed against her clit with every motion and that cyclone of pleasure started anew. Full and deep, she loved him until her thoughts were adrift, everything focused on their two bodies joined as one. Her legs began to quiver, so she gripped him tighter, his sounds of pleasure joining hers. She came in a rush of scorching, sensual oblivion. His gentle rocking raced to small thrusts until he growled his release.

Tension left his body and he relaxed against her. She held him to her, her arms around his back, her feet twisted over his calves. They'd done it, done something bigger than either could do alone.

"Wow." It was all she could think to say once she finally caught her breath.

"Amen to that." He lifted himself off her and then moved off the bed.

"Where are you going?" His withdrawal sent a sting between her legs, so she squeezed her thighs together. She heard water running, answering her question. She reached down and pulled the blankets up so she could press her hand to her core, which helped with the discomfort.

Ray returned and pulled back the covers, catching her with her hand down her pants, had she been wearing any. "Aw, babe. I worried you'd be sore."

He pressed a hot washcloth between her thighs and she sighed in relief. The tight muscles relaxed, the pain easing.

"Next time, we'll play more. And you'll tell me when it's too much, okay?"

She rested her hand on his arm. "I was fine until you left. I'm okay, really."

She glanced down at his cock, still thick and full. His was the first erect penis she'd dealt with, so she had nothing to measure him against. She touched the rounded tip of him with her finger and smiled.

"It's a blessing and a curse. I should have asked how long it had been for you."

She shook her head. "You're perfect. Thank you."

"I should be thanking you."

"You did all the work." She propped herself up on one elbow and admired how amazingly handsome he was. She could stare at him the way art lovers did paintings in museums.

He handed her a dry washcloth and held out his hand as if he expected her to give him the wet one. It went beyond intimate.

"Babe, I had my tongue inside you. I can handle a towel."

She cringed as she handed it over and then settled down against the pillows. Ray joined her beneath the covers. He reached for her and she went to him, resting her head on his chest, listening to the strength of his heartbeat. He stroked her hair and she sighed.

He cleared his throat. "Would it be weird if I said I think I could be perfectly happy to just stay here and not share you with the world?"

She placed her forearms on his chest and grinned up at him. "Definitely stalkerish. But I feel the same way. I don't know that I'll ever have enough of you."

Chapter Nine

Ray kicked the cabin door shut, balancing the plate of breakfast burritos on his coffee mug. He hadn't realized he'd never had coffee with anyone in his cabin until he found himself at his door, a mug in each hand, and was faced with the puzzle of how to open it.

He set their breakfast on his nightstand and took a step back. With the length of his double bed against the wall, Jacy had been trapped between the wall and him. She'd tried to creep out of bed at dawn without waking him, but he'd caught her mid-sneak. Good morning was an understatement.

As fun as that had been, he should probably build another nightstand and turn the bed. He plopped down hard on the mattress. He needed to slow his roll. Because she was in his thoughts twenty-four seven, it felt like he'd known her much longer than a week. She had that something, something he couldn't name, and it drew him like a pig to mud.

He scratched the back of his head, trying to get his mind to slow down and just let things happen. But he'd always been the type to take action rather than wait around. The sound of the shower running flooded his imagination with her delicious curves, warm and slick from the soap. The water cutting off didn't help. Snapshots of terry cloth on bare skin and all that naked flesh left him barely holding on to his control.

Next time she visited, she wouldn't be showering alone. There'd be no reason to leave him to check on horses, and Deke could cover his chores instead of babysitting colts. He was still awed by the way Jacy had handled the mare, and that both of the twins had made it through the night. When he'd gone to get breakfast, he'd caught his old man happier than he'd seen him in years. That made two of them.

Jacy opened the bathroom door, and his gaze drifted to her on instinct. With her hair wrapped in a towel, she walked barefoot into the room, wearing a cream dress that looked like old lace and showed off her long legs. She froze, one hand on the towel and the other on the wide leather belt cinching her waist.

"I smell coffee." Her Venus smile hit him full force. She probably had a hundred different smiles, and he wanted to know them all by heart.

"I know you don't like to be undercaffienated." He sat on the bed he'd made before heading to the house.

She undid the towel and damp strands of her red hair fell around her shoulders. "Lucky for you, Deke brought me my first cup while I was checking on the boys." She folded the towel and placed it on the bench by the door. "Before Rick names them, I do want it noted there were no twins on Bonanza."

"I don't think he cares. My grandpa started that, and I think Dad keeps it up in his honor. But I can pass on suggestions."

She stepped to the bed and then stood there staring at it. The scent of his soap on her skin was a heady thing. She looked innocent. Fun. Beautiful.

"Babe, we went over this last night. It's the only place we can both sit."

She waved him off with her hand. "It's not that. I, well, I don't know how to sit in a dress."

"Okay." It wasn't as if he had any pointers.

"I should have packed jeans like I'd wanted." She undid the belt buckle and hung the belt on his footboard. "And I'm not going to be able to drive with that squeezing me. Hand me a pillow."

She hopped up on the bed and scooted until her back was against the wall. The hem of the dress rode high on her thighs. She snatched the pillow from his hands and placed it on her lap before letting out an exaggerated sigh. “That’s better.”

“Don’t cover up on my account.”

She quirked a brow at him. “I have to get out of here within the hour. If we start something, I’ll be late.”

He shrugged. “Be late.”

She shook her head. “Give me the coffee and no one gets hurt.”

He handed her the mug. Her soft smile as she inhaled the brew reminded him of her innate sensuality. He reached out and wrapped his hand around her bare calf.

“Ray, if I could be late, I would be.” The regret in her voice made him release his hold.

“Breakfast burrito?” He set the plate between them.

“Now I feel bad for leaving.” Her smile disappeared and she sipped her coffee.

“So don’t.”

The silence stretched as they drank their coffee. He knew he was asking too much. She had an established career, in a whole other county, and she’d only known him a week. That fact didn’t change how much he wanted to seduce her into a few more hours.

“I’ll be back Monday night.” Her voice had a pleading tone that had him wondering if she felt it too, this war between what his brain knew and what his soul felt.

“You’re really coming right back?”

“Those twins are in a precarious situation. They have to be monitored closely. The partners at my clinic can fill in for me while we wait and see how strong the colts really are, and how well Candy does with nursing them. We might have to take them to a hospital facility, but I want to avoid that since the stress could cause a snowball of problems. If they make it a week, we might want to think about taking the story public. I could bring down some vet students, so they can see it is possible, and you could get publicity for the ranch."

"We, huh?"

"Are you going to play hard to get right now?" She tried to give him a schoolmarm stare, but her eyes were laughing. The girl had so many tells, it made him think how fun she'd be at strip poker.

"Not with you."

Ray stepped in the front door of the main house. "Ma?" he called out as the screen door snapped shut behind him. He glanced down at his boots and decided they were clean enough to make it to the kitchen. With his brain still reliving last night with Jacy, he'd volunteered to collect lunch. He was too preoccupied to be useful for much else. He grabbed the heavy cooler off the counter and turned to leave.

Only his gaze stalled on a giant black medical bag sitting on his parent's coffee table. He called out for his mother again, because something was up. He left the cooler in the kitchen, and by the time he made it into the family room, he knew without a doubt it was Jacy's bag, and his mother had some serious explaining to do.

Lynn appeared, a blue bandana tied over her grey curls and dust covering her navy sweatshirt. "What's your emergency? I'm in a groove upstairs cleaning."

"What is this?" Ray lifted the heavy bag, noticing Jacy's business card on the back in a clear pocket.

"It's Jacy's. She left it in the tack room last night, so I brought it in for safe keeping."

Anger stabbed at his chest. "You know I have no patience for lying. And she had the bag this morning when she drew blood samples. So try again."

She held up her hands. "Fine. I took it this morning so that she would come back for it. Or you could take it to her."

"Did you happen to think that she'll need this today? That she probably showed up at a call and didn't have what she needed? Why would you want her to look unprofessional?" She had calls to make today, said none of the horses would be as exciting as the lot here. "I loaded some things in her camper. She probably thinks this is one of them."

His mother cringed. "No. None of that came to mind. Just that we like her and you like her and she likes you, so yesterday when she said she wouldn't be back for two weeks, I wanted to help."

"I don't need your kind of helping. We're adults, not teenagers playing a game. If we want things to work out, they will. But having you steal her medical bag? That does not make me look good."

"I'm sorry." She shook her head. "I really am. I should have just left it alone. I just want you to be happy."

"I was happy. But now I have to drive an hour to bring her back her bag and explain that my mother wants to be a matchmaker." He brushed past her on his way to the kitchen and grabbed the phone. He lifted the bag onto a barstool and looked at her business card.

Opal Creek Farm Animal Hospital

Large Animal and Food Animal

Jasonda Weston, DVM, FAVM

541-555-5555

Opal Creek, Oregon

He read it twice. Weston. Maybe the website had gotten that wrong, but Opal Creek was three hours of winding highway from here. He turned on the computer and logged on to Notmy1stRodeo.com to double check her profile. Jacy West, Douglas County, Myrtle Creek.

He closed his eyes as his stomach pitched and rolled. She wasn't real. She wasn't real at all.

"Okay, we're alone." Carly pushed herself up to sit on the wooden countertop, her excitement filling the kitchen. "Dish."

"Dish up the deviled eggs?" Jacy pulled open the refrigerator door and stepped so it blocked her view of her best friend. She'd been able to hold her off with last-minute party details, and then the dozens of people currently in the back yard, laughing and drinking in celebration of her thirtieth birthday.

"Don't make me hurt you."

"Pretty sure I can take you, so bring it." Jacy took the last plate of deviled eggs from the fridge and set them on the counter. The last time her dad had added on to the main house, he'd built her mother's dream kitchen. The size of the space, coupled with the white cabinets and oversized everything had kept Jacy out of the room as much as possible ever since.

"After all I did to make you sexified for your big night, and you're not going to tell me how it went?" Carly pulled a pout a five-year-old would be proud of.

"Well, your dress is ruined." Might as well start with the basics.

"That could happen to you on a random Tuesday. I'm pretty impressed you only have a bit of dirt on this dress." She brushed an offending spot on Jacy's hip and then smacked her ass. "Did you get your birthday present or not?"

"Lots of them." She grinned and tilted her head to the side. "I thought we were talking about Ray?"

"Yes, Ray. You did all this running around so you could sleep with him and not have to be a thirty-year-old virgin. So tell me, did he get the deed done or do we need to find a replacement candidate on the website?"

It felt wrong to talk about their night like it was a game they could review on a play-by-play. Like a wish, holding it tight in her heart made it more special.

Three slow knocks rapped against the cabinets behind them. Jacy turned to see who might have overheard and her heart stopped cold.

Chapter Ten

Ray's stomach clenched in pure, unadulterated fury. Good thing he knew how to roll with the punches, because that had been quite the blow. All this deception to sleep with him. Sleep with anyone really. Just so she could check off her virginity as if were an item on her to do list. She might be cold enough to think it didn't matter, but knowing it had been her first time, her only time, would have meant the world to him. Not that she cared.

He held up her bag and then let it drop to the floor with a satisfying thud. "You left that behind. I don't want you to have a reason to come back to my ranch ever again."

Jacy winced, but he didn't care. She'd stabbed him in the heart, and now he had to get back on his bike and spend the next few hours driving through a forest, figuring out a way to tell his parents the ugly truth.

"What the hell?" A brunette hopped down from the countertop, ready for battle. She wore a green polka dot dress that looked ridiculous outside of a fifties diner.

"Carly, please, give us a minute." Jacy cast her gaze at the ground, which wouldn't do. He wanted her to look him in the eye and tell him why. "Keep them out if you can."

Her friend picked up a tray of eggs and shot a glare his way. "Can't promise you that. But don't worry about a mess, honey. Two thousand acres has plenty of places to hide a body."

He stepped aside as green dress walked past him, her nose in the air. He made his way to Jacy, crossed his arms over his chest and rooted himself to the spot. He needed answers. Now.

"How did you get here?" She asked somewhere over his left shoulder.

"I'm the one that needs to explain? Really?" He watched as panic dawned in her hazel eyes before she lowered her gold-tipped lashes and wrapped her arms around her middle. "Fine. I have nothing to hide. You left your bag, and you weren't answering your phone. I looked at the business card on the bag and found out it belonged to someone else. I dialed the number and found out you'd been to the office and left for your birthday party. Your receptionist actually gave me directions. I got here, and the first person I saw is my buddy from college, Slade. Just a couple months ago, I was up this way and we had a few beers. I told him about an online dating site. He probably would have walked me in, but his boy needed a boost into a tree. Amazing how short a story is when it's the truth."

"Ray." She didn't even open her eyes. "I know this looks bad, but—"

"It doesn't look bad. It is bad. What you did is despicable. You not only manipulated me, but my family. And I bet there's some rule against practicing medicine under an assumed name."

"Slow down." Her voice shook and she held up her hands. She managed to look him in the eye, her hazel eyes glistening. "I never meant to lie to you."

"The hell you didn't." His temper erupted in a white hot flash. He clenched his fists to keep from reaching out and shaking her. "This is how deceit works. It starts small, with something you don't think is all that bad. And then you're building more lies on top of it. If you didn't mean to lie to me, you wouldn't have. But you meant to, and you did."

She nodded. "I wanted to tell you so many times. But I wanted to find the right time, when I could explain and you would understand. I was going to tell you tomorrow."

"Sure you were."

"I told you I was coming back tomorrow night. I planned on telling you then, when it was just us."

"I don't believe you. You weren't coming back for me. You wanted to glean some kind of publicity from the twins. You already got what you wanted from me. But really, kid, I shouldn't be anyone's first time."

"I didn't sleep with you to lose my virginity. I did it because I love you." Her voice pitched up an octave and she wiped her eyes with the backs of her hands. "You have every right to be angry—"

"Well, thank you for that."

She clenched her jaw and fisted her hands at her sides. "I know I made up parts of my profile on the site. I went about it wrong, but because of it I found you. Doesn't that count for something?"

"I'll give you all the credit for lying. On the site, to my face, to my parents, all of it."

"I'm not a liar. I only changed a few things on the site because who I am wasn't working for me."

"I can see why. Tell me, is your ex-husband at your birthday party, or did you make him up too?"

"Damn it, Ray, we wouldn't have been matched if I hadn't joined the site and changed the area I lived in. And if my last name had been Weston, anyone in this state that's ever had anything to do with the annual Fourth of July Buckaroo would know—"

"That Weston Ridge is the main benefactor. Yeah, I know that. Your dad was also very generous with the university. He spoke in some of my classes, about expanding your brand and growing your property."

"Exactly. You're friends with Slade. Would you have gone out with his sister?"

"Not without asking."

"He would have told you no. All of my brothers want me to live in this perfect fairytale bubble. I can't get out as long as I'm within their reach. So I had to move myself into an area they weren't so damned intimidating in."

He shook his head. "You're the one spinning tales, not them. You know what's crazy? We even talked about people who lie on their profile. You could have mentioned what you'd done right then."

"You just said you wouldn't have gone out with me if you'd known who I was."

"That's not what I said. But you didn't think honesty would matter, right? Because you did all this, the lies and the driving and pretending to be what I wanted, you did it just to toss away your virginity like yesterday's trash."

Her throat undulated as she swallowed, anguish marring her delicate features. She knew how to put on a good show. "I wanted to find someone who would see me and not the girl from Weston Ridge. I didn't think I'd ever find that. I was getting to the point where I even accepted it. I'd focused all my energy on becoming a vet while others looked for boyfriends and husbands. Most of the time, I prefer animals to people anyway. So, yeah, I wanted to have sex and know what I was missing. Didn't you sleep with any of the other women you met on the site?"

He blinked and an icy coldness spread across his chest. Dear God, she had no idea what she'd done. "You're right. But I never pretended to be making love to any of them."

"Ray, I wasn't pretending." She reached for him then, but he snatched his hand away before she could touch him. "You were right there with me. You know I wasn't. I've never been more me than I am with you."

"Well then, I don't think you know who you are." He shook his head, so disappointed he'd made the same damned mistake twice. "Have a nice life, Jasonda Weston. Stay the hell out of mine."

"Jacy what *are* you doing?" Slade stood in her doorway, shaking his head as if she were a kid he'd caught with matches.

She didn't pause, just layered clothes in her duffle bag. Carly always joked about how limited her wardrobe was, but she'd always figured T-shirts, jeans and hoodies were the most practical things to wear. Maybe she ought to not pack at all and just go shopping.

"Tell me you're not going to go chasing after Ray."

She cast him a glance and instantly knew. "Carly told you."

He nodded. "Everything."

She wanted to throw up. How could she have embarrassed herself with this many people at one time? "Did Mama start crying?"

"Carly didn't make a family announcement, she pulled me aside." He came into the room and sat on her bed.

Her mind stalled, trying to remember the last time he'd been in here. It was before puberty had changed his hair from blonde to brown, so at least twenty years.

"Listen, Jace. Things aren't going to work with you and Ray."

"Stop. I don't want to hear it. I don't want you to try and keep everyone who might hurt me away. I'm a grown woman. I can slay my own dragons."

"Fine. You go ahead. But it's not going to matter what you say to Ray. He's done, honey."

She clutched a flannel shirt to her chest. "You didn't call him, did you?"

He shook his head. "I know him. I've known him a lot of years. He has a heart of gold and would give you the shirt off his back, but he doesn't take too well to being lied to, not anymore."

"This is more complicated than that."

"No, it's pretty simple." Slade drifted a hand over her quilt before meeting her gaze. "Let me break it down for you. Ray got married the year before I did. I thought he and Kendra were solid. He even encouraged her to go to school, so she'd spend the week in Corvallis at the university and the weekends at home. Until there weren't as many weekends. Hell, he was proud of her for studying so hard. And for his birthday, she gave him a pregnancy test and he was over the moon happy."

She sat on her bed, knowing the crash lay just ahead.

"Only she didn't count on ranchers knowing more about fertility cycles than the average guy. And they're sitting there at the ultrasound, and he finds out it's a boy, and that she's a month farther along than she said. And right there in that moment, he went from having it all to being completely flattened.

"He no sooner got rid of that problem and his dad had a stroke and lied about being cleared to ride again. Then he got thrown and had another stroke. Ray's only bright spot for a long while is how well the ranch has done."

"But what I did was stupid, not malicious. He's just angry. When he calms down—"

"Jacy, I love you, girl. No matter what crazy thing you do. But Ray is never going to forgive you. He just doesn't have it in him anymore. Don't embarrass yourself more by running after him."

"I have to try. If I'd been the one to tell him, he would have been mad, but we would have talked it through. When we were together, it was the best I've ever felt."

"This was just your first rodeo, with the pounding heart, sweaty palms and excitement of the new chance at love. You'll see, it's always like that at first."

She shook her head, because while she might not have a lot to compare it to, she knew. She'd been raised by two people who loved on a soul level, and she knew when she'd found hers.

"It's not the heart-racing-away kind of thing. It's like, when I'm around him, I can breathe deeper and relax more. He treats me like an equal, not like someone who needs his help or he wants to impress. He never spews out false compliments or pushes me to do things I don't want to do. With him, I don't just feel special, I am."

"That's Ray. But trust me, sister, you blew it."

Chapter Eleven

Stillness surrounded Jacy as she stepped out of her truck. No longer night but not yet sunrise, a time of eerie tranquility in the country. She walked softly on the gravel, every step too loud for her ears. Her stomach pitched and rolled, her skin covered in a clammy sweat of regret and determination.

Eight hours and more than two hundred miles later, Ray's words still played in her mind. Carly had said any sane woman would write him off as an ass, and Slade had warned Ray would never give her the second chance they needed. But she'd been raised by a man more stubborn than any other. Surrounded by brothers who saw the world as right or wrong, and thought all reasons were simply excuses. Even though she understood, it didn't make it right. But then, neither was what she'd done.

She'd waited for the rest of the house to fall asleep before heading out, not wanting to explain herself. She knew the only chance she had to get through to Ray before he tore down every connection they'd made was to corner him and make him listen.

Hell, she sounded like a crazed stalker. And it wasn't exactly sane to be here. But she had to try. The only hope she had to go on was that he wouldn't have been that angry if he hadn't been deeply hurt. And that meant he cared.

After grabbing her bag from the storage box, she headed towards the stable, needing to busy herself until she knew Ray was awake. The soft clicking of hoof beats in the distance grew louder until she spotted Hoss thundering across the pasture. Her eyes widened as she saw Ray racing towards her, hopefulness and dread flooding her with anxious anticipation.

He didn't slow until they hit the gravel of the drive, and then just barely. They approached like a shadow in the twilight, and an ominous trepidation circled her the way the horse did before Ray pulled him to a stop.

"What the hell are you doing here?" The anger in his voice shook the stillness.

She swallowed past the tightness in her throat and looked up at him. He sat upon the horse like a king on a throne, his aura of control and powerful body made an intimidating and sexy combination.

"I told you I never want to see you again."

"You said a lot of things, but you were too angry to listen to what I had to say. I came to apologize, to tell you how sorry I am about not coming clean with you sooner. And for the way you found out."

"Sorry doesn't change that you knew all about me and never let me know you." Hoss lowered his head and Jacy reached out. Ray jerked the horse's head up before she could touch him.

"You know the real me, the parts that don't change the way addresses and even last names can." She set her bag at her feet and slid her hands into the back pockets of her jeans. "If I hadn't done it, I wouldn't have found you or this place."

"My life would be a whole lot better if we'd never met."

She shook her head to clear the troubling thought. "You don't mean that. You're just angry."

"Hell, I don't even know who you really are."

"You know me, Ray. I am not my name or my nearest map dot. I'm just me, and you're you, and I'm asking you to forgive me. Tell me you can, that we'll learn from this. Because if you can't realize it was a mistake and love me through it, you aren't half the man I thought you were."

He let out a cruel laugh. "Let me get this straight. You make up an ex-husband, change your name and lie about where you live and even where you're going when you leave, but I'm the one in the wrong here. You have a lot of nerve."

"Damn it, Ray." She clenched her fists but managed to control the urge to stomp her foot. "Get down off your horse and talk to me."

"Whatever game you're playing, lady, I'm out. You got what you came for. I don't know what you're doing here now."

"I'm trying to explain."

"You did. This started with a lie, and you kept right on doing it to cover your tracks. And since your first story didn't work, you're probably here to sell me another. But I'm not buying."

She stared out at the horizon, pinks and oranges peeking over a distant mountain. She was Cinderella at the ball, and the sunrise was her midnight. "That's it. That's all this meant to you. And now I've disappointed you, you can just turn it off like a switch." She wrapped her arms around her middle, needing to hold herself up. "I'm standing here telling you I'm sorry. I know I should have told you."

"See, by your own admission, you knew it was wrong when you were doing it. I don't think you're sorry at all. I think you're sorry I caught you."

Her throat constricted, her traitorous eyes swelling with tears. She willed herself not to blink, not to let him see her cry. "You make it sound like I did some horrible, dirty thing."

"I've been down this road before, and I'll be damned if I let you drag me there again. You're thirty years old. It's time to grow up and stop playing these selfish games."

The word hit her like a slap. He could claim he didn't know her, but he knew exactly where to kick her when she was down. She squeezed herself tighter. "I can't believe this is happening."

"Yeah, that's how I felt earlier. You'll get over it."

"Yesterday, I had everything I'd ever wanted. I'd never been that happy." She swiped an errant tear, but they seemed to multiply without end. "You're making a mistake. I think we're meant to be together, and I just did it wrong."

"I've made this mistake before and learned from it." Derision chilled his voice. "Have a nice life, far away from here."

She turned her back to him and picked up her bag. Her body felt cold, hollow, foreign, as if it belonged to someone else. She took a step towards the barn.

"Where do you think you're going?"

Gravel crunched beneath her feet as she turned around. "I'm going to check on the twins."

"The hell you are." He moved Hoss between her and the stable. "I don't want you on my ranch."

"Those colts aren't out of the woods yet. They could die without proper medical care."

"Our vet has already been out twice. Don't give my horses a second thought."

"My God, you really want to hurt me, don't you?" She had a connection with those babies, and he'd cut her out of their lives like a surgeon with a scalpel.

"What I want is for you to go."

And so she did.

"What a difference a day makes, huh, kid?"

Ray nearly fell as he dismounted Hoss. "Dad, where the hell did you come from?"

He leaned over the half-door of Candy's stall. "I'm on colt watch. Which means I'm in earshot of this bullshit."

He wasn't ready to explain, not so soon after Jacy's surprise appearance. "I'm not talking about this."

"By all means, let's wait and let it fester."

"Just let it lie." Instead of pretending to be working, he should have grabbed the whiskey bottle he kept in his cupboard and drowned his stupidity.

"I see. You can call me out when I'm being a coward, but you can't take it when I do the same."

Ray spun on his heel to face his father head on. "You don't know what you're talking about."

"I know you're not hurting any less for hurting her. You thought it would help, but now your stomach is so twisted you want to puke. And I know that if you leave things like this, it will be your biggest regret."

"You don't have the whole picture here." He led Hoss to the paddock, wanting his old man to let this conversation wait a few more hours. Years even.

"Of course not. I'm just a father looking at his son hurting and wanting to make it stop. I'm not telling you to be with this girl. That's your choice. But you had her so high up on a pedestal, she couldn't help but fall. You thought she was perfect, and it turns out, she's as flawed as the rest of us."

Seemed like everyone wanted to turn this on him this morning. Whiskey sounded better all the time. He looked past his dad to the horses, all probably awakened by the commotion. The colts nursed while Candy drank from her trough.

"It's easy to give up. This is hard and messy and damned uncomfortable. But I've never known you to back down or turn tail and run."

Oh, hell no. "I don't run."

"No, you just drove back here instead of letting her explain. And then when she catches up, you throw her out. Which is your choice, I suppose. But a woman sorry enough to drive through the night to apologize might care more than you think."

"You're supposed to be on my team. My whole life, I've done everything step-by-step, just like I was supposed to. Got good grades, did my chores, finished college, work the ranch, got married. I checked the boxes, Dad. And what did it get me?" He shook his head. "The world doesn't work like that anymore."

"I'm your biggest fan. Your mom and I wouldn't have been able to stay home after the fall if not for you. And you're a smart businessman. This place has never been so profitable. You're a good man, Ray. I just wish you could forgive yourself for not realizing what Kendra was doing. Maybe then you could remember how to forgive other people."

"I didn't do anything wrong. And I'm not having another woman who lies like she breathes in my life."

"You can't talk about Kendra and Jacy in the same sentence. One married you so you'd put her through college while she carried on. Jacy lied about what? Her profile on that dating site you found her on?"

"And she kept building the lies. I don't even know why she came here. She hadn't told her family that she was seeing anyone. I was just a game she played on the side."

"Fine. She was just some girl your mom made you go out with. You told her that, right? That you went out with her as a promise to your mother?"

"That doesn't matter now."

"You're probably right. It's a tricky thing, trying to know when to cut your losses and when to hold on tighter and weather the storm."

"I know what you're trying to do, but I don't know why you're so sure I'm the one fucking this up."

"I'm not." He sighed and returned to his chair in the corner of the stall. Blaze folded to the floor beside him. "I just know that for a week, it was as if your heart had never been broken."

Chapter Twelve

The tree-lined fields darkened to a dense forest before Jacy was forced to pull over. Crying and driving was a dangerous mix. Her only win was that she'd made it to the highway before the ugly cry started. Her head pounded and her face felt both tight and swollen. She wanted to run into the forest and scream as much as she wanted to curl into a ball and hide.

Spending quality time in the fetal position won out. She didn't even leave the truck, just pushed aside the back window and pulled herself into the camper. The main space stored enough medical supplies and specialty equipment to keep her prepared in most any veterinary emergency. Pure practicality.

The bed in the cabover was pure indulgence. She climbed up into the soft, cozy space and squeezed a pillow to her chest. She slept here more than she'd ever expected to when her folks had given her the rig as her graduation present. In a job with such crazy hours, grabbing a nap or sleeping on site proved vital at times.

Now, it provided a safe place to soothe her frayed nerves and shattered heart. She took off her boots and slipped beneath the pink camouflage comforter, the chill of her failure seeping into her bones. She should have listened to Slade, to Carly. They had far more experience at the relationship game than she did. It would have spared her pride. But not her heart.

As much as it pained her to know that her error in judgment had been a fatal blow to their relationship, it hurt deeper to know she'd wounded him so deeply. Later, Carly could help her find the anger, show her how to be offended instead of gutted. But for now, she needed the release of a good cry.

Somewhere in the midst of it all, she drifted off. The sound of footsteps circling the truck jolted her awake. Jacy had a satellite phone because she often found herself in places outside of cell-service range. Plus, she had a loaded shotgun in the cabinet beside her bed. Country girls were more prepared than Boy Scouts. Whoever this idiot checking out her rig was better head out quick, because she wasn't in the mood to shoot the fool in the leg.

Peeking out the windows by the bed didn't give any clues, so she slid out of bed and onto the bench. Her feet had barely touched the floor when she heard her name, so loud the sound jumpstarted her heart. She recognized Ray's voice and froze on the spot.

He had the nerve to try the door. The sound startled her into action. She crossed the camper and opened the door.

Yellow streaks of sunlight shone through the trees, highlighting the curl of his light brown hair. He'd changed into a denim shirt, a few shades lighter than his eyes. Bloodshot eyes, which had probably had even less sleep than her own. She looked past him to his motorcycle parked sideways behind her.

He gave her a half smile and then shook his head. "Can I come in?"

"No, I'm having a pretty nice life in here."

He nodded. "I deserved that."

"You think?" She stayed in the doorway, wanting him to come in but not wanting to feel more of his rage.

"Listen, I'm not exactly proud of how I spoke to you this morning. I thought I had a couple hours to figure out what to say here, but you weren't even a half-hour away." He rubbed the back of his neck, his bright blue eyes pinning her in place.

"You wanted to talk. I'm here to listen. If you changed your mind, I'll go."

"I don't know if I can believe that."

He cast a glance at the sky before returning his gaze to hers. "I said I would, and I don't lie."

"But you do get stuck on one point and ignore the rest. And you want me to carry baggage I didn't pack."

His eyes narrowed and then softened as he caught her meaning. "Fair enough. Do you want me to listen or not?"

She stepped aside, the tight space closing in around them. It wasn't a recreational camper, so there was only one seat. She offered it to him and perched on the bench. She checked her watch, surprised to find half the morning gone.

Ray leaned toward her, bracing his forearms on his strong thighs. "So you made up an ex-husband to join NotMy1stRodeo.com."

She nodded. "It's not for singles, and the one I was on before wasn't working for me. Slade had talked about it, so I checked it out and signed up."

"To lose your virginity."

Heat spread across her cheeks and down her neck. "I know that you don't get it. Somewhere along the way, I turned off that side of myself. I was so busy with school and wanting to not just pass my courses, but to truly understand what I was doing. I took advantage of every opportunity that came my way, and meeting guys wasn't even on my radar. It wasn't until I turned twenty-nine that I realized how far behind I'd fallen."

His expression was blank, unreadable. She sighed, deciding to keep going. "And guys now want to talk about sexual history over the bread basket. And then my lack of experience became the only topic of conversation. Some couldn't get away from me fast enough, others wanted to help me out."

"Why didn't you let them?" He leaned back in the swivel chair bolted to the floor.

She shrugged. "I didn't want to see any of them naked."

A grin flickered across his face. "Fair enough."

Her breathing deepened and the tightness squeezing her chest loosened up a bit. "They didn't want to sleep with me either, not really. They'd hit Google before we'd go out and usually know the size of Weston Ridge and see dollar signs. Guys that grew up anywhere around us didn't want to go near me. I mean, you know my brothers, they're not what you'd call warm and friendly."

"At least not where their sister is concerned."

"I wanted a chance to find someone who wanted me, not a place on the ranch or as a virgin novelty. To do that, I had to get out of the county, away from the name. I could be me and have sex if I wanted. And if it was awful and I embarrassed myself as I usually do, I could just go back to my regularly scheduled life."

He rubbed his hands over his jean-clad thighs. "Your logic is flawed. You know that, right?"

She nodded. "I can see where you'd think that, but I see the value in it."

"In telling people you're something you're not?"

"No, in wanting to find someone who liked the awkward vet who would rather spend the day with animals than people, who rambles when she's nervous and doesn't know how to sit down in a dress."

He pushed a hand through his hair. "You said you did it to have sex."

"When I signed up, that's what I wanted. I wanted to be brave enough to go through with it, but I doubted I would be. It's hard to go from celibate to sex kitten overnight."

He leaned towards her, bracing his forearms on his thighs once more. “Why didn’t you tell me?”

“When? If I told you on the first phone call, you would have thought I was crazy. And after we met, I didn’t think you knew me well enough to understand. Plus, you said yourself, if you’d known I was a Weston, you would have asked Slade for his blessing. And he wouldn’t have given it.”

“Why not?” He sat up straight, vertical lines pressing into his forehead.

She swallowed, not wanting to say something that might hurt him more. But he had a thing for the truth. “Our folks have always said that marriage is the union of two people who are great at forgiveness. And that’s not you.”

He pulled his hand down his face, his expressionless mask returning. “He’s right. I'll never forget what you did.”

“I know.” Her future spiraled down the drain in front of her. Ray wouldn’t be here unless he wanted to try, she just needed to give him a reason. “I’ll never forget the way you kissed me after we got caught in the rain. I’ll never forget your confidence in me when Candy was foaling. Or how you kept me company during my drive home, and how I got that shirtless selfie out of you.”

He groaned and closed his eyes and she wondered if maybe, just maybe, he remembered it all too.

“Most of all, I’ll never forget how gentle you were with me. And how in that moment, nothing else existed.” Her throat tightened, her lashes wet as she blinked. “It was amazing, being together like that and knowing that you loved me and I loved you. It made something better than either of us.”

The silence stretched, the whirring sound of passing cars on the highway punctuating how long it had been since either of them spoke. Jacy closed her eyes and focused on anything else. The window against her back, the bit of comforter hanging off her bed that rested behind her head. If he wanted to go, he needed to be the one to leave.

"I can't forgive you today."

She opened her eyes at the sound of his voice. When he stood, he filled the space completely. She lifted her gaze to his and forced a smile. "I know."

"I don't think I will tomorrow either."

Dear God in heaven, if he was going to get mean now, when she'd been so vulnerable with him, she was going to have to jump up and get her gun. She wouldn't shoot it, but the thing was heavy and it would hurt like hell when she hit him with it.

"And I know I won't be able to trust you until I forgive you."

Not sure if she should ready herself for the fatal blow, she tried to read his eyes, finding only naked emotion. He seemed as confused and scared as she was.

"But I do know that I loved you yesterday, and you loved me, and it was the best I've ever felt in my life. And in an instant, it was all taken away. I don't know if I can handle someone having that much control over my life."

"That's the part that sucks for me right now." He was damned lucky she'd learned how to save her tears for privacy, because holding back now wasn't easy to do. "I don't think either one of us are getting out of this whole."

He cleared his throat and hooked his thumbs in the pockets of his jeans. "I know I don't have much place to ask, but can you give me a few days? I'm so angry with you right now, and I don't want to make a permanent decision while I'm seeing red."

She sighed, her heart still leaden but her burden easing. "Okay. So this is a don't-call-me, I'll-call-you thing?"

He knit his brows together. "No, I mean come home with me. You cleared a few days because of the twins anyway, right?

We can talk and fight and try to figure out where we go from here."

"You want me to stay with you so we can fight?"

"It could happen. Probably will."

She nodded and stood in front of him. "I'll go home. With you. To make up. We can talk or fight or whatever you want, so long as we make up after. I'll do anything it takes to get us back to yesterday."

He reached for her and took her hand in his. "I hope we get there."

She stepped closer and wrapped her arms around him, resting her head against his chest. His steady heartbeat beneath her ear soothed the parts of her soul still aching. He pulled her close, tightening his grasp around her.

"Maybe if we both hold on tight enough, it won't unravel." His husky whisper warmed her as much as his big body surrounding hers did.

"I love you too much to let go." She loved the scent of him, all clean man and hard work.

"But you have to." He tilted her chin up to meet his gaze. He brushed his lips against hers in the faintest of kisses. "You have to drive home."

"Home is wherever we're together." She pulled him to her and his lips found hers. For a moment, she forgot about apologies and forgiveness, future worries and past regrets. He tasted like crisp autumn and fresh mint, his kiss melting into hers as if they belonged together. Which they did.

He pulled away when she slipped her fingers between the buttons of his shirt. "I'm going to like making up with you, babe."

"Making up, making out, making love, making sandwiches..."

"Sandwiches?"

"I have a big appetite."

His warm, rich laugh filled the space with hope. "You and me both, babe. You and me both."

Epilogue

Seven months later

Jacy tried not to fidget too much in the passenger seat. She hadn't spent this much time in a car with someone else driving since before she had her drivers permit.

"Relax," Ray said for the third time, reaching out to rub her jean-covered thigh. "We're almost there."

"I'm trying, but this is a big deal. And if we do it wrong, it's going to be..." She flailed her hands about, making explosion sounds.

"You mean I can't open with Happy Mother's Day, we're pregnant?" Ray laughed, the warm sound like music to her soul.

She swatted his arm. "You're on thin ice with my mother already."

"She'll like me again once the baby's here. Babies make everything better." He squeezed the thigh and then returned his hand to the steering wheel. Ten and two. He'd been obsessed about safety for the last five weeks. The day they'd seen the plus sign, he'd gone out and bought the car because he didn't think a car seat would be safe enough in either of their trucks.

Jacy twisted the engagement ring on her finger. "If your parents hadn't already guessed, I'd wait until the wedding to tell them. It's only three weeks away. Lots of people wait until the second trimester before they announce."

"They're going to figure it out." Ray rubbed his knuckle against her breast. She glanced down at the new cleavage and sighed. "Unless you want to cop to a boob job."

"They do look fake." She crossed her arms over her chest and squeezed. So far, adding two cup sizes was her only symptom.

"They don't."

"Like you're some boob judge. They could totally be fake."

He shrugged. "There's a class guys take our freshman year of college. How to spot who got a boob job for high school graduation 101."

"Ah, yes, I must have been too busy at how to tell if your guy is full of shit 102."

"You aced your class, I aced mine."

She glanced down at her cleavage again. "They're too big for my body."

"You're going to grow into them. If I get lucky, they'll stick around. If not, we'll just have to have another baby. And another."

"That's hot," she deadpanned.

"Three is the magic number."

"Two. Maybe. We have to see how this one goes." She rested her hand below the waistband of her jeans. "You're going to have to figure out how to keep condoms from breaking, or we'll go back to the birth-control method I used before we met."

"You didn't... Ah, I see what you did there. Clever. Never going to happen, but clever." He cleared his throat. "Are you going to tell anyone the condom broke? Because I'd rather Bubba never know that. I mean, I wasn't even back from the bathroom and you had your legs up the wall and were talking about when the baby would be due. It's an oops, but not with a capital O."

"It was an ideal time to get pregnant. The holidays are a slow at work and January is a good time for me to take a month off. I'm a practical girl, that's where my mind went." She rested her head on the seat back and smiled his way, the edges of his profile lit by the afternoon sun. "But don't worry, no one in that house wants to think of us having sex. My mom's just going to be disappointed because this is exactly why she doesn't approve of living together before marriage."

"We're staying the night so we can get the marriage license in the morning before we head back home, so we can get married in her county, at her house. Still, my money is she makes me bunk with your brother, even after we tell her about Bubba."

No way would she take that bet. She rubbed her fingers in the newly shorn hair at the nape of his neck. She liked it a bit longer, but the Mitchells had a Mother's Day haircut tradition. "I want her to like you, and right now you're really not her favorite person."

"I'm not going to apologize for something we're both happy about. Personally, I don't care what she thinks. But if she's upset, it will bother you, and you're busy making a baby, so I'll jump whatever hoops she wants me to. What did you say this week is?"

She took his hand off the steering wheel and placed it on her belly. "He's the size of a grape and his heart is dividing into chambers."

"Exactly. You're busy. No one needs to hassle you with their judgments." He stopped the car and yanked it into park. He turned to her with a megawatt smile. "Let's do this thing."

He leaned in for a quick kiss and then circled around the car to open her door. He offered her a hand in this chivalrous way he had. She always took it, because when she did, he pulled her up right beside him.

"Babe, no matter what, I'll back you up. If you want to go in there and pretend you found some new supersizing bra, I'll go with it."

She wrapped her arms around his waist and grinned up at him. He hadn't shaved since morning and a light shadow covered his jaw. Right here, in this tight little circle, she had what she needed. “Leave our stuff in the car. If Mama doesn’t want you to stay with me, I’ll bunk with you at Slade’s.”

He kissed her forehead and took her hand as they walked up the steps. He held open the screen door while she walked inside first. As soon as the screen door slammed, her mother came running the rest of the crew behind her. Jacy squeezed Ray's hand tight, tighter.

“Happy Mother’s Day,” she said as her mom wrapped her up in an embrace. “We’re having a baby.”

About the Author

Jenna Bayley-Burke is known for her fun, sexy romance novels, baking banana bread and over-volunteering. She thinks she has the best jobs in the world—mother, wife and author. When she's not lost in her latest story, she can be found pursuing whatever hobby her characters are enamored with—photography, yoga, shoes, gardening, crafts and cooking up a storm. For more on Jenna check out her website www.jennabayleyburke.com.

Look for these titles by
Jenna Bayley-Burke

Now Available:

Her Cinderella Complex
Par for the Course
Compromising Positions
Pride and Passion
Private Scandal
For Kicks
Drive Me Crazy
Just One Spark

Under the Caribbean Sun
Caribbean Christmas
Caribbean Casanova
Caribbean Crush

Print Collections
Tempted

CPSIA information can be obtained at www.ICGtesting.com
Printed in the USA
BVOW04s2219070615

403460BV00001B/34/P